The Very Thought of You

Carolann Camillo

CRIMSON
ROMANCE

F+W Media, Inc.

This edition published by
Crimson Romance
an imprint of F+W Media, Inc.
10151 Carver Road, Suite 200
Blue Ash, Ohio 45242

www.crimsonromance.com

Dedication

THIS BOOK IS DEDICATED TO JULIE, LINDA, AND PHYLLIS
FOR THEIR INVALUABLE SUPPORT.

Chapter 1

The vanity license plate bolted to the black hybrid read N MAN 1 when it should have screamed TR UB LE. A rainy night rush hour flat tire on the freeway kind of trouble. That's what Molly Hewitt expected when she approached the not-for-profit medical clinic where she served as administrator. Otherwise, why would Nick Mancini's car squat in the twenty-four minute zone—ticket territory? He had his own parking slot at the other end of the block, alongside the trailer he used for a construction office. It wasn't as if he were inside the clinic making a killer donation. The odds on that were as slim as men and women flip-flopping on the Mars/Venus thing.

The morning from hell already landed on Molly's doorstep. She'd overslept, burned her toast, and forgotten to plug in the coffeemaker. Now, hungry and caffeine deprived, and with Ms. Cranky lurking inside her and ready to stomp on her usually placid disposition, she had to maneuver through a *tête-à-tête* with the San Francisco condo king. Were the Furies tap dancing on her head, or what?

She shoved her defenses into high alert, pushed open the clinic door, and stepped into the small waiting room. She'd expected to find the builder ready to pounce from one of the six mismatched chairs aligned beneath the Golden Gate Bridge poster, but there was no sign of him. Still, she sensed he prowled somewhere nearby. She shot a glance toward the closed door of her equally undersized office.

"He's not in there." Cynthia Wells brushed aside a long strand of maroon-tinted hair and stepped out from behind the third-hand desk that served as a reception center. "When I told him you hadn't come in yet, he decided to go for coffee. I offered ours, but he turned it down. I guess he didn't want to feel obligated."

"That's assuming he feels anything at all." Molly headed into her office. To make the cluttered space more tranquil, the pale lime walls held a quartet of scenic Monet prints that bled all her favorite pastel colors. She flipped on the fluorescent overhead lights and dumped her faux Kate Spade handbag and worn leather briefcase onto her desk. The tantalizing aroma of freshly brewed coffee settled in around her.

It surprised Molly that it had taken Mr. Mancini a week to accuse her of poking her nose into his business—a possible million-dollar poke at that. She'd found that out from Mrs. Zamoulian who lived in that wreck of a building Mancini had recently bought. Since the building sat smack in the middle of his new condo project, he planned to demolish it. Sure, the building screamed for demolition anyway, but not without substantial compensation for the tenants. Apparently, Mrs. Z has caved under the third degree from her new landlord and ratted out Molly, whose only crime was to express an opinion on how *she* would handle his cheesy buyout offer should she ever be in Mrs. Z's shoes.

Cynthia leaned in her office. "What will you say when he comes back?"

"Hmm. What I'd like to say is so X-rated my lips would have to do penance for a month. So I'll stick to the PG version." Molly dug a tin of Altoids out of her purse. Unlike some of her friends who hit the gym or the fast food counter when under pressure, Molly stuck to Altoids. Less pain . . . less gain. She offered some to Cynthia, then popped a couple into her mouth. The spearmint flavor burst on her tongue and began to soothe her rattled psyche.

"How can anyone look so gorgeous and be so rotten?" Cynthia said from the open doorway.

"Who knows? Maybe he suffered some deep childhood trauma."

"You think so?"

Molly shrugged. "Anything's possible."

"Well, inside, he might be decayed meat, but outside he's a dream."

"Yes, but what good are looks if they mask a whole laundry list of defects?"

Cynthia grinned. "Where should I start?"

Although Cynthia was usually focused, today she wore a bemused expression, which suggested Nick Mancini still occupied her attention. Barely two years out of high school and fully invested in guys who gave her "jock shock," looks still mattered to her.

Molly was almost a hundred percent certain Mr. Mancini had been the one in the dress shirt, tie, and pressed slacks she'd spotted the other day leaning against the hybrid's hood and talking with several hardhats at his construction site. If so, even she had to admit he deserved her highest rating—three mochachino raspberry grandes—two point five more than she awarded each of her last two boring dates.

Molly changed the subject and glanced in the direction of the two examining rooms located at the rear of the building. "Have the doctors come in yet?"

"Huh?"

"Are the doctors in?"

It took Cynthia a few seconds to refocus. "Dr. Ed is with a patient. Dr. Jake is on late call today."

At precisely that moment, the front door opened and closed. Molly offered up a silent prayer for it to be someone seeking medical attention, but one look at Cynthia's lips forming the words "it's him" and her belief system crashed.

As soon as Cynthia cleared the doorway, Nick Mancini filled it. Yes, he was the man she'd spotted with the construction crew. Only today he'd opted for khakis and a forest green T-shirt. The short sleeves banded well-toned muscles, which placed him high on her totally buff list. Add those to the hard pecs and abs held prisoner beneath the fabric that stretched across a broad chest, and he easily qualified for triple blue ribbon status. Molly swallowed, and what remained of the Altoids slid down her throat.

When she had cruised by his building site the other day, he'd glanced over, which had forced her to speed up. Now she stood close enough to better fit the pieces of his face together: strong chin, full mouth, and a nose flat enough at the bridge to make it interesting. Perhaps he'd fallen off a ladder and broken it. His dark hair, worn long enough to separate him from the "looking forward one day to retirement" crowd, ramped up his sex appeal. *Look, but don't touch.* Molly bit down on the outer edge of her bottom lip. She'd hate herself in the morning but, what the heck, she piled on an extra mochachino.

"You must be Ms. Hewitt." Two long strides brought him into the middle of her office. The air bristled with the high-octane energy that rolled off him. His deep voice boasted a full complement of male hormones—not exactly gruff, but not musical, either. Whatever the quality, it was in direct proportion to the rest of him: exceedingly male.

"You are . . . ?" Molly obeyed the urge to feign ignorance. After all, why give the impression she attached any importance to his complaint about her meddling?

"Nick Mancini." His eyes drilled into hers like a bit swiveling through a redwood plank.

Still, she remained rooted to the vinyl floor, exactly three feet from N MAN 1. "Yes, I'm Molly Hewitt." She extended her hand. "Nice to meet you." Which it wasn't, given the circumstances, but maybe the "nice" would take some of the charge out of his battery.

His gaze drifted over her royal blue knit top and ivory linen knee-length skirt. The tightly bunched muscles in his face relaxed.

"We need to talk." He took her hand and applied what felt like friendly pressure when, probably, he'd like to snap all five fingers as if they were swizzle sticks. His skin texture suggested the reverse side of an emery board—barely abrasive. Why not, since he no longer had to climb up on a girder and bang away at a helpless board anymore. The hired crew carried out the heavy duty stuff.

He withdrew his hand and began to fire questions at her. "What's your connection to the tenants in my building down the street? In what capacity do you represent them?"

"I don't—"

"What are you, another wannabe lawyer?" That brought him one step closer.

"I'm not a wannabe anything." Molly jumped in quickly before he accused her of having her hand in the latest economic downturn. "Nor do I represent your tenants. Several are patients here at the clinic. That's my only connection to them."

Standing five feet nine and a half in her three-inch wedge sandals , she brought her eyes closer to Mr. Mancini's. They shared basically the same color—sort of a smoky caramel brown. She was never wild about the shade, but he made it seem almost . . . exotic. Due, no doubt, to the contrast with his dark lashes. Hers were redhead-light and needed a double application of mascara from any brand on sale at the local drugstore.

"You're advising them on a matter that doesn't concern you."

It took another moment to drag her eyes away from his and cajole her brain into thinking mode again. "Actually, I didn't offer any advice."

"That's not what I heard."

Poor Mrs. Z. He'd probably threatened her with the twenty-first century equivalent of the rack. "Well, I did offer a suggestion or two." A small, dark mole that looked more interesting than dangerous sprouted near the outer edge of his left eyebrow. *Maybe Dr. Ed should take a look at it later.*

"That's not giving yourself nearly enough credit. My guess— you offered a lot more than *two* suggestions. That's why they've formed a tenants' association." He held up a hand before she had a chance to contradict him. "Don't bother denying where the idea, along with the inflated buyout demand, came from. Now there's talk about circulating a petition."

"I don't recall the police carting anyone off to San Quentin for that."

"I suppose tomorrow you'll advise them to walk a picket line in front of the building."

A picket line. What a great idea. She might mention it to Mrs. Z so she could pass it on to the others at the next tenants' meeting.

"All my permits are in order. They can collect a thousand signatures and leaflet the entire South of Market area. It won't change anything. They'll never stop my project from going ahead."

They'll give it a heck of a try, though. Maybe they could interest enough people to see the justice of their cause. San Francisco was rife with citizens' groups agitating for the have-nots who were always getting the shaft from the have-it-alls.

"You never know," she said. "Sometimes good things happen when least expected." His aftershave brought a refreshing hint of the outdoors into the small, windowless space. Nice. After he left—and it couldn't be soon enough—she hoped the scent would linger.

"They've had more than enough time to relocate, nearly twice what the law requires. You *advised* them to stay put." He stabbed the air with one long finger, almost as if conducting a discordant symphony. Molly beat off the urge to lean back, since that might suggest she'd given up ground. Unless her little patch of terra firma crumbled, she was determined not to part with an inch.

"Several tenants asked what I'd do in their situation, and I told the truth. Having practically no resources with which to make a move, I'd absolutely stand pat."

His eyes narrowed at the poker term, as if he'd just awakened to the possibility that he was dealing with a con artist or at least someone accomplished at bluffing. Nothing could be further from the truth. Sure, most Friday nights Molly played poker with her Aunt Vi and cousin, Dominique. She never bluffed, though, and wouldn't know how to con anyone.

"I made a very generous cash offer. One any landlord would consider overly generous."

His skin tone ran toward olive and blended well with an eye-catching tan. One of the perks of outdoor work. Even lathered with sunscreen, she couldn't avoid burning through the entire pink to red spectrum if she exposed her skin to the sun for more than thirty minutes.

"You consider twenty-five thousand dollars per apartment unit generous?"

"When you don't have to work for it, yes."

"Sorry. Not even close. Especially for people who live on or just one notch above the poverty line." She tried to temper the censure in her voice but failed.

"I suppose *suggesting* they hold out for a hundred grand instead wasn't the same as giving them advice."

"That's not how I see it."

"I get it. *You* would hold out for a hundred." That brought him in maybe fifteen more inches. Another fifteen and he'd leave his shoe print on her sandals and spray-on tan toes.

"If I were in their situation, sure I would."

"You don't consider a hundred grand greedy?" He shook his head and a lock of dark hair nudged his brow, further ramping up his sex appeal and breaking God only knew how many scientific laws of nature.

Molly took a few moments to clear her head of the kind of thoughts that could turn a woman into Play-Doh. If he were any other man, under any other circumstances . . . She sucked in a deep breath and had to kick start herself to refocus on greed.

"No." She exhaled in a whoosh of air. "To expect a generous buyout isn't greedy. It's just plain common sense. When's the last time you checked out the economy?" She sidestepped around her desk, opened the center drawer and dug out a hand calculator. "Hard to imagine where you think those people are going to move to in this city on twenty-five thousand dollars. You probably have a team of financial advisors who do nothing all day but figure out ways to make you piles of money. For your tenants, though, a savings account is probably the best they can expect. That's one step up from a cookie jar." She tapped numbers into the calculator.

"Let's assume twenty-five thousand times a measly two point five percent in a money market, which assumes it's tied up practically for life. That only comes to . . . "

"Six twenty-five." He spit it out, with hardly a hesitation, as if he had an adding machine implanted in his brain. "Even without the interest, the principal should last for years if they're careful."

"You mean if they use it as a supplement and add it to the amount they pay for rent now."

"That's the idea. They'll have a financial cushion to bridge the gap once they relocate."

"Except in today's market and in this city, that should last about . . . "

As her fingers again danced across the instrument's key panel, his hand reached out and clamped onto hers. He snatched the calculator with his other hand and dropped it onto her desk.

"You know, I'd love to sit down with you sometime and crunch numbers or whatever, but right now I'm running late for an appointment."

She pulled her hand away. "That sounds like just another way to say the argument has gone against you, and it's time to retreat."

"Were we arguing?"

"Weren't we?"

"I hope not." He smiled for the first time. At least he proved he had the capacity and wasn't all just rugged good looks. The smile softened his strong features. Molly supposed plenty of women jumped out of their lace thongs at the slightest encouragement from him. Even if she wore a thong, she didn't foresee adding her name to the list. Not even if she prevailed and he encouraged.

"Well, disagreeing, then."

"I understand your point, and yes, I'll admit it will take some effort to relocate where rents are cheaper. But those kinds of units do exist."

"Really? Maybe in the Yukon . . . and even there, there must be a waiting list."

The smile dropped a notch. "There's no need to go that far. Low rent apartments can be found right here."

"Not to my knowledge." Also, if the rumor proved true, he might gobble up the seedy real estate—perhaps even the clinic—at her end of the block and no one would make a buyout offer to her. No other San Francisco landlord would give the clinic the kind of break on rent her current "angel" offered—a dollar a month. She would love to pump Mr. Mancini on any future plans but decided against a two-pronged assault.

"In my business, I've gotten to know the city pretty well. There's affordable housing available right now if you know where to look. Do you want me to prove it to you?"

"Do you really think you can?"

He slid his cell phone from its sheath and gave it his attention for a few seconds. "I can free up some time this afternoon to prove there are inexpensive units out there—given my tenants will have a windfall to work around. We'll check out a few. Then once you're convinced, we can both get on with business."

It had been far too long since a determined man invited her inside an apartment for *any* reason—she didn't count the octopus who'd earned a squirt in the eye with hand sanitizer when he'd decided to take inventory of her body, and in a public lobby. Or the blind date with the comb-over that didn't quite hide the double-sided tape. Even though *this* man had a face and body that could take a woman's inhibitions and shred them into confetti, she wasn't about to drive around town with him so he could try to prove a non-provable point. "That sounds like a waste of both our time."

"I can make time."

"Sorry, but I can't during work hours on a Friday or any other weekday. So why not just take a good look at the classified ads in the *Chronicle* or check out the Internet? You'll see what's available in the rental market." *That should settle it.*

His gaze bored into her like a laser primed for maximum penetration. "You're backing down."

"Absolutely not."

He braced his hands on the edge of her desk and leaned in several inches, which brought his eyes practically level with hers. His arm muscles flexed, and a second later, her toes curled. Which would be understandable if he were her type, which he wasn't, but he *was* TR UB LE. Oh, yes.

"Ms. Hewitt . . . ?"

"Huh?" Great. Now she was channeling Cynthia.

"Why don't you just admit you're wrong?"

For heaven's sake, why didn't he just throw down a glove and challenge her to a duel? Obviously, mere words would never change his mind. He needed physical proof, so she figured she might as well relent.

"I admit nothing of the kind. Also, I don't have an overblown ego that forbids me to acknowledge a mistake." A dark brow—the one with the mole—rose. Her dart had hit a bull's eye. "To prove my point, I'll take a look at what you *imagine* is available."

He nodded. "Okay, then. Why don't I drop by your place and pick you up tomorrow at ten?"

That was the time she'd set aside to cruise around the city and scoop up gift cards donated by several high-end restaurants for her upcoming auction event. Afterwards, she had an appointment with the producer of the funky smash revue Beach Blanket Babylon. They'd discussed the possibility of squeezing in the highest bidder somewhere between Louis the Fourteenth and the dancing poodles.

"I have appointments tomorrow, but I could finish by two." Free from there on, also. All she had on tap for Saturday night was to curl up with a glass of Chardonnay and a good murder mystery.

"Doesn't work for me." He went back to his cell phone. "How's

Sunday afternoon around three?"

She figured that morning he'd be sleeping off a big Saturday night frolic. He didn't sport a wedding ring, but that didn't mean he didn't frolic with a wife. "Not possible then, either. Sorry." Her cousin Dominique had agreed to drop over around four to help with the proposal Molly planned to submit to the Bill and Melinda Gates Foundation. She would cancel except for a looming deadline.

He nodded his head. "See, you're trying to avoid a showdown. You know I'm right."

"You're wrong on both counts. I can meet you tonight around six." That would turn tonight into the second Friday in a row she'd have to bail out of the poker game. But she wanted to get this search over with, like quadruple ASAP.

"Can't make it."

"Well, then, I guess that only leaves Sunday morning. Or perhaps now you'd like to postpone this indefinitely."

The mouth that had smiled so invitingly only a couple of minutes before sank into a frown. "I . . . okay, I can try to squeeze it in."

"Thank you." She managed to get the words out without too much sarcasm—which, where Nick Mancini was concerned, didn't come easily. If he was going to have an overnight guest, too bad. He'd just have to kick her out of the sack early.

"All right, where do you live?" he asked.

"Why do you want to know that?"

The broad shoulders under his T-shirt slumped, and he blew air out through his mouth. "So I can pick you up."

"Oh." At least he refrained from adding "stupid." "I can meet you here. I don't give out my address to people I don't know."

He stared at her for such a long time she wondered if he'd had some sort of seizure. What luck they were in a medical office.

"Right. We'll meet here Sunday morning at, say, ten. Does that fit into your schedule?"

"Yes, fine."

"Good. We'll settle this, and then maybe you can stay out of trouble for a while. Or at least not cause any more."

"Really? Not cause trouble for whom?" She figured the "whom" stared her down from across her desk.

"I had my tenants in mind. Who did you think I meant?"

"You. Who else?"

"Uh-uh." The corners of his lips tipped up and his facial muscles relaxed. "Usually, when trouble heads my way, it has little to do with business." Between the slow drawl and the sensual look that bumped his expression into *approach at your own risk* territory, a patch of heat sprang into her cheeks. To her credit, she kept her mouth from dropping open.

"Your face is flushed." He reached across the desk and tapped her lightly on the chin with a bent finger. "Do I make you nervous?"

At this juncture he did, more so than when he'd practically laid siege to her office.

"No, of course not." Lax, lately, about practicing yoga, Molly made a mental note to review the Alternate Breath Technique. She had a feeling that, on Sunday morning, she would need the benefit of its promised natural tranquilizer.

"Okay, then. I'll stop by for you Sunday at ten." No more smiles. He just turned and left the office.

Once the front door closed, Cynthia buzzed in. She set a mug of steaming coffee on Molly's desk. "You sure held your own with the big bad builder."

Molly let out the breath held far too long. She swept her dog-eared copy of *Grant Writing for Dummies* and a pile of empty file folders off her chair and plopped down onto it. "Do you think so?" She fanned her face with her hand. Either the cooling system had failed, or Mr. Mancini had vacuumed up all the air.

"I know so. Wow, I would have crumpled."

"Yeah, like poor Mrs. Zamoulian." It pained her to think about the woman going up against N MAN 1. She hadn't stood the tiniest chance. Well, on Sunday morning, Molly intended to show up with enough evidence to prove low-rent housing was even scarcer than a fogless summer in San Francisco. Then, hopefully, after their apartment hunt, Mr. Mancini would realize his cheesy twenty-five thousand dollar buyout offer wouldn't stretch from here to the corner.

Would he admit it, though? She guessed he hardly ever confessed he was wrong, even when faced with incontrovertible proof. Speaking of which, she wondered how much he was going to require and if just a few hours would be enough to prove her point.

That put a prickly thought into her head. She wouldn't have to do this more than once with him, would she?

Chapter 2

"Molly, you remember my friend who works at the Hall of Records." Vi Phillips dealt from a deck of cards whose backs were emblazoned with a faithful image of a young, slim Elvis. "She helped you out by telling fortunes at your carnival event last year."

Trudie, aka the mole. Molly shuddered inwardly. "You didn't volunteer her for my auction, did you?" At the carnival Molly had sponsored the previous summer, she'd overheard the mole reading the palm of one of the city's most prominent men. She predicted he'd find a Playboy Bunny in his bed that night.

"Of course not. Although you kind of hurt her feelings when you closed down her booth. She did you another favor."

"What?" Apprehension colored Molly's tone. "I haven't asked for any favors." She took a quick glance, then slapped her cards down onto the speckled green tin tabletop. Her aunt was into everything retro, including the chairs they occupied—stainless steel tubing with red vinyl seats. Ferns sprung from every corner of the kitchen and provided a tropical effect for the macramé birds that swooped across one wall. Before it became chic, she'd shopped at vintage clothing stores, which accounted for the floral bell-bottoms she wore that night—bell-bottoms almost identical to the ones she'd bought Molly for her last birthday. Those were secreted in a dark corner of Molly's closet and worn only when she was coerced into accompanying her aunt to the annual Love Parade.

"I know you didn't, dear. I did."

"Aunt Vi . . . " What had started as apprehension swooshed into alarm. "What are you up to?"

Vi flipped one of her brown gray-flecked braids over her shoulder. "When we spoke earlier, you said you wished you knew something more about Mr. Mancini, other than the plan to evict his tenants."

"He hasn't evicted them, at least not yet. Anyway, how does that concern Trudie?" Molly cast a suspicious glance across the table. "Oh, my God." Her aunt hadn't christened her friend the mole for nothing. Buried deep inside the Hall of Records, Trudie had access to all sorts of personal information.

"Your Mr. Mancini is thirty-six years old and was born right here in San Francisco at St. Luke's Hospital. His birthday is April twenty-ninth. He's a Taurus."

"That's the kind of useless information I don't need." Molly gathered her cards. "It would help to know what he's like inside." She'd already decided the outside could stand up to anyone voted the Sexiest Man Alive.

"Taurus is a bull, sweetie." Vi propped her elbows on the table and leaned toward Molly. "Either ride him until he's spent or chance getting gored by his horns."

Molly frowned. What kind of advice was that?

"Did Trudie find out if he's married?" Dominique asked.

"What difference does it make if he's married?" Molly picked up her cards.

"Have you checked out the lack of availability of thirty-something eligible men in San Francisco lately?"

"No. Also, Aunt Vi, looking up that kind of information is an invasion of privacy, if not against the law. Tell Trudie to quit."

"No problem. Anyway, if he were married or divorced, there's no record of it, at least in this county. Nor is there a deed for a private residence. We assume he's a renter, or worse, lives in the 'burbs. That's all Trudie could ferret out about him. Unless you want her to call a friend who works at the IRS."

"Absolutely not. Trudie is liable to get you both arrested over information that's of no possible use." Except, maybe, for his tax return. A peek at that would be as good as striking gold, but Molly kept that thought to herself.

"Molly is right, Mom. What's more important is finding affordable housing for Mr. Mancini's tenants. Once that's accomplished, who knows? She might take a second look at him then—if he's single."

"Forget it."

"Well, he sounds like a better deal than your last few dates. Remember the airline pilot?"

Molly had excised that particular loser from her brain. Not only had he taken her to a cheap restaurant, he'd made it very clear what he expected for dessert. She left him sitting at the table with a shit-eating grin on his face.

"Just don't limit your options," Dominique added. Molly groaned and switched her attention to the local newspaper she'd brought along. In between poker hands, she perused the unfurnished apartment ads in the *San Francisco Chronicle*. She had highlighted a few of interest with a felt tip pen.

"Listen to this." She tapped the folded newspaper at her elbow. "Here's a one bedroom in the Tenderloin advertised for eight and a quarter. A find, if you weren't mugged almost every time you left the apartment."

Dominique, who worked as a law librarian at a prestigious San Francisco firm, and who had promised to research the city's eviction laws, ran her fingers through her short-cropped dark hair. "On Sunday, drag Mr. Mancini to all the way-out-of-their-reach places first. Then head for the Tenderloin. The shock might force him to up the ante."

"Did you broach the subject of the rumor he might have designs on your end of the street?" Vi asked.

Molly turned her attention to her poker hand—a pair of twos

and junk. It looked like she'd end her day just as it had begun. She was already in the hole for eighty-five cents. "The mood wasn't conducive to multiple problems."

"I wouldn't wait too long to find out, not if you'll need to relocate the clinic. Unlike his tenants, you'll be offered zilch."

"Mom's right. Sometimes it pays to be up front. Maybe the rumor is false."

Molly shook her head. "I don't think so. Except for his condos, the rest of the block looks ready for a bulldozer."

Dominique tossed a dime into the pot. "Speaking of down-on-your-luck, is the Swaying Palms, that motel a couple of doors from the clinic, a hot pillow joint? I know I wouldn't lay my head down there."

Molly kept her pair and added the rest to the discard pile. "No, it's legitimate. It just needs maintenance. The lights have quit in half of the fronds *and* the P. Now it reads Swaying *alms*. It's ripe for demolition."

Vi dealt Molly three cards, Dominique two, and herself one.

Dominique checked out her cards, then laid them face down on the table. "I'll bet a dime. Anyone want to see what I've got?"

Molly frowned. There was nothing she could do with a pair of deuces. "I'm out."

Vi folded her hand. "Ditto for me."

Dominique raked in the pot and dealt the next round. "Let's play seven card stud. Threes and nines are wild and fours give you an extra card."

Everyone anted up a nickel.

"So you think the rumors are true." Vi peeked at her two hole cards.

"Eddie, the manager of the Swaying *alms*, caught Mr. Mancini taking pictures from across the street. Not only of the motel but the hole-in-the-wall Chinese restaurant, the clinic, and the costume/novelty shop. He wasn't sure about any of the other properties on the block. Ever since the economy tanked and the mayor put the kibosh on the Halloween hijinks over in the Castro, the costume store has lost business. Eddie wasn't sure if the building that used to house the coffee shop next door to us at the corner had fallen victim to the camera. The units above it have been unoccupied for at least six months."

Dominique dealt herself a four, which entitled her to an extra card, then dealt her mother a nine and Molly the inevitable deuce.

"The building department had almost a hundred years to find out those units were out of compliance." Molly bet a nickel since she already had one deuce in the hole. "Now they've caught up to the current owner, you can bet he's anxious to unload the property. Perfect for Mr. Mancini but a nightmare for the clinic."

Vi added her nickel to the pot. "He'll make a tidy profit when he finishes his condos and sells them. Enough to expand. The rumor is probably true."

Molly wondered if the mole could do a record search to find out if any deeds had recently changed hands. She'd wait a while and see what else developed. If the clinic seemed in jeopardy, she'd ask her aunt to contact Trudie.

Dominique continued dealing. "His profit wouldn't be so big if he had to fork over a hundred grand per unit to his tenants. You didn't suggest that on purpose, did you, Molly?"

"Suggest what?"

"They turn down his twenty-five thousand and hold out for a hundred."

Molly shook her head. "Of course not. Why would you think that?"

"It'll cost him a million dollars if they refuse to move for less. That would take a nice bite out of his profit margin."

Molly sat back and stared at her cousin. "Oh, you have a wicked mind." She laughed.

"What? You don't?"

"Not on a million-dollar scale. It never entered my head to

try to stop the Mancini bulldozer. His tenants deserve a fair deal. When I offered my opinion, I thought only of them."

"Maybe you should think of yourself more."

"He can't buy up another chunk of the block for a million dollars."

Vi picked up her mug of mulled cider. "It might be enough to float a bank loan for the motel and Chinese restaurant."

"Or the costume store and clinic," Dominique offered. "Maybe even the building that housed the defunct coffee shop, too. A triple whammy. He could anchor the block with new condos."

"Ask him on Sunday," Vi suggested.

Molly nodded. "First chance. I promise. Although, on Sunday it's important to keep his attention on his tenants."

Dominique dealt the last face down card. "Did he strike you as a man with a limited attention span?"

"Not in the least." Molly didn't find him limited in any respect other than his cavalier attitude.

She perused her cards. Even with all the wild threes and nines, she could only muster two pair.

Vi laid down a royal flush helped by three wild cards and raked in sixty-five cents.

Molly slumped in her chair. "Why couldn't he have built on some other city block? God knows there are enough in need of a wrecking ball." She pushed away from the table. "I've gotta go." She grabbed her newspaper and marker. Just talking about the builder brought on a headache. Spending hours with him on Sunday was going to totally wreck her karma.

Chapter 3

As soon as Nick entered his apartment, he pulled off his tie, yanked open the top button on his shirt, and shrugged off his suit jacket. He tossed the tie and jacket onto the sofa, then headed into the kitchen and rescued a cold beer from the refrigerator. At the rehearsal dinner that night, the prelude to his brother's wedding the following evening, champagne had flowed as if from a gusher. He hated champagne. It gave him a headache. Ordering a beer at the dinner, however, was apparently tantamount to committing a mortal sin. Since the affair was semi-formal, his mother had given him the usual orders: suit, tie, and no beer bottles on the table. Shit.

He popped the cap on his brew and sauntered back into the living room where he didn't bother to turn on a light. A street lamp and a perfectly full moon gave off enough illumination. He found his Faith Hill CD and slipped it into the player. While the music drifted low in the background, he sipped his beer and opened the sliding glass door. Now that many parts of the country were preparing for the briskness of fall, the fog that shrouded San Francisco all summer had finally dissipated, ushering in balmy weather. He never minded the fog. It was one of the many features, along with the hills and cable cars, that made the city so unique.

He stepped outside onto his small balcony, leaned against the rail, and gazed out over the bay. Lights blinked in every direction. The Golden Gate Bridge stood out in stark relief and spanned the inky-dark water.

"Hi, Nick. Great night, isn't it?"

His neighbor Serena—or was it Sabrina—greeted him from her balcony less than thirty feet from his.

"Yeah, it's okay." He could think of several ways it could have been better: bottled beers at dinner, a black hole swallowing Ms. Hewitt, and Serena/Sabrina canning the conversation.

"You're out late tonight." She flipped her Sheena, Queen of the Jungle jet-black hair over a shoulder. "I missed you earlier. My gym has a promotion—two free months for newbies. Interested?"

He wanted to ask if she kept a running account of his movements—which he suspected she did—but knew any encouragement would only lead to a drink invitation.

"Uh . . . not at this time."

"I get a free month if you sign up. It's worth a dinner . . . on me. Can I change your mind?"

The woman was a piranha. He waved her off.

"Well, the dinner invitation still stands. You're not dating right now, are you?"

He wasn't, but before he let her know that, he'd take a header off the balcony.

"How about—"

"I have no time right now." He cut her off without the addition of "maybe in the future." That courtesy had once landed her within fifteen seconds at his front door.

"Well, think about it."

He stepped back a couple of paces, which put a three-foot portion of a side wall between them.

His apartment building sat midway up a steep hill in Pacific Heights and afforded one of the best views of the city. He glanced down over the rooftops and wondered if Molly lived somewhere within sight. He'd been unaware of her until last week. When he'd asked around about the clinic, he'd found out it had been open for almost two years and operated on a sliding scale from free to whatever a person could afford. Obviously, a shoestring operation. One story high, the building was squeezed into a narrow slot that fronted a sidewalk littered with soda cans and assorted paper debris. The steel door kept it safe at night. No window faced the street, probably for the same reason.

Somehow, Molly must earn a living from it. When he'd walked into her office that morning, he'd expected a woman somewhere between fifty and retirement age with bad hair and narrow lips and who wore polyester and no-nonsense orthopedic shoes. A bulldog. What he found instead was Molly—with a jumble of rust-colored curls that ended midway down her neck and looked as if they'd stick out all over like heating coils after a night of steamy sex. That is, if nosy do-gooders even engaged in steamy sex, which he doubted. He also figured a couple of decades would pass before she saw fifty and left behind her strappy shoes and knee-length skirt. The pale fabric had hugged a slim waist and nicely shaped hips, the kind he usually didn't mind wrapping his hands around.

Although plenty of attractive women lived and worked in the city, she scored well above average. That should take some of the sting out of spending Sunday morning apartment hunting with her. And if she kept her opinions stuck permanently on pause, the sting might disappear altogether.

Fatigue settled in. His day at the construction site had been a bitch. What had once seemed doable—building five floors of live/work lofts on a space occupied by an empty warehouse, a ten-unit apartment building, and a vacant lot—had become plagued with problems. As the guys had dismantled the last warehouse wall, he'd said "go easy" so many times he sounded like a damn monk spouting a mantra. Oh yeah, and they'd had an audience. Five people from the apartment house had carted out folding chairs and watched them chip away at the wall. It had taken a lot of persuasion to convince them to move back to a safe distance. He didn't need a lawsuit if a stray brick connected with someone's head. He'd also expected Molly to steamroll down the street in support of the tenants, but she hadn't. Too bad. He'd like to check her out again and see if the sun turned those russet curls flaming red.

He finished his beer and hit the kitchen for another. Inside the refrigerator, along with three bottles left over from the six-pack, there was a half brick of cheese, a carton of milk, and something that had rolled toward the back and vaguely resembled an apple. His mother had dropped in recently, poked her head into the refrigerator, and thrown out everything but the beer. While she'd delivered sheets, towels, and cutesie sofa pillows—none of which he wanted or needed—she'd given him the usual sermon about his being single.

"You still live like a traveling salesman. Your sisters are all married and your brother will be soon. You need a wife."

She must be on the same wavelength as Serena/Sabrina. Thank God the women had never met. Maybe someday he'd need a wife, but right now he'd settle for more action in the sack. If he told his mother that, she'd race to the nearest church and start a novena. He knew any time he wanted sex, he'd find it where single women congregated after work. After springing for a couple of drinks and dinner, he'd have a bed partner. But a one-night-only collision with a stranger usually held little appeal.

Last week, his mother had nagged him again, this time about not bringing a date to his brother's wedding.

"You'll be the only one on the dais without a partner. There's still time for you to meet a nice girl"—*girl*, as if he were still in high school—"and invite her to accompany you." Maybe jump in and make it a double ceremony while he was at it. But he'd let her ramble on.

"God forbid you stay a bachelor forever, like your Uncle Richard who lives with a houseful of cats. You'll wind up talking to yourself, and that won't be the worst part. People will think you're eccentric or, God forbid, peculiar." Why didn't any of his relationships last more than a few weeks? Maybe if he found the right *girl*.

He'd stood back while she'd sprayed Windex on his kitchen counters, which were almost spotless since he never cooked. Pizza,

Chinese, and Mexican take out got eaten right out of the carton at the coffee table in the living room while he watched the late news or a ball game. He couldn't remember ever bemoaning the fact that there wasn't a wife and an overdone roast waiting for him after work. Lonely wasn't a word that occupied space in his conscious mind. As for his recent relationships, he didn't have the time right now for the kind of attention women demanded.

He ambled back onto the balcony with his beer. Serena/Sabrina had abandoned her post, which made it safe to walk to the railing. Almost midnight now, fewer lights glowed in the surrounding homes and apartments. He wondered if Molly lived alone or with some guy—another do-gooder or Mr. Success. Yeah, he wondered who she slept with and if she slept *au natural*. His last girlfriend had slept in the nude, which had been convenient. But when she'd paraded around the apartment like Eve in Eden, much to the delight of his neighbor with the telescope, he'd figured it was time to move on. That was eight months ago.

He couldn't imagine Molly Hewitt sashaying around in broad daylight in the buff. Even if she were married. She wore a ring on her right hand, a small amethyst set in gold. So maybe a husband wasn't in the picture yet. However, it wouldn't surprise him if a boyfriend lurked in the background. If he was going to bird-dog her, he didn't need any complications from Mr. Right. He didn't need any complications, period.

He thought about how she'd meddled with his tenants and started getting pissed all over again. He finished half the beer and pressed the cold bottle against his forehead. When he'd first met with the tenants and offered a buyout, he'd assumed they'd grab the money and resettle in the time allotted. But somewhere between then and now, Molly, with the pouty lips that made a man want to grab her and plant a big wet one on them, had entered the picture. In a nanosecond, twenty-five thousand had become little more than taxi fare. He was stretched thin. Dangerously so. He'd already taken out a second on the small office complex he owned on Sutter. Shit, did he look like Donald Trump with money cascading out of his nostrils? He owned a small company. In nine years, he'd completed four projects, and this was only the second time he'd had to deal with an occupied building.

What had puzzled him about his tenants was how organized they'd become—at least, until he'd met little Ms. Greedy.

A picture of how Molly had filled out the sleeveless knit top she'd worn that morning floated into his mind. Yeah, she scored pretty high on the "cute-as-all-hell" scale and had enough sex appeal to catch and hold the attention of a healthy male. Him, for one, to be honest about it. Along with looks and a body that could get a man to think about doing the nasty tango with her, he guessed she also possessed some pretty well-honed organizational skills.

What he'd discovered at the clinic that morning was she might look like an angel, but she had an I-bar up her butt. She didn't bend. He'd bet his building permit *she* was the de facto head of the tenants' association. He'd have to go through her in order to reach a settlement with them. So yeah, dealing with Molly Hewitt would require strategy. He'd start by throwing a little charm her way. Once he knew her better, he could find out what curled her toes and brought a smile to those sexy lips.

Maybe he'd come on a little strong that morning. Instead, he should have taken some time to figure out the best way to nudge her toward a compromise. How much of a man-eater could she be, running a not-for-profit clinic? If he worked at it, he thought he could convince her to sign up for his team. That shouldn't be impossible. He possessed some pretty fierce organizational skills himself. When a situation called for persuasion, shit, *he was the man*. He was definitely up for a little one-on-one with her and might even get some fun out of it.

Yeah, it was time to introduce Ms. Hewitt to Mr. Charm.

Chapter 4

When Molly pulled up outside the clinic on Sunday morning, Nick Mancini's hybrid was already parked at the curb. She wondered how long he's been sitting there and if he was an early bird, the kind who rose at five a.m. and needed only a few hours' sleep. Or maybe he was trying to make a good impression. Of course, she'd arrived early, too, and that had nothing to do with impressing him. For once, she hadn't had to spend an excessive amount of time taming her hair so it didn't resemble something you slapped on the end of a pole and used in place of a Swiffer.

She dragged herself out of her car and walked to the passenger side of the hybrid. He popped the lock, and she slid into the seat beside N MAN 1 and engaged her safety belt. Today, he wore tan slacks and a black T-shirt that more than accomplished its job of defining his impressive set of pecs, abs, and prize-winning biceps. She figured him for a gym rat.

"Good morning." He greeted her with a smile and a drink container from Starbucks that looked exactly like the one in his hand. "I didn't know if you had time for coffee, or even if you drank coffee, or what kind you liked. I took a chance on a mochachino raspberry grande. Is regular okay?"

Was he telepathic? Mochachino raspberry grande, four of which she'd already awarded him for his looks, was her very favorite. She rarely sprang for a grande, though, and regular was the only way she drank her coffee. A needed jolt most days.

"Thanks." She smiled and didn't have to force it. She parked her purse in her lap along with a couple of folders that contained unfurnished apartment ads from the *Chronicle* and tips she'd gleaned from Craigslist and other Internet sites. She also brought along a couple of local independent publications that advertised rental properties. She pried the top off her container. The subtle aroma of chocolate mixed with the robust blend of coffee made her want to moan with pleasure. She put that on hold and took a few sips before replacing the lid.

"I see you came prepared with ammunition." Nick shifted position so he partially faced her. He placed his hand on her seatback, and his fingers brushed her hair. She wondered if that was deliberate or if her hair stuck out too much and he couldn't avoid contact.

She followed the direction of his eyes to the newspaper ads that peeked out from the folders under her purse.

"I figured we needed someplace to start. Or did you already have somewhere in mind?" Maybe he'd tucked similar materials away in the glove compartment. The interior of his car was spotless. Not even a gum wrapper. Unlike hers. Half-filled water bottles, running shoes, a windshield sun visor, and assorted materials related to her fundraisers cluttered the backseat and floor.

He drank from his coffee container for a few moments. "I'm curious about the clinic. Who funds it?" His hand moved and brushed her hair again. "I'm curious about you, too."

She edged slightly forward and turned toward him. Not to avoid his fingertips, which caused a pleasant little buzz of electricity to swarm around her head, but so she could make eye contact when she spoke. A lot could be gleaned from a man's expression, oftentimes more than from his words.

"The clinic is strictly treat and release. We keep a small supply of prescription medication on hand—most of it donated by medical salesmen. Our most serious procedure is usually setting a broken bone." She took a sip of coffee and savored its sweet, robust flavor. "The city contributes a small percentage toward the salary of our senior doctor. Since most of our patients have no health insurance, my job is to find enough financing to cover everything else. One way I do that is to stage events."

"How many doctors staff the clinic?"

"Just two. In order to work with us, our younger doctor temporarily gave up the opportunity to practice medicine in the Amazon. Luckily, the grant I wrote to cover a portion of his salary came through."

"You're good at it, aren't you?"

Molly blinked. "At what? Oh, you mean grant writing. My cousin helps me with that."

"No, I meant rounding up financing, separating people from their money." His smile and jovial tone didn't quite jibe with his words.

"I do okay."

"I'll bet a lot better than okay."

Molly shrugged. "Most people are very generous when approached for a good cause. I don't twist arms or anything, and I rarely just ask for donations. I always plan something interesting and fun. I much prefer that to grant writing, which is such a hard slog and so technical. Also, I never meet the people I address."

"How many grants do you have in the pipeline?

"I'm writing one to fund a dentist a few hours a week. That's the only way to squeeze it into the budget. Ours is tighter than Washington's at Valley Forge. I don't suppose you'd care to contribute?"

He draped one arm over the steering wheel and settled into a position that brought his right knee closer to hers. "I'm tempted, what with the expectation of . . . fun . . . and all." He tapped a long finger against the wheel. "What did you have in mind?"

His expression slid from sensual to carnal and hot enough to make her want to weld a Yale lock to her panties.

Mind? Molly's was bereft of thought. She could only shrug.

"Hmm. Well, it doesn't matter. As much as I'd love to contribute, right now I could use someone to write a grant for me."

He secured the lid on his coffee and set it in the drink holder behind the gear shift. Then he reached into the glove compartment—as noticeably tidy as the rest of the car—pulled out a pair of aviator sunglasses, and slipped them on. As if he didn't have enough sex appeal before, it did a steady climb up the heat index chart and almost blew the top off. Either Molly's coffee still steamed, or somehow Mr. Mancini had the kind of effect on her not even her last three boyfriends put together ever had. At least she'd never experienced a tingle in her toes *and* heels before. Hopefully, the little beads of moisture that broke out along her scalp would settle down once he activated the air conditioner.

He turned to face forward and eased the car into the slow stream of traffic. "Who pays your salary? If that sounds like prying, just tell me and I'll stop."

Molly sat back. Blessed air pumped through the car's interior vents, and her body returned to a more recognizable state. "No, that's okay." If she answered a couple of questions about herself, she might root out some further clue to his personality and any future plans he had for expansion. "I'm paid through the fundraisers I sponsor each year. That's really the main part of my job and mostly the only way to keep the clinic open."

"Do you live in the city, since your budget is so tight?"

"You mean have I found low-rent housing for myself?"

"Yeah, like the kind you're so sure doesn't exist."

Molly laughed. He was good. She'd like to ask what man cave he holed up in at night, but for now she'd satisfy his curiosity. "I get a big break on rent. I live on the top floor of my aunt's Victorian."

He turned onto Third Street and headed north toward Market. "Your aunt sounds very generous."

"She is. My mom died when I was eleven and shortly after, my dad and I moved into the flat. She helped raise me."

He hung a left, caught a light, and turned his head toward her. "You live with your father." There was a flatness to his tone, as if he thought her social development had skidded to a halt somewhere between puberty and the legal drinking age.

"My father remarried a few months after I graduated from college. He and my stepmother live in Palm Springs." She finished her coffee and looked around for a place to set the container.

"Here, give me that." He took hers and added it to his. They approached the corner, and he pulled over and glided to a stop alongside a narrow space that separated two parked cars. The driver's side window slid down.

God, was he going to throw them into the street?

He leaned outside the window and tossed the empties over a car trunk and into a trash receptacle. A perfect three pointer.

Oh, he was Mr. Neat all right. Or maybe he was just plain fussy. Which didn't seem to mesh with his rating four mochachino grandes. Everything about the man remained a mystery.

"So, you have a whole floor to yourself." He eased back into the stream of traffic. "That's great."

He was digging again. Why should he care if she shared the flat with a girlfriend or even God's answer to a maiden's prayer? It wasn't as if he planned to date her.

He shot across Market, turned left, and then veered right onto Franklin. Several minutes later, they were well into an area affordable only for people that earned six figures and up.

"Don't you think we're headed in the wrong direction?" If he hoped to prove his point, he'd never do it in this neighborhood. The area would still be far beyond the reach of his tenants, even if he broke down and offered the hundred thousand. "Rents around here start at a minimum of twenty-five hundred a month." She tapped a folder. "If you like, I can show you."

"Not necessary."

Molly shrugged.

He slowed for a red light. "I promised to stop by my folks' house for a few minutes."

"Oh."

"There was no way I could bail out. And, given the scheduling problems we'd faced, Sunday morning seemed the best possible time for us to get together. Trust me, a quick in and out. I hope you don't mind."

"I guess it's okay." She wondered what kind of people raised him. Did they have any inkling that the new condos their son was building required the displacement of tenants who couldn't afford to rent garage space in such an upscale area? Since she didn't expect to stop in with him, she'd never find out. Just as well. She didn't have the energy to condemn a whole clan. Dealing with their son took enough.

*

Nick cruised by his parents' house, the one he'd grown up in, a two-story white stucco with pitched red tile roof. As usual, there were no parking spaces anywhere near it. He circled the block and the adjacent streets. Nada. That left the one available spot in his parents' driveway. His aunt and uncle had parked to within inches of the garage set beneath the house. He could just about squeeze in behind the car with Arizona plates without blocking too much of the sidewalk. It shouldn't cause a problem since he and Molly weren't staying long.

Every time he dropped by the house he was reminded how lucky he was to grow up in a close-knit family. His father, an engineer with Bechtel, earned a good salary so his mother could stay home and take care of him and his siblings. Weekends had always been reserved for whatever activities he and his brother and sisters were involved in. Nick remembered all the ice hockey games they'd attended when he was in grade school and thought life revolved around a hockey stick and puck. The same thing had happened in high school, when his interests changed and he was never far from a baseball and bat. There'd been no time for sports during his four years of college at UC Berkeley, much to his regret. He'd become a spectator, which wasn't the same, but better than nothing.

Yeah, he was one of the lucky ones, never had to head home with a house key tied around his neck. There'd always been more than enough food on the table and money for a small allowance. He'd enjoyed the attention and camaraderie back then. He still enjoyed the camaraderie, but too bad his mother sometimes forgot he'd grown up and didn't need fussing any more.

He pulled in and turned off the motor. His mother gazed down at him through one of the living room windows. No, not just gazed at him, but at them—and then not so much at them, as at Molly. She wore the biggest smile since she'd suckered him into taking her friend's visiting daughter sightseeing and to dinner. That was six months ago. He'd brought a *girl* home to mama now. Why hadn't he seen that train wreck looming on the horizon. He yanked off his sunglasses and tossed them onto the dashboard. Then he slid out of the car and walked around to open Molly's door.

"Come on." He extended his hand. She glanced at it as if it dripped acid and made no move to offer him one of her soft, delicate ones.

"Come on what?"

He kept his eyes on Molly's face. That way he didn't have to deal with the drama that was surely playing out up in the house. Just to make sure he didn't glance in his mother's direction, he dropped his eyes to Molly's cream-colored blouse with the ruffled V that wasn't nearly deep enough to show off more of her light tan. He let his eyes wander over her short brown skirt to her legs. Long, bare, tan legs. She must have figured on a lot of walking, as she'd traded Friday's strappy sandals for flat-heeled shoes. It didn't matter. Even if she wore combat boots, Molly Hewitt was the kind of woman who encouraged a man's heartbeat to break into a sprint. There were extra ticks in his now. He bent and leaned in closer.

"Come on inside. I have to make an appearance. It's a brunch for the out-of-town relatives who were at my brother's wedding yesterday. I'll give them a quick hello and good-bye. Twenty minutes tops, and we're out of here."

"That's okay. I'll wait in the car."

A covert glance at the house told him that would work about as well as a hammer without a head. He'd never intended to leave her outside. Jeez, why couldn't he just show up with a woman who landed a one-two punch to his gut and made him hot but who wasn't "the One" or even sleeping with him?

"You'll make me look like an a-ho . . . a jerk if I leave you here." He plastered a smile across his face—the kind that rarely failed when beamed at a woman.

"You could have stopped by earlier."

"I didn't want you to stand around and wait in case I got hung up." He took the folders from her lap and dumped them on the floor. Then he caught hold of her arm. With his other hand, he unsnapped her seat belt, clasped her tightly around her waist, and almost lifted her out of the vehicle.

"Well, *okay*, if it's that important." She showed as much enthusiasm as if he were about to introduce her at a nudists' convention. And she hadn't even spotted his mother yet. She slung her purse over her shoulder, straightened the neckline of her blouse, and fiddled with her belt. The sun hit her hair and gave it an interesting copper sheen. He caught the subtle scent of strawberries.

"Don't worry. We won't stay long."

He led her along the flagstone path that paralleled the strip of garden that bordered the front of the house and up the short flight of concrete steps to the porch. His mother met them at the front door, her eyes hopeful. He hated to drive a nail through her heart, but he had to do it. Quickly.

"Hi, Mom." He bent and kissed her cheek. "This is Molly. We . . . "

"Oh, what a lovely name." His mother reached out and drew Molly into an embrace. "It's so wonderful to meet you." Her eyes swiveled to his and held them. She looked ecstatic. No, more than ecstatic. She looked fulfilled.

"Mom, we can only stay a few minutes." He peeled his mother's hands off Molly. "We . . . " He caught himself before he started to explain they needed to check out apartments and were pressed for time. That would have brought out the champagne for sure.

"You'll stay for something to eat."

He spread his fingers across Molly's upper back and felt fragile wing bones. His palm grazed her bra strap. For an insane moment, he wondered how she looked without either the bra or the blouse. Or without both. He killed the thought. A wonder like that could cost him a million dollars. He reminded himself to keep his mind on business and guided Molly into the house in his mother's wake.

A large white crepe paper bell hung from the middle of the living room ceiling. Matching streamers, anchored to the moldings atop the high walls, floated out from it and tented the off-white sofa, coffee table, and familiar brace of maroon velvet wing chairs. His mother made a shooing gesture toward him, then took Molly's hand.

"Go say hello to your father and your aunts and uncles. You won't see most of the relatives again until we have another wedding." Her look said she expected it to be his. "Or a death, God forbid." She touched the gold cross that dangled from a slim chain around her neck. She escorted Molly toward the archway that led into the dining room.

His mother saw only what she wanted to see. Forget reality. She had it wrong about Molly, and he didn't know how to set her straight. Maybe he'd call her tomorrow. That way he wouldn't have to look her in the eyes while he crushed yet another hope that he'd finally found his ideal woman.

Chapter 5

Molly cast a last glance at Nick as he disappeared into a circle of men. When one reached out and hugged him, he returned the gesture. He looked comfortable being hugged by another man. She liked that about him. Also that he brought her coffee and kept his promise to his family to drop in at the brunch. It showed a sign of warmth. Warmth showed promise vis-à-vis her crusade to wring more money out of him for his tenants. Also, there was the show of good citizenship when he'd disposed of the coffee containers properly. He smelled good, too. The scent of his aftershave was subtle but not so insipid that it was practically unnoticeable. It reminded her of the woods after a rain shower.

If he'd raise the ante in his buyout offer, she could possibly see him as something other than a greedy moneymaking machine. Just as important, he had to keep his wrecking ball away from the clinic. If she pressed hard enough, maybe she'd find a way to bring up any expansion plans before the day ended.

Nick shook hands and made the rounds of the other men. Someone said, "The baseball game is on in the family room," and the circle moved as one toward another part of the house, taking Nick along with it.

Molly followed Mrs. Mancini into the dining room. A large table covered with a white lace cloth and laden with chafing dishes sat against one wall. A white frosted cake, edged with a ring of icing and creamy pink roses, occupied the center of the table. A banner, adorned at each end with Cupids, spanned the wall and read "Congratulations Tom and Beth." The bride and groom, apparently. Sunlight spilled in from two large windows and turned some of the chandelier crystals into prisms, which made an already bright and cheerful room more so. Several well-dressed people clustered near the table; most sported white hair. The out-of-town relatives Nick mentioned earlier. Everyone held plates of food.

"This is Molly," Mrs. Mancini announced. "She came with Nicky."

Nicky. A name left over from childhood, no doubt. In spite of the warm greeting, she wondered if Mrs. Mancini suffered from separation issues. Maybe that was why he was still single. She decided he *was* single—otherwise, a wife would have met them at the door or been glued to him like an insect strip in the front seat of the car.

And she wasn't really *with* Nick, in the sense his mother seemed to have assumed, as much as he just dragged her along.

"So, Molly, do you live in the city?" Mrs. Mancini released Molly's hand and selected a white china plate. At least a quarter inch of gold circled the rim. She began to place food on it.

"Yes. I live on Haight Street, about a block and a half from Golden Gate Park."

"Haight Street. You don't remind me of a hippie." This was said in a tone completely devoid of censure. Although if this woman, impeccably dressed in aqua silk, ever saw Molly's Aunt Vi, whose hair hung in braids as if she channeled the old Willie Nelson, the tone might have changed considerably.

"No, I missed the hippie era." Though, Molly had the privilege to relive it most Friday nights when she went downstairs for the poker game.

Mrs. Mancini handed Molly the plate now heaped with food. "How long have you and Nicky known each other?"

Molly was about to tell her she and her son had met for the first time about forty-eight hours before when a woman who seemed about Nick's age and who resembled Mrs. Mancini right down to the dark hair and eyes and flawless complexion approached.

"Mom. Aunt Rita and Uncle Ed are ready to leave for the airport. They're looking for you."

"Must they go so soon?" Mrs. Mancini gave a wistful sigh. "Well, we don't want them to miss their flight." She patted Molly's arm. "You'll excuse me, dear. I'll leave you with Barbara for a few minutes."

"Oh, sure." Molly eyed the slice of quiche that nestled against two plump prawns and what resembled a crab meat stuffed mushroom. The seafood aroma along with that of egg and bacon made her almost swoon in anticipation. However, this was no time to shovel food into her mouth, not with introductions imminent.

Mrs. Mancini left the room. The young woman smiled at Molly. "Hello, I'm Nick's sister."

"Hi, I'm Molly." It wasn't possible to offer a hand, not when hers held a plate and fork.

"You're with Nick."

She gave a quick shake of her head. "Well, actually, I'm . . . ah . . . not really *with* Nick."

"Oh, I thought you came in together."

Molly hated it when, at least on limited occasions, she came across like a dork. She should have just said yes and let everyone draw their own conclusions. "We did . . . ah . . . come in together." She sneaked a forkful of quiche into her mouth.

"You look familiar." Barbara wrinkled her brow. "Were you at the wedding last night?"

Molly swallowed the quiche, the best she'd ever tasted. "The wedding? No."

"I didn't think so. My mother tried to persuade Nick to invite one of his old girlfriends, but when she rags on him like that, he runs the other way."

"A natural reflex." Molly nibbled on the vegetable frittata and thought about all the guys Dominique tried to push on her. Also, the bit about girlfriends confirmed it—he was single. Not that it mattered.

"So, how do you know Nick?"

Why couldn't they have met over a puddle? It would have been so much easier to explain.

"We . . . ah . . . met near where his condos are being built." *Or not.* "I supervise a clinic on the same street."

"That's it." Barbara snapped her fingers. "That's why you look familiar. Your picture was in the Bay Area section of the *Chronicle* about two or three months ago. You auctioned off a five-hundred-dollar bottle of wine. That's something not easy to forget. It was to raise money for a clinic."

"Actually, it was a raffle. The wine was donated along with a number of other expensive bottles. The event I put together was a wine tasting. I'm doing an auction, though, this Thursday evening. I usually do four events a year." Molly speared a plump strawberry with her fork and bit into it. She wondered if she and Nick would stay long enough to sample the cake. She had a sudden craving for sweet, fluffy icing.

"That sounds like fun. Where will you hold it? Can anyone attend?"

Molly didn't have the heart to say her fundraisers were by invitation only and limited to no more than one hundred. That sounded snobby. She could always squeeze in an extra person.

"If you're interested, I'll leave your name at the door. The auction is at the Grill House on Van Ness. The owners volunteered the use of the upstairs party room. We'll start around eight. I have an extra list of donations somewhere for you to browse." She set her plate on the sideboard and rummaged through her purse and found a copy. She handed it to Barbara who made a quick perusal. Molly picked up her plate and rewarded herself with another bite of quiche.

Barbara folded the list and slipped it into her skirt pocket. "Thanks. I've never been to an auction. I'm looking forward to it."

Molly managed to stick a cold asparagus tip in her mouth when a boy of about ten burst into the dining room. He slowed down as he skidded toward her.

"Are you with my uncle Nick?"

This was weird. It wouldn't surprise her if next thing, someone asked where she was registered and if she'd picked out her china pattern.

"Yes, she is." Barbara smoothed back the boy's auburn hair and adjusted the collar of his white dress shirt in what seemed like a motherly gesture. "Speaking of which . . . here comes the Martian twin now."

Nick entered the room, and Molly could have sworn the light rose in intensity. He kissed his sister on the cheek. "Don't listen to her. She's called me a space monster ever since the day I played Commando with her dolls."

Commando.

"You cut off all their hair." Barbara brought her hand up like she wanted to swat him.

Nick raised both of his as if to ward off an impending blow. "You can't charge into battle with flowing locks. If you wanted to join the Commandos, you had to surrender your hair." He laughed in that deep, masculine way but with an ease of a man who rarely had to force it. "Right, Joey?"

"Right, Uncle Nick." The kid performed a quick karate chopping motion.

"You're twins." Upon closer inspection, Molly saw the resemblance. Only Barbara seemed to possess a certain kind of gentleness Nick distinctly lacked. She was sweet, sticky lollipops and ruffled pinafores. He came across more like a chainsaw and boxing gloves.

"I'm four minutes older."

His sister patted him on the shoulder. "That made you top dog."

"Oh yeah, all that meant was I had to jump in the middle of everyone's squabbles and whip the rest of you guys into shape."

The Commando in action. Molly wondered if he planned to whip her into shape once they started apartment hunting.

Barbara smiled and nodded as if in acknowledgment of the role he played in their childhood. "Do you have any brothers, Molly?"

"No."

"Sisters?"

She shook her head.

"That's too bad. In spite of how we sound, we're all pretty close. Maybe next time you come around you'll meet my younger sister. As usual, she's late."

Next time? Molly didn't think so.

"My other brother is on his honeymoon. He's the normal one." She gave Nick a tap on the arm that seemed to suggest it was time he married and went on one, too.

A lopsided frown pinched his face as if he heard that one too often. He took Molly's plate and set it on the deep ledge of a breakfront. "Listen, Barbara, we have to leave. Did you see Mom?"

"I think she went outside to say good-bye to Uncle Ed and Aunt Rita."

He put his hand on Molly's shoulder. Top dog marking his territory? Not likely. It couldn't have been more innocent, but in everyone's eyes, it probably came across as if she were invited to brunch as his date. Usually, when a man she hardly knew touched her, she backed away. So she couldn't account for her shoes becoming Krazy-Glued to Mrs. Mancini's deep green plush carpet or explain the aura of heat that seemed to envelop her.

As they headed out of the dining room, she reminded Barbara about the auction.

"What auction?" Nick asked.

Barbara pulled out the slip of paper detailing the items up for bid. "It's Molly's fundraiser. She's auctioning off fancy dinners, a balloon ride in the Napa Valley, vacations in Carmel, and seats to the Giants opening game next spring." She handed Nick the list and pointed to the baseball item. "If you change your sinful ways, I'll bid on that one for you." She turned to Molly. "Nick is a rabid sports fan, especially the Giants. He never misses opening day." She plucked the list out of her brother's hand.

Nick steered Molly to the front door. They stepped outside

onto a small brick and concrete porch where Mrs. Mancini waved at a couple as they pulled away in a taxi. He dropped his hand the moment his mother turned their way. Molly didn't blame him. Not with all the matrimony that floated in the air.

"Mom, we've gotta go."

Mrs. Mancini stepped over to Molly and clasped both her hands. "So soon? Did you have enough to eat?"

"I had more than enough. Thank you." Although Molly was sorry no one cut the cake. "Everything was delicious."

Mrs. Mancini shrugged. "It was catered. They did their best." She released Molly's hands and glanced briefly at her son. "Have Nicky bring you over for a home-cooked dinner sometime."

He pressed his lips together and gave his mother an enigmatic smile. Whatever she expected—yes, maybe, or when hell turned out to be the only place to achieve Nirvana—she received no response from him.

"Do you like seafood, dear?" Apparently not a woman often thwarted, Mrs. Mancini turned a beatific smile on Molly.

"I love it."

"Good. Then you two decide when, and Nicky will let me know the date."

Separation issues? *Au contraire.*

The exchange seemed almost surreal with this lovely woman inviting her to dinner. Nicky, whose bank account she planned to plunder, gave a good imitation of a man who did everything possible to stave off cardiac arrest. Too bad. She liked his mother and would love to sit down with her and maybe even the whole Mancini gang and dig into a big crab or lobster feed or whatever the woman had in mind. That was never going to happen, though. As soon as they were back in the car and out of this high-cost area, Molly expected to prove to her son nothing talked like money. Especially his paltry twenty-five thousand. It not only didn't talk, it barely squeaked.

Chapter 6

"Thanks for coming inside with me. I hope it wasn't a hassle." As soon as they settled in the car, Nick engaged the motor.

Molly retrieved her folders off the floor and fastened her seat belt. "Not at all. I love brunch food whether catered or otherwise. It was great. I enjoyed meeting your sister and your mom, too, of course."

"My mother has a tendency to overdo the hostess thing when someone new comes over to the house." He shoved on his sunglasses and buckled his seat belt then backed out of the driveway and onto the street. "I hope she didn't embarrass you."

Molly figured his explanation was a subtle way to warn her not to take his mother's invitation to the fish fry seriously.

"I'm never embarrassed when someone exhibits warmth. The world would be a much better place if people showed more of it."

"You mean me?" He whipped a right and headed down Chestnut.

"I meant in general."

"Well, generally speaking, no one's ever accused me of a cold nature. Just the opposite." He shot her a quick glance and a smile that contained enough wattage to light up a mineshaft.

She decided it best for now not to bring up his tenants. Maybe by the end of the day he'd live up to his exalted opinion of himself.

As they approached the corner of Chestnut and Gough, the light turned from green to yellow. He floored the gas pedal and roared across the intersection. Molly's head jerked back and her purse and folders flew off her lap. She grabbed the armrest anchored to the passenger door and braced her other hand against the dashboard.

Nick's arm shot in front of her and lightly grazed her breasts. His palm cupped her far shoulder and pinned her to the back of the seat.

"Sorry." He eased up on the gas. "Trying to beat the yellow is a bad habit of mine. I hate it when the light changes just when you hit the corner." He let go of her and clamped his hand back onto the steering wheel.

Molly pushed a lock of hair out of her eye.

"Do you always run the yellow?"

"Not always. Well, too much of the time. I hold back, though, if it seems anyone's about to enter the intersection."

"Well, thanks for the consideration."

"Don't worry. You're safe with me."

Safe? Molly had her doubts, and it had little to do with traffic. Except that he played hardball with his tenants and posed a possible threat to the clinic, she couldn't find a single thing wrong with him.

"I'll bet you collect a lot of tickets."

He shrugged. "I do my share to keep the city solvent."

"You must be at the head of the class in traffic school."

"I do that over the Internet. I have it down to thirty-eight minutes."

Molly straightened her blouse. The heat from his palm had come right through the silk fabric and still lingered on her skin. He had large hands. She tried to remember if the size of a man's hands went along with something more intimate. Or was it big feet? She had to force her eyes to stare straight ahead and not take a detour where they had no business.

She gathered up her purse and the materials scattered around her feet. With everything back in her lap, she opened a folder and glanced at a sheet that contained a listing of apartment rentals. Earlier, she'd circled three that fell within the thousand to eleven-hundred-dollars-a-month range. Studio apartments probably little bigger than a typical one-car garage. None in a particularly desirable area, either. What else could you expect in San Francisco for such a low price? Those apartments were still way out of range for Mrs. Z and the other tenants, which should more than prove her point to Nick.

"Maybe we ought to set some ground rules, like which areas to avoid. We won't waste each other's time that way."

"Ground rules." He hunched over the wheel. "You mean like a lot of don'ts." His vibe changed from pleasant to the kind that usually came her way when she accidentally cut someone off in traffic. A vibe that clashed with the rampant sex appeal that oozed from his pores. "Then, again, you're probably right. Yeah. Why don't you lay out a few?"

Talk about a quick change in attitude. Could she have misjudged him all along? She didn't think so but appreciated his effort to appear agreeable.

"Okay. We should only consider apartments within a one to two block distance of a supermarket and close to public transportation. Mrs. Z told me none of your tenants own a car." Molly worried about them traveling to the clinic for medical attention. Forget taxis. They'd have to hop on a bus even if they were minutes away from a heart attack or ready to upchuck last night's dinner. "Forget skid row or any area screaming for a cop on every corner." Contrary to Dominique's advice, she'd decided to avoid the Tenderloin. "Your tenants need to know the area is safe."

He gave her a quick glance. "Do you think I'd put them at risk?"

Did she? He'd chopped the hair off his sister's dolls . . . Okay, so he'd been a kid playing Commando. She wondered if he still played it. If so, she hoped it wasn't with people's lives.

He paused at a stop sign, pulled off his sunglasses, and tossed them onto the dashboard. He leaned toward her. "Well, is that what you think?" His dark eyes turned into twin thunderclouds.

"I can't make that judgment." *Not yet.* Was he ever touchy.

"Then let me make it for you. I'm one of the good guys." He managed to sound hurt and defensive, like her opinion of him mattered. "Really. I am. Trust me." The thunderclouds scattered under a sunny smile.

"Well . . . okay." He still had to prove it.

"I can't think of any law that requires me to offer a buyout. There are plenty of property owners who serve eviction notices with the understanding their tenants either move in the time allotted or find their belongings in the street. I'd never do something so callous. Certainly not to that down-on-their-luck bunch who live in my building. With the buyout offer, we can all come out winners."

Molly preferred his smile to a frown, so she didn't contradict him. Later, while they viewed some dump, she'd remind him of recent history. Since the economy had nosedived straight into the toilet, his buyout sucked.

As they left the Marina District behind, the streets grew grittier. Leafy trees gave way to telephone poles strung with exposed wire. A city bus lumbered by, the back panel tagged with graffiti. A diverse cross section of people—some well-heeled, others not—ambled along the sidewalks. Nick pulled the car into a No Parking zone and killed the motor. He pointed to a building diagonally across the street.

"I told the owner we'd meet him outside at eleven thirty." He checked his watch. "We're a few minutes early."

Molly leaned forward to peer around Nick and gazed out the driver's side window. Rising four stories, the building's brick façade looked in need of an immediate power wash. Shades were drawn in some of the windows. Cheap curtains framed smudged glass in the remaining ones. Someone in a ground floor apartment had balanced a couple of clay flowerpots on a window ledge. A few tired-looking sprigs of green peeked up over the rims. The front door looked as if you needed a battering ram to enter the premises.

"Is that a transient hotel?"

"No."

"Are you sure?"

"Yes. It's an apartment building."

"It looks shabby."

"What? I suppose *my* building reminds you of the Fairmont."

She caught another whiff of his aftershave. Damn if it wasn't the exact one that came as a sample sheet in the latest issue of *Cosmo*. Rugged, yet seductive, or so the ad claimed. Rightly so. She wondered if a woman had bought it for him in hopes he'd put that heady scent to work on her. If it weren't for their million-dollar disagreement, Molly might consider taking a turn on the receiving end. He'd have to drop the attitude and really prove he was one of the good guys, though. What were the chances he'd morph into a prince? She hoped not as unlikely as being dealt a royal flush *sans* wild cards.

Mostly commercial buildings lined the block. A deli occupied one corner, a bar and launderette the other two. The ubiquitous hole-in the-wall Chinese restaurant clung to the fourth.

"How did you find this place?" She sat back and opened one of her folders and did a quick scan of the ads to see if she'd highlighted the address.

"A guy who works on my condo project touted me onto it. He lives here. Said he pays in the low seven hundreds."

A construction guy. Well, it never hurt to have a little muscle on the premises. The low seven hundreds? He must hole up in a jail cell-sized room with a hotplate, mini fridge, and bathroom privileges down the hall. If true, it ought to blow a hole in the Mancini Proclamation.

Nick angled his body into the corner created by the driver's seat and door. The expression that settled across his features said the attitude was out and the sex appeal was back in. He raked a dark lock of hair away from his forehead while his eyes did a quick survey of her body.

"So how does a woman like you wind up running a not-for-profit clinic?"

A woman like *who*? And what was the "wind up" supposed to mean? "The clinic was the mayor's idea. He broached it at a meeting two and a half years ago when I worked for the city in social services. There weren't any facilities in the area for people to seek medical help. The nearest hospital, San Francisco General, is miles away. Anyway, the emergency rooms are always jammed. I wasn't sure if he was serious, but without thinking it through, I jumped up and said I could get something like that off the ground and keep it operational."

"Yeah, I figured you for a do-gooder."

The way he said it made her feel like a Mother Teresa clone. Was that how he pigeonholed her? Sexless and on the fast track to sainthood?

She frowned. "There are worse things than trying to make a difference in peoples' lives."

"I agree. Absolutely. Like you said, the world would be a better place . . . " He gave her a lopsided grin that pulled one edge of his mouth up. His strong, chiseled features relaxed. His eyes gazed into hers with a kind of warmth she hadn't noticed earlier.

Molly's annoyance crumbled like a slice of month-old bread. She smiled back.

"I didn't mean to interrupt you. That's another bad habit of mine."

She supposed "bad" pretty much covered all his habits. Except maybe sex. She suspected he was very good in the sack.

Although the air conditioner was off for less than five minutes, heat began to climb inside the car. She blamed N MAN 1 and not Mother Nature.

"You were telling me about the clinic. How you became involved with it."

"There's not much more to tell. I interviewed with the deputy mayor who liked my proposal on how I'd operate the facility and keep it funded. So he set up an appointment for me with the mayor."

"What did you tell the mayor?"

"Pretty much the same as his deputy. Also, I made it clear I refused to spend half my time cutting through all the bureaucratic crap that came with working with another city agency. Or some such words." She'd also told His Honor she was a self-starter and good at handling unexpected situations. She'd praised the mayor for his understanding of the needs of the city's less fortunate and his efforts to do something constructive. She decided not to let on to Nick about the compliment, though. He'd probably accuse her of kissing the mayor's *derriere*. "I knew how to keep the clinic on track. I expected some oversight, but I work best with a minimum of interference. The mayor had no problem with my conditions."

"They must love you at City Hall."

"They should. I don't make many demands on them."

"You saved those for me." He grinned and his sex appeal—the kind that could have a woman naked in less time than it took to say "strip, baby"—climbed into the active land mine zone.

"You find me demanding?" Molly resisted the temptation to fan herself with a file folder.

"That sounds a little strong. Let's just say—determined."

The very word she'd used to describe him to her Aunt Vi.

He uncrossed his arms. One settled along the upper curve of the steering wheel, the other across his seat back. Corded muscles flexed under the sleeves of his T-shirt. Ditto where the cotton fabric stretched across his chest. The car didn't seem ample enough to contain his broad shoulders and long-legged, well-proportioned frame. His gaze held hers, and she didn't need Dominique's Ouija board to prove that, under other circumstances, she could become hardcore attracted to him.

"What's wrong with determination?" she said.

"Nothing, if it isn't taken to extremes."

His upper and lower lips were equally full. Like the Michelangelo sculpture of David. The one with what seemed like a larger than life hand. She couldn't remember how far the sculptor went with the shepherd's other parts.

"Do you?" she asked.

"Do I what?"

"Take things to extremes?"

"Sometimes. Especially in my work."

At the mention of work, his eyes became animated like a chocoholic's might when about to dig into a taxi-sized Hershey bar.

"How did you get into building condos, if you don't mind my asking?"

"It was a natural progression."

"Starting when?"

"It started when I was a kid. My folks stored some lumber in the basement. One day I dragged it outside into the backyard. I built a fort—worked at it every day after school and on weekends."

Of course. What good was a Commando without a fort?

"I always liked using my hands."

Her gaze flicked to his long fingers. They appeared strong enough to wrestle with a steel beam. Probably, they could be gentle enough, too, with a woman.

"It still amazes my parents and just about everyone who knows me that I traded in a business degree for a hard hat and a tool belt. I tried the office route for two years and found it suffocating. I liked the freedom of working out in the open." He shrugged. "I still like to crawl around a building site, but creating new projects excites me much more these days."

Molly thought about her little cubbyhole of an office. Most of the time she was so busy, she never noticed the limited proportions. She couldn't imagine Nick stuck in a room even twice as big in size.

"Obviously, you enjoy building. How else do you become a condo king?"

His mouth opened and a frown pulled at his brows. "Where did you get that from?"

"The *Chronicle*. Last month, an article outlined how building green caught on really big in the city and ways in which it protects the environment. Your name was mentioned a couple of times. It's an interesting concept. I read recently where Pacific Gas and

Electric has started a drive to erase our carbon footprints."

"Going green is the future. Not just in San Francisco. I intend to incorporate whatever aspects are available to use in my current project. The one you'd like to torpedo." He grinned as if a sunny smile could take away the sting.

She let it pass. "What aspects?"

"The plan is to collect rain water for use in the air-conditioning system, use recycled wood and coated glass to keep heat in and solar radiation out. It's more expensive but worth every cent in the end. It's not only environmentally friendly, it cuts down on monthly bills for the prospective buyers. Don't get me started on any aspects of building green, though. It's one of my passions, and I tend to go on too long. Condo king is an exaggeration. It's nothing I aspire to, anyway. My main goal isn't making money."

"No?"

"My goal is to find out what people want and need and then provide it. I never gouge the tenants on my rental properties. I keep the rents affordable, rarely raise them, and hardly ever lose a tenant. The city has changed and, in many ways, for the better. I just want to take a small part and create a more enriching future for people who choose to live here. I'd like to make urban living a little more pleasant and a lot more available."

The man certainly had a passion, not only for sparing the environment, but for his work. Now if he could only extend that to Mrs. Z and the other occupants of his apartment building.

"What about your tenants? They can't afford condos."

"True. That's why we're on the prowl today. To find out what's affordable."

"Exactly. Since we're on the subject of what is or isn't affordable, there's a rumor floating around on the block . . ."

"There is? Hmm. For some reason, I never would have taken you for a woman who put much stock in rumors."

"Well, generally, I don't."

"Or spreading them."

"I never do."

"Good. Neither do I." He checked his watch. "It's almost eleven thirty. Maybe we should wait across the street. I'd hate to miss this guy. He said he owns a couple of other buildings, too. If he has a few more vacancies, it could turn into a big plus. We can network."

The way he so effectively quashed her mention of a rumor led Molly to believe it contained some truth. For sure, she'd better find a way to bring it up again later.

At the first break in traffic, Nick exited on the street side. Molly slung her purse strap over her shoulder, put her folders on the floor mat, and opened the passenger door. By the time she swung her legs out Nick stood at the curb and offered a hand. His fingers grasped hers and he gave a gentle tug that brought her up and out of her seat and into his arms. One arm, anyway, since he still clutched her hand. They stood like that for what seemed like an unnecessary length of time. Close enough, too, for the tingle to shoot back into her heels. It marched up her legs and, somehow, she found the good sense to quash it at her knees.

Finally, he stepped back and released her.

Her heels screamed for additional gratification, and she dug them into the sidewalk.

He ignored the crosswalk at the corner. When there was a lull in traffic, he took her arm and jaywalked her quickly to the opposite side of the street. When they arrived at the apartment building, he led her into a narrow setback formed by the front door and two shallow walls. Chips in the dark paint exposed an undercoat of gray. Candy wrappers, an empty soda can, and assorted flyers and newspaper flotsam littered the floor.

"Listen, I think there's something I better tell you before this guy shows up."

The words, coupled with the tone of his voice, put her internal radar on alert. "What's that?"

"He . . . ah . . . " He bit down on the inside of his lower lip and appeared to wince.

"Yes?"

He came up slightly onto the balls of his feet, then set his heels down. "He thinks we're married."

"What?" Dim light suffused the doorway, and she gazed up at him through a web of shadows. "How did he get such a weird idea?"

"When I phoned him, he asked if only I was interested in the apartment, or if I planned to move in with a wife. Before I had a chance to think, I said I didn't have a wife. Then I remembered you."

"Me?"

"Yeah, we'd be checking it out together. After I screwed up the 'no wife' bit, I wasn't sure how to explain you."

"Was an explanation necessary?"

"I thought you might think so."

"In that case, you could have told him I was your sister."

He cocked his head, pressed his lips together, and frowned.

"Okay, he wouldn't believe we were related."

"Not even for a second." His featured relaxed, and he shrugged and smiled.

"Why didn't you say you were bringing a friend?"

"Listen, I didn't have a lot of time to come up with anything creative. I thought it was important to protect you."

"Really? How?"

"I didn't want to give him the impression you were a . . . a shack up."

"A shack up?"

"Look. Landlords aren't stupid. They want to know how many people will occupy their units. Once he saw us, he'd assume we were both moving in. I thought you'd be more comfortable showing up with a man you'd only just met—me—if the guy thought we were married instead of . . . you know . . . living together. You having worked in social services and running a clinic, I wasn't sure about your views on, eh, shacking up. So I said we'd just gotten back from the honeymoon, it was all so new I forgot for a second we were married." Innocence flickered behind his eyes. His bottom lip curved down as if in apology.

Molly leaned against the slots cut into the metal plate that protected the mailboxes. He was right about the shacking up part being a bad fit. Three boyfriends back, she'd almost been pressured into it. When she'd said no, the boyfriend took a hike.

"Maybe I made a mistake. If the owner mentions anything, I'll say he must have misunderstood."

"Great, and then I'm left with being your shack up and getting leered at by some oily slumlord."

"Look, I'm sorry I goofed. But the guy wants to rent this apartment. He'll know better than to leer. Why would you assume he's a slumlord?"

"Well, just look at this place."

Nick rubbed the back of his neck. "Would you rather wait in the car?"

"No."

"Don't you trust me?"

She let him glean the answer from her expression.

"Okay. Lack of trust noted." He checked his watch. "It's your call. You better make it quick. Either we took a trip to the altar or we've slept together without the benefit of marriage." Molly felt her eyes roll up in her head. Any farther and there was a chance she could have examined her own brain. She groaned. "Maybe we should scratch this one."

"It's too late."

"We could check out some of the possibilities I've come across." She took a step toward the sidewalk.

He grabbed her elbow and reeled her back in. "Are you always so stubborn?" Impatience flared in his eyes.

"No. Well, almost never."

"Look, don't you think for, maybe, twenty minutes you could act married?"

"You mean to an almost perfect stranger?"

He brushed a corkscrew curl off her cheek and tucked it behind her ear. "I don't consider myself a stranger. Or perfect."

That was for sure.

His impatience died under a self-effacing grin.

"I'm anything but an accomplished actress. In third grade, I played a gumdrop in the class production of *Hansel and Gretel*."

He braced his hand against the wall directly above her shoulder and leaned in. "That doesn't matter. I'll take the lead."

"Oh, you know how? Why? Are you married?"

He shook his head. "No. Never came close. You?"

"No."

"You've considered it, though. Am I right?"

Molly frowned and shook her head. What did he care if she'd had one foot at the marriage altar?

He let go of the wall and took both her hands in his. He laced his fingers through hers and held her arms steady at her sides. The touch of his skin against hers sent goose bumps along her arms and a different kind of shiver down her back, the kind that resulted from contact with a gorgeous hunk of a man. Wouldn't you know it? In this case, he was the wrong hunk of a man.

"We can pull this off," he said.

She tried to free her hands, but he held them captive. "I have many doubts. As in too many."

"What we need is a practice run." Humor lurked behind his irises.

"Practice?"

"Sure. To make it convincing, like we've been together a while, like we've been . . . close . . . you know, intimate. Remember the honeymoon?"

She wondered if he'd smoked something funny at his parents' house. Except everyone there looked like they'd just flown in from a papal convention.

"Are you making this up?"

His soft laugh filled the small enclosure. "Sweetie, I wish I were. But I'm not, so let's cement the deal." The humor left his eyes, and his mouth descended on hers.

Molly made a concerted effort to free her hands, even as she parted her lips. His mouth felt warm against hers, and the way he kissed showed he was not at all self-conscious about doing it practically in public. Then he let go of her hands and slid his up her sides. That sent a flutter into her stomach. She shivered as his long fingers ranged over her back and onto her shoulders. Right about now her "stop" button should have screamed like an alarm gone berserk, but it jammed just about the time he got her lips farther apart and slipped in the tip of his tongue. The remnants of something sweet lingered. Pepsi, maybe. He probably drank some at brunch.

Her skin prickled as his fingertips slid along her neck and through her hair. He cradled her head in a gentle grip, one she probably could have squirmed away from if she wanted to, but she didn't want to. Heat slid down her chest and into her stomach and folded into a tiny corner where she stored those kinds of stimuli.

Molly placed her palms against his chest. Muscles bunched under his T-shirt and proved steely-hard beneath her probing fingers. His mouth moved against hers, and she gave in totally to being possessed. His breath touched her cheek, hot and steady. His tongue slid against hers and sent her body heat into a torrid zone that lately had existed only in her imagination. Talk about adding a few extra z's to sizzle. This was insane. She was standing here practically in full view and kissing an almost total stranger and letting him do whatever he wanted with his hands, lips, and tongue. From her scalp to her toes, Nick lit her fire. If he didn't quit soon, all he'd find was a small pile of ash where she once stood. A moan come from deep inside her. When had she become such an easy target?

He ended the kiss. Her eyes were Elmer's glued to his. Her lips felt like they were pumped full of some sort of puffy stuff.

"See, you're a better actress than you thought." The honey-smooth seduction in his tone turned her breathing into an Olympic-sized operation.

His breath continued to warm her cheek and the glow didn't stop anywhere near there. It moved in waves throughout her body. She touched her upper lip with the tip of her tongue and almost expected a puff of steam to billow from the spot.

Had she gone along so as not to cause a scene? She didn't think so. Not with the depth of emotion she'd put into the kiss. She never even kissed on a first date, which she didn't consider prudish, but smart—just in case the guy didn't call again. So why had she locked lips with Nick Mancini like they were two dates short of being anointed a couple? What kind of woman did that? The words "needy" and "dumb" came to mind. And since *he'd* ended the kiss, she added "vulnerable" and "weak."

She tore her gaze away from Nick's. She figured him for a player. Why else would he have kissed her like that without a good reason, without *any* reason except he wanted to? Molly hated to think what might have happened if he'd tried to get more intimate. Also, forget protecting her reputation or any of his other baloney about putting up a good front for the landlord vis-à-vis their supposed marriage. *Marriage.* As if it weren't bad enough that she'd enjoyed the kiss, and wouldn't have objected to a longer one, he *knew* she'd liked it.

Oh, he was a player all right. Which posed the next question: Where would she find the fortitude to kick him off limits if he wanted to play with her again?

Chapter 7

"You must be the Mancinis."

Nick angled his head toward the sidewalk. A man of average height, weight, and skin tone stood in the doorway. No gangster-sized cigar sticking out of his mouth, or rumpled suit. He spoke in a clear, businesslike tone. Although the building needed repairs, he didn't put this guy together with Molly's conception of a "slumlord."

"Yeah. Nick Mancini. I spoke with you yesterday on the phone." He extended his hand. "This is Molly."

"Mrs. Mancini. Pleasure to meet you." The landlord ignored Nick and steered an outstretched hand in Molly's direction.

She barely managed a nod, no less a handshake. Her lack of enthusiasm didn't seem to faze the landlord who gave her a slow up and down body search with his eyes. Nick stepped in between them and cut off the man's view just as it began to descend again from the V in Molly's blouse. Still, who was he to cast blame? He'd taken a little body inventory of her, too, along with the liberty of a kiss. At least he never leered.

He cut a sideways glance at her. She still had something of a bedazzled look in her eyes, as if she'd engaged in more than just a one minute kiss. A kiss she'd clearly enjoyed. Her hair, recently home to his fingers, had a bed-head look, which halfway answered the question about any post-coital coif. Her lips remained parted, and her breathing showed continued signs of some pumped-up heart action. A few minutes before, he'd experienced a little pumped-up action in the area south of his belt, when she'd sucked his tongue. On second thought, maybe she hadn't. Anyway, her response surprised him. She could have given him a knee in the groin. Instead, he'd gotten some passion from her.

Oh, yeah. Little Miss Stubborn went up against Mr. Persuasion, and the result couldn't have been more satisfying. It went something like quarterbacking a Niners' game. He'd not only kept possession of the ball but ran it forty yards for a touchdown. Or at least he'd kicked a field goal. Whichever. It held promise for when they finished the apartment search. After she admitted he was right about affordable housing, they'd go someplace quiet and negotiate the hundred grand. Worst-case scenario, he'd bump his end up to twenty-eight five. Then maybe after dinner they'd snuggle in his car outside her aunt's Victorian, and he'd find out if Molly ever got hot enough to suck a guy's tongue. Like he was hot right now at the thought of it.

"The elevator's toward the rear." The landlord reached into his pants pocket and produced a ring of keys. He unlocked the front door and led the way into a small dim space that masqueraded as a lobby. Weak light escaped from a pair of cheap sconces anchored to the wall. Paint peeled in a long swath off a portion of the ceiling. The air smelled dank. Molly, who had finally come out of her near trance, shot him a glare that said she planned to memorize every rotten feature and prepare a list of minuses to throw at him later.

They followed a narrow hallway. The linoleum underfoot buckled in spots, which made navigation somewhat tricky. Nick took hold of Molly's arm. Her skin was as smooth as stone washed by endless sprays of sea spume. After a shower, she probably poured on body lotion. Right away he pictured her naked, which, of all images, was the wrong one to invoke. He refocused his attention on the hallway and dropped his hand.

"Watch your step." The landlord held the elevator door open.

Nick entered the confining cage behind Molly. Weak light seeped through a crack in the glass inset above his head. Some literary aspirant left his mark in crayon on the wall, singing the praises of Sonja with the big knockers and other body parts that shocked even him. He turned Molly a few degrees toward the opposite wall. He hoped she hadn't noticed it. He'd come in for a lecture that anything less than a jackpot-sized payoff would doom his tenants to an obscenity-laced cave.

"I wasn't sure what you folks had in mind." The landlord punched a button and the elevator began a shaky ascent. "Like I told you, I have a couple of vacancies, both one bedrooms. The apartment in the rear is quieter, but there's not much to look at, just the back of another building. It's more private, though. Since you're newlyweds, you two might appreciate some privacy."

"It sounds exactly like what we hoped to find, isn't that right, sweetheart?"

Molly rolled her eyes and gave her head a shake. The curls danced like a burnished halo. He thought back to the kiss. Damn if that halo hadn't crash landed. He held the key right in his hand to easing his tenants out and his condos built. Yeah, the kiss was the right move. He hadn't even planned it, which said a lot for spontaneity. She was a sun-ripened peach, ready for plucking.

"The front unit has a nice view of the street, but it's noisy."

Nick gave Molly a self-satisfied nod. "A little noise shouldn't cause a problem for us. What do you think, darling?"

"I'm sure it's a regular Eden." The face Molly made at him brought her eyes to within a hair's-breadth of crossing.

The elevator jolted to a stop. Molly lost her footing and made a grab for Nick's T-shirt. He clamped his palms onto her hips—for the sake of balance—and felt bone under a feminine swell of flesh. Since she didn't let go right away, neither did he. Her eyes stayed focused on his chest. He preferred to think she enjoyed his touch, rather than she worried the elevator might take an unscheduled dive into the cellar. He had no complaints either way. Just as long as he remembered the hands that clutched his shirt were the same ones that declared open season on his wallet.

The elevator door slid open with a groan. Nick stood back to let Molly exit first. As she stepped into the hallway, the sway of her hips earned her another leer from the landlord. Nick considered decking the guy. Except a fist to the jaw would lead to a lawsuit, and he didn't need another hand in his pocket. He'd pull the man aside and give him a verbal one-two punch if he tried it again. At six feet two, weighing in at one ninety, he knew he could appear intimidating.

Low wattage bulbs burned in sconces along the hallway, making it as dimly lit as the ground floor. When they arrived at apartment 3D, the owner pushed a key into the lock and opened the door. A rancid odor immediately escaped. Holy hell. Nick shot a glance at Molly who crinkled her nose. He'd have to deal with the smell later, too.

"Come on in, folks."

Once inside, Nick glanced around but couldn't find much "in" in the cramped space. The whole apartment couldn't measure more than five hundred square feet.

"Someone must have left raw meat on the counter for at least a week." Molly's voice wafted from behind him.

"No, no. The unit's been empty for over a month. We just need to let in some air." The owner stepped to one of a pair of windows that overlooked the street and cranked a lever. As he forced the metal casement out, traffic noise flooded in.

Molly, who'd moved into the center of the room, couldn't have looked more out of place in this dump. Nick wanted to take her hand, scrap the crummy elevator, and hustle her down three flights of fire stairs to his car. From there he'd head straight to Fisherman's Wharf where they'd stroll around like tourists and eat fresh crab and prawns out of paper cones. He gave the idea serious thought, then quashed the impulse. First, he had to prove his point: Low rent units existed in San Francisco.

The temperature inside the apartment must have been close to ninety degrees. Molly lifted the back of her hair with one hand. With the other, she peeled the collar of her blouse off her neck and exposed skin that glowed with a pink flush. Nick knew better than to blow cool air right below where she held up a fistful of russet curls. Curls he'd discovered were infused with the scent of strawberries. Curls that invited him to plow his hands through right now.

"The apartment could use fresh paint." A few steps took Molly to the kitchen doorway. She peeked into the miniscule space beyond. "Also, someone needs to scrub the stove or, better yet, junk it." She turned away and let her hair fall back into place. "The whole apartment needs new carpets, and those windows . . . " She shrugged and her nose twitched.

She couldn't have said it any clearer. The place was a hellhole. Still, Nick might be able to convince her that, if spruced up, it could become livable. Even better, at a little over seven hundred a month, clones must exist in other parts of the city. They could discuss it over lunch at the Wharf. His confidence rose.

"This here's the bedroom." The landlord pushed open a door and entered a room little bigger than a tool shed. He began to wrestle with the lone window. He banged on the wooden frame and coaxed it up.

Nick sidestepped around Molly and took up a position in the doorway, which blocked the entrance. No way would he allow this guy—okay, slumlord—to maneuver her into a room with the word "bed" attached to it. She moved close behind him and he glanced at her over his shoulder. She stood on her tiptoes, which brought the top of her head even with his ear. Her breath brushed the side of his neck. While she checked out the room, he checked out the sudden increase in his heart rate.

"I'd say *bedroom* is a misnomer, wouldn't you?" she whispered.

"No, I wouldn't."

"It's hardly bigger than a shower stall."

"It looks adequate. How much time do people spend in a bedroom anyway?" Like her, he kept his voice low.

"In a dinky room like this one, I'd say not much. Stuck in there, a person could develop serious claustrophobia."

He'd made his own checklist, so he guessed where she headed. First the paint and carpet, then the stove, now the rotten dimensions of the bedroom. It surprised him she hadn't brought up the cacophony that blasted in from the street.

"Another person might consider it cozy." He figured the "cozy" angle was worth a try. Maybe she'd give it a second look and view it, not for its deficiencies, but as a valuable piece of real estate.

She leaned closer. "A child would find it minuscule. You couldn't even cram a double in there, not if you wanted to add a nightstand and a chest of drawers."

His gaze cut sideways to her eyes. Such serious eyes. Maybe he should try to lighten her up a little. Otherwise, how could he ever elevate this hellhole into practically move-in condition?

"When you say 'double,' I suppose you mean a bed?"

She tilted her head back and scrunched her eyebrows in a way that said she couldn't believe he was so dense. "What else?"

"A lot of people who live alone don't require anything bigger than a single." He wondered about his tenants' sleeping accommodations. Only six out of the thirteen were married.

"Get serious. Only kids sleep in singles."

"Some grownups do, too."

She shook her head in denial. "No."

He nodded in assent. "Yes."

"What makes you so certain?"

He shrugged. "I'm as certain as a thinking man can be. Lots of people live in studios, share apartments. It's a space issue."

She rested her hand on his shoulder. "Do you?"

"Do I what?"

"Sleep in a single."

That brought him around so fast he almost fell over her. She lowered her heels and gazed up at him. He tried to find something suggestive in her eyes. Instead, they were wide open and clear, without any hint of guile.

What the hell? She started it. "No, I don't sleep in a single."

"That's what I imagined."

He backed her up a couple of steps. Had she thought about

him? Or more to the point, had she thought about his *bed* and imagined him in it? Could such a thought have credibility? Maybe she wondered if he slept in pajamas or *au natural.*

"Why do you want to know?"

"Why do you think I want to know?" She barely mouthed the words.

He could maybe detect a little seduction in her tone. If he wanted to stretch it. If circumstances were different, if she weren't the woman he couldn't risk offending, he'd ask her if she'd like to come home with him and see firsthand what his sleeping accommodations were. Maybe even try them out.

He opted for caution. "I haven't a clue. Would you like to tell me?"

She gave him a wilted smile. "Sure. I just believe whatever is good enough for you should serve as the norm for your tenants."

"Hey, folks, why don't you talk it over while I go next door for a couple of minutes? Woman needs a new washer in the kitchen faucet." The landlord headed for the front door. "Take your time. I'm not in any rush."

As soon as he vacated the apartment, Molly planted her hands on her hips. "Ha, I'll just bet he isn't. Wouldn't that guy love to rent this dump? I wouldn't offer him more than five hundred a month. I'd make him toss in a new stove, as well."

Nick supposed that signaled the end of bedroom talk. It was back to stoves and carpet and the kind of serious money required to rent an adequate apartment.

"I think it has potential. At least now you know something is available in the low seven hundreds."

"Who's Sonja?"

"What?"

"There's an ode to her in the elevator. The cretin who wrote it must live here. That's the kind of person who inhabits a dump like this."

"What does it matter? Your fan club isn't moving in. We just ran a test. It passed as far as I'm concerned. Case closed."

"It's a rat hole."

At least that had a better ring than hellhole. Although it *was* a rat hole, it seemed like one with possibilities. He might still find a way to bring her around.

"Look, I'm not into interior decorating or whatever, but I'm sure some fresh paint and a major clean-up in the kitchen would more than satisfy anyone looking for a bargain."

"The whole place should be gutted and turned into a studio. At least then a tenant wouldn't feel like it was impossible to take more than five steps in any direction."

"You're exaggerating. You just don't want to admit you're wrong."

Molly made a slow three-hundred-sixty degree turn. "If Martha Stewart were to take a gander at this place, she would probably instruct one of her minions to toss in a bomb."

Nick wondered how often the mayor had to deal with her. Maybe too often, which would account for all the time His Honor spent away from City Hall.

"Anyone with enough savvy could decorate, which is what I suggested earlier. A few bucks for paint. Carpet just needs a cleaning . . ."

Molly pressed her lips together and shook her head.

"So, folks, what do you think?" The owner had slipped back inside.

Nick glanced around the small space and nodded. "I think it's a steal for seven something a month."

Molly folded her arms across her chest and stared at the ceiling.

"Who told you seven?" The landlord jiggled the keys in his pocket. "You can't rent anything around here for that price."

"A fellow I know has an apartment in this building. He told me he pays around seven."

"How long's he lived here?" The owner closed the living room window. "If it's long-term, he's under rent control and gets away with robbery. I'm only able to raise the rent a lousy two percent a year." He turned back toward Nick. "This unit's priced at a thousand fifty. Only way I can jack up the rent is when someone does me a favor and dies or moves out."

"A thousand fifty?" Molly's lips tipped up into a smile. "At the moment, that's beyond our budget. Isn't that right . . . *darling?*"

That's for damn sure. Nick frowned.

Molly left the apartment and headed for the elevator. After the landlord locked the door, Nick took him aside.

"Can't you do a little better on the rent?"

"Are you kidding? You wouldn't believe how some of my tenants bleed me like leeches."

"Yeah, I know a little something about that myself."

When they caught up to Molly, Nick said, "You mentioned you own a couple of other buildings in the city. Would you have anything more affordable in one of those?"

The landlord pushed the elevator button. "I got a vacant studio. If you folks are interested, I could let you see it today. You look like a couple of nice kids. I'll let you have it for eight seventy-five, first and last month's rent plus cleaning deposit. You do any necessary painting and clean-up."

Eight seventy-five. A slam dunk. Nick congratulated himself for his ability to make champagne out of flat beer. While he patted himself on the back, the owner geared up to give Molly another quick once-over. She seemed clueless that her body stirred up more libidinous thoughts than the peep shows in the Tenderloin. He raised one eyebrow and shot the landlord an "I wouldn't try that one again" husband-like glower. It stopped the guy in mid-stare.

When the elevator car arrived, Molly stepped inside. Nick followed, but this time he didn't have to hide the expression of lust etched into the wall. Now she'd seen it, she turned away. They descended with a lurch, and he reached over and cupped her elbow when she lost her balance. She let his hand stay there until the elevator clunked to a halt on the ground floor and the door opened. She took her loss pretty well. He could almost feel the sun on his back as if they already strolled along the Wharf. He could even imagine the taste of the fresh seafood. First, though, they'd check out the studio, and he'd make sure not to gloat.

"The only problem with the studio is there are no closets," the landlord announced as the threesome headed for the front door. "You gotta find room to squeeze in a couple portables."

Nick swung back toward him. The guy might just as well have declared that San Francisco had broken away from the mainland and floated out to sea. *No closets*. What kind of shit was that? It was the kind engineered to force him to really hike up the twenty-five grand buyout figure. That's the kind of shit it was. He really needed to pour it on at the Wharf if he expected to limit the raise to twenty-eight five.

"Listen, Molly . . . " He turned toward where she last stood, but she'd evaporated. He kicked open the front door and charged outside in time to see a flash of leg as she jumped into a taxi.

"Son of a . . . " The cab zigzagged through traffic and disappeared down the street. Nick jammed his hands into his pockets, then threw back his head and laughed. In the space of twenty minutes, Molly had changed from sculptor's clay, pretty darn near molded by him, to a million-dollar challenge. He should feel pissed but, oddly enough, he didn't. Instead, her little charade energized him. Okay, the apartment was a bust, but he had no plans to leave town. Neither, presumably, did she. Now he had her in his sights, he intended to keep her right there, so close, they'd breathe the same lungful of air.

"So, I'll be back," he growled in a perfect imitation of the state's body builder/movie star/ex-governor. "Yeah, I'll be back, Ms. Molly. You can count on it."

Chapter 8

Molly rummaged through the box of earthquake supplies she kept under the kitchen sink—flashlight, battery operated radio, bottled water, and granola bars—until she found the utility candles. She brought a pair, along with two candle holders and a book of matches, into the living room. Dominique had already cleared some of the framed pictures and assorted knickknacks off Molly's glass-topped coffee table. In their place, she set a box containing her Ouija board. The lid bore the logo OUIJA Mystifying Oracle; a shadowy figure, cloaked in black, floated above the words.

"I was thinking about something." Dominique picked up her glass of Chardonnay. "Remember what Mom's friend, Trudie, found out about Nick?"

Molly grimaced. "You mean all the worthless information she dug up? I didn't need to know any of it. All I'm interested in is his building plans for my end of the block and if he's going to cave on the twenty-five thousand he offered his tenants. I'll never find another 'angel' and no other landlord will give a future clinic, if we're forced to open another one, any break at all on rent. If I didn't already know it, I figured that out this afternoon. Eight seventy-five for a studio with no closets. Whatever Nick decides will affect a lot of people—not just his tenants, but anyone in need of pretty much free medical care."

"Some of what Trudie said had value."

Molly inserted the candles into the holders. "I can't think of one piece of information I could put to good use."

"I can think of several. For instance, Nick is just the right age for you. Also, Taurus is a perfect match for Capricorn. You're both Earth signs."

Molly wrinkled her nose. "Forget it. Anyway, you know I don't believe in that stuff."

Dominique had her chart prepared every year by some guy with the tattoos and piercings of a debauched rock star. Molly considered it a waste of money. She didn't believe in Ouija, either. However, Dominique had brought her board with her and insisted that, after they worked on the grant, they have a session. Especially once she'd heard the full scope of Molly's two encounters with Nick.

"People born under Taurus and Capricorn have a lot in common and usually think alike. Of course, on the down side, they're both stubborn." Dominique sipped her wine. "I don't have to tell you who'll come out on top in a clash of wills. Think horns."

"I will never again spend time clashing wills or anything else with Mr. Mancini."

"Don't be so sure. From what you told Mom and me on Friday, plus what happened with him earlier today, he sounds like a pretty determined guy. Am I right?"

Molly thought for a moment. "Yes, he comes across as determined. At least, he isn't belligerent." Belligerent men were obnoxious. They were the kind who bellowed like thwarted bulls. The kind who lost their temper right from the get-go. She couldn't remember Nick Mancini raising his voice. If he had a temper, he kept it hidden deep inside that toned body.

"You said he's cute, though."

"No, I didn't." Molly formed a mental image of his face. "He's definitely not cute. That's a guy with a buzz cut and pug nose. He's rugged. Some women might even consider him . . . handsome. Not that it matters if he's handsome or cute or if he's often mistaken for a Troll. My business with him is over, finished, deader than yesterday's news."

"Well, he can't be any worse than the guy you dated last April whose goal was to become a househusband."

A frown pinched Molly's brow. "I never dated him. It was a

one-time fix-up, courtesy of your husband. You'll notice, after that, I swore off flying blind forever."

"Maybe that's why you're still single at twenty-nine. At your age, a woman shouldn't narrow her focus."

"I'm perfectly happy with my life. I'm not the kind of woman who'll eat a whole shopping cart full of Twinkies if she doesn't have a Saturday night date."

"If you can't drum up any interest in Mr. Mancini, I wish you'd reconsider the techie Rob plays squash with on Friday nights. Okay, you'd have to wear flat-heeled shoes if you dated him, but he *is* cute."

Molly groaned. "Forget him and anyone else on Rob's reject list." She lit the two utility candles. "I don't understand why we need *illumination*." That was Dominique's preferred reference to candlelight.

"It sets the right mood."

"Why did I let you talk me into this?" Molly picked up her glass of Chardonnay off the coffee table and took a few sips. Dealing with Ouija worked better for her if she had a slight buzz. She settled against the plump navy blue pillow in the corner of her white wicker sofa and kicked off her shoes.

"Although it's not an exact science, it practically borders on the supernatural. In case you haven't heard me mention it before, like a hundred times, I'll remind you again. The supernatural has been proven to exist."

"Proven? Ha. I doubt it."

Dominique lifted the Ouija board from its box and placed it on the table. A black cat with flattened ears and spiky-furred arched back hovered above two rows of alphabet letters at the top of the board.

"You believe in the subconscious, don't you?"

Molly nodded. "Yes, but not mental telepathy and mind reading."

"That's not the principal behind Ouija. It communicates through the subconscious. Almost everyone is curious about where their life is heading. Aren't you?"

"I suppose so." Molly had to admit she was guilty of drifting lately. However, she doubted Ouija could make the path clear.

"If you have questions, Ouija will provide answers."

"How can a board game predict the future?"

"It isn't a game, and Ouija doesn't predict. It's an aid to unlocking deep-seated thoughts and desires. Haven't you ever wondered *why* when you did something out of character?"

"You mean like what happened earlier today with Nick?" Molly still felt the imprint of his lips on hers.

"Exactly."

"I suppose impulses rattle around in the backs of our minds. Sometimes we act on them without thinking it through. I believe that much."

"You ought to."

"Why?"

"It's what happened to you when you let him kiss you."

Uh-oh. That was one impulse Molly should never have obeyed; the other was telling her cousin about her lip-lock with Nick. "I didn't exactly let him, and it wasn't like he bothered to ask permission."

Dominique smiled. "You wanted him to kiss you. When he did, you enjoyed it. Think of it as your subconscious at work. He could have used mental telepathy on you, too. He might have programmed you to kiss him and he didn't have to utter a word."

Molly sipped her wine. "You think it's possible someone can make you do something you ordinarily wouldn't do?"

"Well, maybe not commit a felony."

"You think that's what Nick did? He programmed me into kissing him?"

"He sent you a message, and you responded without conscious awareness. Or maybe you *were* aware. You know, mental telepathy works both ways."

"I know I didn't influence him."

"Then the desire sprang from deep in your subconscious. When he used a little thought transference on you, you fell right into his arms."

"Thought transference? Please. Where did you learn all this stuff? I didn't fall into his arms." Tripped, yes, but fell? No way.

"People have bent minds for centuries."

Molly frowned. Was it possible? Was that why she let him swoop in on her, for heaven's sake, right there practically on a public sidewalk?

"No. I don't believe in thought transference. Or that Nick Mancini needs to program a woman to kiss him. He just does it because . . . " She glanced up at the ceiling, at a loss to explain what motivated him to kiss *her*.

"Yes, you were saying? He does it because . . . ?"

She shifted her gaze to Dominique, " . . . because he can, and I'll bet he doesn't encounter much resistance. He just zeros in for the kill."

"Isn't that every woman's dream? To be killed by a French kiss from a fabulous-looking guy?"

Molly sighed. "I suppose there are more painful ways to meet the Grim Reaper."

Dominique removed the planchette—a palm-sized triangular object perched on three small knobby legs—from the box and placed it on the board. "Okay, let's put the mysterious message indicator to work."

Molly picked up the planchette and peered through a small glass circle cut into the wood. "What's so mysterious about this?"

"It acts like a medium. You ask questions and it reveals answers."

The sun had completed its descent. Lit only by the candles, the room slid into semi-darkness. Shadows brushed against the pale yellow walls.

"What if I have no questions?"

"Believe me, you do." Dominique scooted her chair close enough to Molly so they could balance the board on their knees.

Molly replaced the planchette and took another sip of wine. Maybe if she mellowed out more, she'd become less resistant and unlock the deep-seated desires Dominique insisted swam around in her brain. She set her wineglass on the adjacent white wicker end table.

"I'll ask the questions." Dominique moved the planchette to the center of the board and placed her fingertips along one edge. She instructed Molly to do likewise.

"You're serious, aren't you?"

"Absolutely."

Molly groaned. "I don't have your faith."

"I think you're afraid of what you might find out."

"Wrong. I'm not afraid. I'm skeptical."

"We'll see how long your skepticism lasts. Now, take a minute and totally clear your mind."

Molly drew in a deep breath, held it for a few moments, and then let it whoosh out. What harm could it do to go through the motions? They'd share a couple of laughs, finish off the wine, and then she'd hit the sack early. Tomorrow night would probably turn into a killer, since she promised Mrs. Z she'd drop in at their association meeting. Tuesday and Wednesday she had to run around the city and collect the last of the donated items for her auction on Thursday night.

"Ready? Is your mind empty?"

Molly tried to create a vacuum in her brain.

"Let's have a practice run to help you get used to the movement of the planchette."

Practice. That's what Nick had suggested just before he zeroed in for a kiss. Also, why was it every time the kiss came up a pocket of heat settled in her chest? She could put Ouija to the test, but she already knew the answer: The way she connected with him *had* affected her. She enjoyed it and deserved to have "traitor" branded onto her forehead.

"Remember, let your subconscious guide the planchette, not your fingers."

Molly nodded.

"Okay. First question. Is your name Molly?"

Molly watched the indicator. She waited for something to happen, but it seemed stuck. In case she'd exerted too much pressure, she lightened her touch. Still nothing.

"It's not working."

"It will. Have patience."

A second later, the indicator began a slow movement and eventually settled near one corner. Molly read the word *YES* through the glass window. Well, that was true.

"Next question. Are you married?"

The indicator showed no sign of activity. Then it slowly circled the board. As the rhythm increased, it slid to the opposite corner and stopped above the word *NO*.

How weird. Not that Molly hadn't yet nailed down a groom—well, Dominique thought it was weird—but that the planchette uncovered the correct answer once again. She had no recollection of prodding it. Molly removed her fingers. "Have you guided this thing?"

"Absolutely not. I don't have to. It's obeying your subconscious. Put your fingers back on."

Molly complied, but not without suspicion.

Dominique paused for a moment. "Are you dating right now?"

Molly waited for the answer to reveal itself, but the indicator stalled again. What difference did it make, anyway? She knew there was no one special in her life. Just when she decided the whole premise was silly, she felt movement. The indicator circled slowly then picked up momentum. For a moment, it appeared as if it might slide off the side of the board when it made an abrupt correction. It skirted along the edge and stopped above *NO*.

"When's the last time you had a date?"

"You already know everything about my love life." Or lack thereof. It made Molly feel like Mary Poppins.

"You're not allowed to answer the questions."

Molly blew air out through parted lips. She found it difficult to focus, to turn her mind into a wasteland. After what seemed like a full minute, the answer revealed itself. The planchette moved letter by letter. *M O N T H S* appeared through the glass window. Had it been *that* long?

"Why has it been months?" Dominique kept her voice low.

The indicator skimmed over the board. *B U S.*

What? Molly never rode the bus. Muni sucked. The buses ran late and some passengers brought along more than a hint of danger. She looked up. There was gentle movement under her fingertips. Her gaze returned to the board. *Y* sat squarely in the viewing window. *B U S Y.* How true.

"Would you like to meet an interesting guy?"

This time the planchette appeared free from its former constraints. It buzzed straight to *YES.*

That was a no-brainer.

"In fact, have you already met one?"

YES appeared in the window.

"When?" Dominique's voice was almost hushed.

Molly followed the path of the planchette as it spelled out *L A S T W E E K.*

That's when she met Nick. This was spooky. She blamed the candlelight. Every minute or so, the flame flickered as if an unseen presence hovered in the room.

"Would you like to be married?"

Would she? The indicator began an unhurried stroll through the alphabet. The first letter appeared. *M.* Quickly, it was followed by *A Y B E.*

She supposed it was true, if she ever met the right man, which she hadn't exactly killed herself to find. If she didn't meet Mr. Right, she didn't foresee it making her bitter. She led a relatively uncomplicated life, in part because she was single. Just last year, two of her friends filed for divorce. She'd been in their weddings. She'd thought they were happy. Now they were statistics and hung out in clubs and dated losers. Something any sane woman would work hard to avoid.

"Let's go back to this interesting man. Does he have a name?"

Dominique's voice reminded Molly to put her brain back on

hiatus. She struggled to empty it of thoughts about marriage and its pitfalls.

While the indicator remained stationary, a tiny thought sprouted in Molly's supposedly comatose mind. Then the indicator took a circuitous route and spelled out *N I C K.*

"Are you interested in him?"

The planchette slid right over to *YES.*

"No." That was Ouija's first slip-up. It didn't matter how she reacted to him, Nick Mancini ranked just below Quasimodo in the "available to date" category. She didn't have to remind herself thirteen tenants and possibly the fate of the clinic stood between her and one of the hottest single men on the planet.

"Does he get you excited?"

YES made another timely appearance.

"Baloney," Molly muttered even as her inner voice screamed, *Liar!*

"Shh. You're supposed to concentrate, especially now things have heated up."

Molly wished she could find a way to chug a little wine without using her hands.

"Okay. Besides interesting and exciting, how else would you describe him?"

Molly blamed herself when the indicator stalled. Thoughts of Nick bubbled in her mind like the chocolate soufflé she'd burned recently. She searched for ways to describe him. She wasn't supposed to, though—description was Ouija's job. She took a deep breath and nudged her mind into a blank state. Just to ensure she didn't cheat, she closed her eyes.

"*S . . . E . . . X . . . Y.*" Her cousin's voice broke the hush in the room.

Molly's eyes popped open as the indicator ranged over another flock of letters. *H O T.*

"Is he really?" Dominique asked.

"Some women might think so."

"Do I sit opposite one?"

Molly shrugged. That was as close to the truth as she'd admit. "Let Ouija confirm it."

It took longer than usual for the answer to appear.

Dominique said, "Don't be resistant."

YES appeared in the window. "See, no resistance from over here. I think you cheated, though."

"If that's want you want to believe, fine. It won't erase the truth. You're attracted to him."

Molly hated to think of herself as just another poodle in heat. Next thing, she'd fantasize about buying a thong and having him peel it off her body.

"Would you like him to kiss you again?"

Molly wanted to bring this soul search to a close. Her mind buzzed from the effort to banish cognition to a dead zone. However, Ouija, seemingly impatient with her balking subconscious, whisked right over to *YES*.

Could that be true?

Dominique leaned closer. "On a scale of one to ten, how good a kisser is he?"

"The earth moved." Molly pulled her hands off the planchette.

"Wow, and with only one kiss."

Molly leaped off the sofa, sending Ouija flying. "No, *right now*."

"Earthquake!" both shouted simultaneously.

Molly grabbed Dominique's hand and pulled her across the white shag carpet that covered a section of hardwood floor. She guided her to the archway between the living room and kitchen. Dishes danced against each other and chattered from behind the cabinet doors. The light fixture suspended from the kitchen ceiling swayed in a slow arc. Outside, car alarms shrieked.

Although Molly had experienced at least a dozen small quakes and one large one, she never got used to the swaying motion that signaled even a slight movement below the earth's surface. Especially since it always came without warning. She held tightly to her cousin's hands until the movement stopped.

"It didn't feel like the big one," Dominique said.

Molly brought her rapid breathing under control. "Thank God it wasn't."

"How would you rank it? Maybe a four on the Richter scale?"

"It's possible. Turn on the TV and see if there's any mention of it. I'll bring in the rest of the wine." Molly headed into the kitchen. A couple of pictures were knocked off center, but other than that, the room showed no visible signs of damage. She grabbed the bottle of Chardonnay out of the refrigerator.

"It's just scrolling now. They think the epicenter is a few miles off the Monterey coast. No major damage reported." Dominique clicked off the TV.

Molly brought the wine into the living room and refilled their glasses. She turned on a light and blew out the candles. A glance into the street showed nothing unusual.

"Can you believe the earthquake struck at the precise moment I asked about Nick? He must have given you one hell of a kiss."

Molly thought for a moment. Maybe it wasn't earthquake-sized, but it came close enough to shake up her orderly little world.

"Do you think half the state might have slid into the ocean just now if he'd asked you for a date?"

Molly shook her head. "Don't worry. He won't. Especially after I bailed on him this afternoon."

Dominique scooped up the planchette and Ouija board and placed them in the box. "Why won't he? He kissed you. He's interested."

Molly turned on another lamp. "He's interested in protecting his profit margin." It occurred to her that while her mind subconsciously enjoyed the kiss, she should have ground her heel into his instep. She'd learned how at the self-defense course she took last year. Protection for when she sometimes had to hike to her car after dark. It hadn't occurred to her then that the technique might also come in handy for warding off men with agendas.

"You think he'd use you?"

"Get real. I know he would. It's not like we shared a romantic dinner and he parted with a hundred fifty bucks for the privilege to sit across a table from me. We stood on the threshold to the apartment from hell."

"So why did he . . . you know?"

Why indeed? Even more provocative was why she let him. "I suppose he tried to prove a point." Also, she'd bet the raise she couldn't afford to give herself it had nothing to do with the marriage thing. *Mrs. Mancini*. Really.

Molly plopped down on the sofa.

"What point?" Dominique carried the blue and white striped upholstered armchair she'd occupied back to its usual place beside the silk palm and sat down.

Molly hoped it wasn't to prove how easily he could manipulate her. Handsome, sexy, interesting men did that to women all the time, usually to lure them into bed. All Nick wanted was for her to stop waving her calculator under his nose.

"Maybe he wanted to show me his warm side. You know, live up to his golden reputation. Maybe then he could convince me to sympathize with his situation. 'Aw, shucks. Here you are, a great guy, held up practically at gunpoint by your tenants, and I'm ready to pull the trigger for them.'" Molly sighed. "The thing is, I don't really believe he's cold. But calculating? I'll bet he could teach a course on it."

"Play his game. Suck up to him. He's attracted to you. Use your body."

"You mean have sex with him?"

"Not actual sex, unless you want to. Just put it out there, get him hot. Then maybe he'll hit his bank and empty out his accounts. That's what you think he did with you to garner your sympathy."

"I can't."

"Then let your subconscious do it, because *it* thinks he's H . . . O . . . T. If you're not up to it, introduce him to me."

Molly stared at her cousin. Was she unhappy in her marriage, too? She'd been only twenty when she married Rob. That was twelve years ago. True, after all that time, ardor was bound to cool a little. Had they hit a patch of ice? Molly didn't know how to broach the subject or even if she should. "Are you and Rob . . . ah . . . having problems?"

"No more than usual. Just minor stuff. Rob and I are perfectly suited to each other. Oh, every now and again, I have to use a little thought transference on him when he says he's too tired for you-know-what." She laughed. "Why, did you think I was interested in an affair?"

"Well, no."

"I was fantasizing. That isn't reserved only for singles." She took a sip of wine. "Don't tell me you never fantasize about sex."

Molly shrugged. Sure she did, but not on anything like a regular basis. Actually, she hardly ever did. Dwelling on sex was nowhere near as fulfilling as the real deal.

"Would it be so hard to fantasize about sex with Nick?" Dominique grinned. "Tell the truth or I'll cart Ouija out again."

Molly took her time and sipped her wine. She let it warm her insides. Her inhibitions would lessen if she drank enough of it.

"It probably wouldn't be hard at all." That's where it would stay. At least she was smart enough not to get into a situation where he could *program* her into the real thing. Since she'd never agree to another apartment hunt, her worries ended there.

All evening, she'd been expecting a call and an accusation that she cut out on him. But then again, she hadn't even stuck around to retrieve her folders from his car. Maybe he took a good look inside and realized she was right about the lack of affordable housing. Maybe he'd given up and accepted the truth.

"Do you have today's *Chronicle*?"

"What?"

"The *Chron*. Where's today's pink section? You haven't thrown it out yet, have you?"

"No. It's on the kitchen table. Why?"

"There's something I want you to read. I just remembered it." Dominique retrieved the paper and thumbed through a couple of back pages. "There, read your horoscope for today." She thrust the sheet into Molly's hands.

It took a moment to locate Capricorn among the other eleven horoscopes. Molly read hers quickly, then read it again.

A certain charismatic person is about to turn your world upside down. Don't even consider running away. You're already under his spell. Enjoy.

Chapter 9

Monday turned into a busier than usual day at the clinic. Patients were lined up at the door by the time Molly arrived. The doctors treated them without a break. She stayed close to her office and worked on updating files and contacting people who showed interest in contributing to her future events. At one o'clock, she ordered a turkey sandwich from the deli around the corner. She ate half then and finished the rest at seven. That was it for food. The tenants' association meeting was scheduled for eight o'clock that night.

At a quarter to eight, she packed everything away and headed for her car. Minutes later, she cruised down the street and pulled over where the beginnings of Nick's construction project loomed behind a chain link security fence. Although a green windscreen was anchored to the street side, it was still possible to vaguely see into the site. It appeared like a dark specter ready to swallow the seedy apartment building that crouched beside it. Work had also begun in the empty lot on the other side of the building and that made up the third parcel. It was also protected by an identical fence.

Molly had her pick of parking spaces tonight, a rarity in San Francisco. As dusk settled on the horizon, all the commercial buildings—with the exception of the Swaying *alms*—stood dark and empty. Their occupants had decamped for the night. Directly across from the construction site, a beat-up van with faded flower decals on the door panel hugged the curb. A nearby streetlamp cast a pale yellow glow. Molly almost whipped a U and pulled in behind the van. Since it could house some latter-day hippies, it might be best to park in front of the apartment building. Instead, she angled her five-year-old pre-owned Chevy into the empty space alongside Nick's darkened trailer. That would make it less conspicuous in an area ripe for break-ins. Six months earlier she'd contributed a CD player to the bad guys.

She turned off the motor and pushed the last bites of a power bar into her mouth. Guilt poked at her chest now as she squatted on Nick's property, as if she were about to take part in some illegal activity. When Mrs. Zamoulian had asked her—no, begged her— to attend their meeting, she couldn't refuse. Not after she heard about the ruckus that had ensued during their initial powwow the week before. She'd already given Mrs. Z a few pointers on how to compose an agenda. Tonight she'd limit her contribution to introducing the tenants to the rudiments of Parliamentary Procedure. She hoped it would make more sense to them than it had to Mrs. Z when Molly first broached it.

So why the guilt trip? She needn't plumb her subconscious for the answer. She'd allowed Nick to kiss her and instead of giving him a knee in the groin, she'd gone right along and fully participated. And according to the infallible Ouija, she couldn't wait for him to kiss her again. Whenever she thought about it, the same tingling sensation invaded her lips as if they were still pressed against his. Now Molly prepared to enter what Nick probably thought of as the enemy's camp.

She tried to kick Nick out of her mind but he'd charged in and taken up residence there. Compared to other men she'd kissed, with his technique—unhurried, deliberate, and full out—he rated a straight A. She supposed she'd have to live on the memory. She had no romantic prospects in the foreseeable future, which was just as well. Alongside Nick, the next hopeful didn't stand a chance of coming off any better than adequate.

She exited her car and double checked to make sure all the doors were locked. She jammed her keys into the outer pocket of her purse and hurried the few steps to the front door of the apartment building. She scanned the name slots, found Mrs. Z's, and pushed the bell. A moment later, she was buzzed inside.

A narrow hallway, lit by two circular opaque glass fixtures mounted to the ceiling, led to a rear staircase. A threadbare carpet of some dark, indeterminate color covered the steps. Its installation probably stretched back decades just like the overhead lights. Someone had made an effort to patch it with black electrical tape, which created a checkerboard effect. Probably Nick. Better to make a temporary repair than have a tenant take a tumble and sue him.

Molly began the steep climb to 3C. Midway up the first flight, she met Mrs. Z on her way down.

"Ah, thank God, it's you and not . . . " Mrs. Z, her gray hair coiled in a bun and clothed in a black dress and laced-up black stout-heeled grandma shoes, squeezed Molly's arm.

A second wave of guilt sprouted like a poisoned weed in Molly's chest. Who else but Nick could Mrs. Z mean? Had he found out about the meeting? He knew about the tenants' association. She glanced over her shoulder and half expected him to burst through the door and accuse her of sedition.

"We're nine tonight, including the big troublemaker from last time. You use your Parliament to keep him in line."

Parliament?

"Oh, what we talked about earlier. Sure." Molly felt strong misgivings, and not for the first time. She never intended to aid in fomenting a revolution. Nor did she consider it her place to act as a mediator in the dispute between the tenants and Nick. On the drive down the block, she'd decided to adopt the role of neutral observer and to limit her contribution to keeping the meeting on track and civil. With luck, that wouldn't prove any more difficult than riding a unicycle. Backwards.

"They're waiting in the apartment." Mrs. Zamoulian, who kept a claw-like grip on Molly's arm, led her up the steps. "Watch where you walk. The whole staircase is ready to fall down—God forbid—and maroon us up there. I told my husband—he should rest in peace—rent something on the ground floor. No, he wanted the exercise." She shrugged. "Now I climb instead."

At the second floor, she paused. "I need to find my breath."

"Take your time. Would you like to sit down?"

"What sit?" Mrs. Z waved away the suggestion. With her tiny stature and beak-like nose, she reminded Molly of a sparrow, its eyes alight with fire. The woman must be at least seventy-five, if not more, but was still feisty.

Another flight led to the final landing. A skylight threaded with chicken wire beamed in enough filtered light to keep alive a small jungle of potted plants. Someone had clearly made an effort to improve the ambiance. Probably not Nick since he intended to tear the place down.

Mrs. Z announced a return to normal breathing then grasped Molly's hand. They proceeded to her apartment. The door to it stood open. Raised voices escaped into the hall.

"You're a crackpot, Duncan."

"And who are you? Albert Einstein?"

"If you continue to threaten Mancini, he'll have the cops haul you out of here on your ass. You might even end up doing time."

"Says who?"

"Says the guy you're threatening. Go on and give him a good reason to kick us all into the street."

"I tried to move this thing along. If he thinks we're a bunch of patsies, he'll rip the roof off right over our heads. Then you'll all be beggin' for his lousy buyout. We gotta show him we're tough. Either he caves or else. So whadda ya care, ya big doofus?"

"I still live here. That's what I care. Watch who you call a doofus."

Oh, great. A pre-meeting rumble.

Molly entered the apartment on the heels of Mrs. Z. A dark purple plush sofa festooned with white crocheted doilies, two overstuffed matching armchairs, and four straight-back wooden ones of the kitchen variety pretty much filled the small living room. An ivy plant sat atop a wrought iron stand and occupied one corner. In another, an electric floor fan circulated dead air through the room. Pictures of bucolic hunting scenes hung on the walls. She wondered if Mrs. Z was the one who'd gussied up the landing with plants.

The occupants, five women and three men, stared at Molly from their respective seats. A couple of the women offered a weak smile.

Mrs. Z rattled off a bunch of names, rendered mostly unintelligible by her accent. Molly recognized a few people who patronized the clinic and remembered them mostly by their ailments.

"Come, sit." Mrs. Z proffered the lone empty chair. "Then we start."

Molly settled into the close-knit circle and couldn't help rubbing shoulders with the man on her left. Was he the crackpot or the doofus? His dark hair was pulled back in a straggly ponytail and he wore a T-shirt extolling the virtues of Kentucky bourbon. The ripped-out sleeves gave him an excuse to expose Mr. Universe-sized toned muscles. He could probably dismantle the entire building if he wanted to. She pegged him as Duncan, the intimidator.

"Okay, I make agenda." Mrs. Z held aloft a piece of lined paper. "First thing we do—"

"I won't settle for no twenty-five grand."

The speaker was one of the two other men in the room. He'd been to the clinic twice over the past year. Hemorrhoids.

"Me neither." A woman Molly recognized as having arthritic knees chimed in.

"What are we? Suckers?"

"No shittin' way."

"I say we get a lawyer."

"Yeah, and who's gonna pay 'im?"

Mrs. Z, who'd either run out of chairs or didn't want one, stood over her little flock and waved her agenda.

"We can discuss . . . "

"Screw 'im . . . "

". . . ten ways to Sunday."

Molly's head swiveled from person to person. This might be

the time to introduce her *Parliament*, as Mrs. Z referred to it. She cleared her throat.

" . . . arrange a little accident."

Accident?

The man sitting beside her, who'd made the threat, could add thug to his resume. Molly frowned. "That's not a very good idea."

Nine pairs of eyes latched onto hers, their gaze so intense it made her feel as if she crashed a local coven.

"What's your stake in this here thing?" Her seatmate, who looked more than capable of arranging an accident, spoke directly into her face. It didn't help that he'd eaten something garlicky for dinner.

Molly twisted away from him. "Mrs. Z invited me to attend." She addressed the other members of the group. "I'm only here to keep the meeting on track." As if it bore any resemblance to a meeting and not a free-for-all. "It would help if, before you spoke, you raised your hand so the chair can recognize you." Was it possible they had any clue as to what "chair," in the context of a meeting, meant, other than somewhere to park their rear ends? "Just don't all speak at the same time."

"Thank you, dear." A woman, who only last week limped into the clinic for a follow-up visit for a severe case of gout, nodded. She always insisted on paying five dollars.

"I hear your frustration." Molly almost choked on the understatement. "There are more productive ways to address your situation than engaging in a physical . . . ah . . . encounter with Mr. Mancini." It felt strange to defend Nick when she agreed with the tenants about not accepting his niggling offer. However, bodily harm? To be fair, he had the law on his side. Legally, he wasn't compelled to make an offer. The whole thing had become way too complicated.

"Says who?"

"Mr . . ." Molly craned her neck so she could look at the nemesis to her left without actually having to move any closer to him.

"Serk. Why don't you call me Duncan?" By way of invitation, he made a clicking sound with his tongue.

"Mr. Serk, it might help your cause if you adopted a more conciliatory attitude. If you showed a willingness to negotiate in good faith, perhaps Mr. Mancini might show more generosity." Nick hadn't seemed receptive to bumping up his offer, but it might rein in Mr. Serk if he thought it possible. Was there some way to warn Nick about Serk's threats and that trouble might be headed toward him— maybe even violence—without admitting she'd met with his tenants?

"I knew Molly would understand," Mrs. Z announced. "She can teach us all about negotiate."

"There's really not much to learn. Just present your side in a calm, clear manner and let Mr. Mancini present his. Perhaps you should consider inviting him to your next meeting."

"No damn way." Duncan Serk stamped his foot so hard the whole apartment seemed to shudder.

"It sounds to me like a very good idea," the arthritic lady chirped.

That garnered several nods of approval.

"What are you people anyway, stupid? You think the army gives away its attack plan to the enemy?" Serk, who possessed the eyes of a ferret and the demeanor of a rhino, glared at the people sitting around the room. No one contradicted him.

Would Serk's "attack plan" land Nick in the clinic, this time as a patient? "Perhaps you might form a negotiating committee. Two or three of you. You also might consider being a bit more flexible."

"What is this flexible?" Mrs. Z asked.

"It means you bargain. Both sides are stuck in their groove right now. You should try to reach some sort of agreement. Be pleasant when you speak with him." The last remark was meant for Serk, but she didn't dare direct it at him for fear of becoming his proxy punching bag.

Mrs. Z nodded. "Just like in the saying, 'You catch more bees with honey. You don't need gun.'"

"Talk ain't gonna get us no hundred grand." Duncan Serk sprang to his feet and pushed through the small opening between his chair and Molly's, almost knocking her off her seat. He stalked toward the doorway. "Talk never got no one nothin'. Only these." His beefy hands curled into fists. "Next thing, you'll be bakin' the asshole cookies. What Mancini deserves is to have his nose mashed into his face." He did a little shadow boxing, then stomped out and headed toward the stairs.

The room fell completely silent.

Chapter 10

Nick pulled his car in behind the van and cut the motor. Across the street, his construction project sat behind the temporary security fence he had erected to keep out the curious and anyone else who had no business on the site. The area no longer resembled a giant black hole. The remaining façade of the corner warehouse had been removed without difficulty and the foundation reinforced. The guys had worked hard to get the ground floor and framework started. Same with the third parcel. If he settled with the tenants in the next couple of weeks, he felt confident he could bring the whole project in without a major delay.

Thinking about the tenants brought his gaze to the occupied building. Of the ten units, only two—1A and 3C—showed any light. That struck him as odd. He checked his watch. 8:47. At their age, most of them should be home watching TV. Two younger men, both security guards, rented apartments on the second floor and worked the night shift. So did the guy who rented the basement apartment. He'd driven by a couple of evenings the week before, and the front of the place had been pretty well lit up. He disengaged his seat belt and exited the car. Someone had parked in the space beside his trailer. Either they were hunkered down in the dark and sleeping, visiting in the building, or otherwise up to no good. Maybe the guy in the van he hired to keep an eye on his construction site had noticed who commandeered his spot.

He walked over to the van and peered through the driver's side window. He expected to see someone inside. Instead, the front seat was unoccupied. Curtains covered the side windows. Even angling his head three different ways, he couldn't see into the entire rear compartment.

Two weeks ago, someone had begun ongoing sabotage of his condo site. Holes had been drilled in exposed studs, building materials destroyed or stolen. A fire had consumed part of the framework of a ground floor unit. The guy who ran the motel had called it in to the fire department. Nick couldn't remember anyone bearing him a grudge, so it seemed natural to focus on some of his tenants.

He assumed the older ones were retired or lived on social security. Or maybe collected small pensions or disability checks. A couple of the younger guys looked rough. He hadn't a clue how they made the rent, but since they did, they must work. Or got money another way, which he didn't like to think about.

He went around to the passenger's side of the van and knocked on the glass. No response. Shit. He'd hired the guy with the expectation he'd stick with the job. When he'd checked last week, the man had binoculars and two cameras, each with a telescopic lens. Now he was AWOL and only two hours into an all-night shift. Nick rapped again. Nothing. He smacked the window hard with the palm of his hand.

He returned to his car and pulled a flashlight out of the glove compartment. He crossed the street and pulled aside an edge of the windscreen and shone the beam through the chain link into the construction site. Building materials, bundled and ready for future use, and a pair of steel beams sat at the far end of the ground floor.

Satisfied everything seemed in order, he moved over to his trailer. He turned the beam on the rear end of the car parked beside it—a Chevy—and illuminated a California license plate. Below it, on the bumper, a sticker read KEEP AMERICA WORKING. Nice touch. He was sure they were grateful in Detroit. However, he doubted the sentiment belonged to anyone bent on sabotage. Buying a domestic car in a market flooded with foreign makes might appeal more to someone like Molly. *Molly.* Driving American seemed to go right along with the way she thought.

He tried to remember what kind of vehicle she'd arrived in when they met on Sunday morning. He'd only become aware of her when she'd approached his car. Once she'd settled inside, he didn't think about what make or model she drove. Now, while he stood here in the dark playing detective, her eyes, her lips, her lithe, slender body flooded his mind. If the car belonged to Molly, she was inside the building—*his* building—and probably pushing a million-dollar agenda at another association meeting.

He snapped off the flashlight and backed up for a better view of the apartments. He scratched off 1A as the meeting place. Raised shades provided an almost unobstructed view of the living room. Empty. That left only the top floor apartment: 3C. Sound escaped through the open windows, but not loud enough for him to clearly distinguish any words. A couple of women sat with their backs to the street. Neither had Molly's style or shade of hair. That didn't mean she wasn't there, leading a seminar on extortion. Maybe he should just crash the meeting. He could give his own pep talk on the ethics of sucking up money when you hadn't earned it.

Before he had a chance to fully commit, the front door opened and a man stalked outside. One of his tenants, the surly one. Serk. As he approached the construction site, he pulled a pack of cigarettes out of a hip pocket and lit up. Nick tightened his hold on the flashlight in case the book of matches flared and arced behind the security fence. It didn't, and Serk continued on his way.

Lights began to glow in the other apartments. Nick crossed back to the van. Again, no signs of life. He decided to wait in his car and see who showed up. He bet on Molly, if indeed she were inside. If the surveillance guy didn't make it back by ten thirty, he'd leave a note on the windshield firing him.

He sat in his darkened car and started the motor so he could pump in air-conditioning. Then he played around with the radio dial until he found an all-night talk station. Only dim light from the street lamps and few apartments kept the area from falling into complete darkness. The single-story commercial buildings across from his project were dark. A few stars poked through the ozone layer. He leaned his head back but kept his gaze focused on the van and the front door of the apartment building.

Molly slipped outside just as his patience began to fade and he thought he might zonk out from fatigue. The sight of her in her knee-length skirt, short-sleeved blouse, and halo of curls gave him a jolt of energy. He cut the motor, grabbed the flashlight off the front seat, jumped out of the car, and closed the door before the ceiling light caught her attention.

Molly headed quickly toward his trailer. Yeah, that was her car parked alongside. He had her pegged—every which way. She had her keys out and in the door lock before he reached the middle of the street. She didn't waste any time but slid behind the wheel and fired the motor.

Nick picked up his pace. Probably, he should have blocked her car with his. Quite possibly, that would have derailed what happened next. As he approached the driver's side of the Chevy, he turned on the flashlight and aimed the beam through the window.

"Molly . . ."

She turned her head and squinted into the light. The sound of a gunned motor reached him a second later, and he had just enough time to dive out of range before the car fishtailed backward into the street.

He sprinted to his car, but by the time he leaped behind the wheel, the Chevy had disappeared into the night. Shit. That was the second time she pulled a vanishing act on him. It pissed him off this time. She was slick all right. If that was how she wanted to play, he was more than ready to arrange some serious one-on-one private time with her. He thought about it for a minute, thought about where and when and how to sandbag her. He preferred to corral her on her turf, but not at the clinic.

He stuck the key in the ignition and waited. Then it came to him like a blessed revelation. Oh, yeah. He rubbed his hands together as an idea took shape. Why hadn't he thought along those lines earlier? The where and when fell neatly into place, and a broad grin spread across his face. He had the perfect surprise in store for her. If it was one of the last things he ever did, he was going to get her alone and win her over to his side.

Chapter 11

At seven forty-five, the private room above The Grill restaurant buzzed with chatter. Molly took a quick head count from where she stood on the raised platform that served as a stage. Only about a dozen chairs remained empty. If they didn't fill by eight o'clock, she'd wait a few more minutes and then start the auction. With the guest list limited to a hundred, she counted on a full house.

A microphone, gavel, and two boxes that contained gift cards for each donated item occupied space on the table in front of her and Dominique. Soft light emanated from wall sconces, illuminating a pair of murals that depicted a Venetian canal spread along one wall and the Italian lakes on another. An abstract painting, ablaze in color, in contrast to their muted tones, sat propped against the front of the table.

Molly watched people's reactions as they approached to examine the canvas. Some smiled while they studied the frenzied globs of paint; others frowned as if perplexed. Molly thought it belonged stashed away in a dark attic. Still, to show appreciation to the artist who'd donated it, she'd gushed over the painting as if it deserved space in MOMA—the city's modern art museum. Maybe it did. Her tastes ran to Impressionists—notably Monet and Renoir. Whether it took an hour or a month to slap together, she counted on it sparking a lively bidding war.

Molly checked her watch. Almost seven fifty. A steady hum filtered throughout the room. The hum escalated when the deputy mayor arrived with a popular supermodel. Molly hoped they wouldn't become a continued distraction and dampen the crowd's enthusiasm for the auction.

Earlier, she'd placed programs on each chair. Most of the guests still perused the three pages of short blurbs that described the items up for bid. Although cool air poured from ceiling vents, pockets of heat skipped like tiny flash fires under Molly's three-quarter-sleeve black rayon dress. She'd picked through her closet and hunted for something suitable—not too dressy but not too severe. The dark shade and tiny metal studs that swirled beneath the neckline accomplished the goal. Still, she should have chosen something lighter in color and sleeveless. She planned to dash home and jump under a cool shower the minute the auction ended.

While Molly fantasized about lowering her body temperature, Cynthia burst through the doorway at the back the room. Maroon hair flew as the young woman rushed down the center aisle. She climbed onto the platform and almost stumbled into Molly.

"He's here." Cynthia panted as if she'd just galloped through Golden Gate Park in her four-inch stilettos. She braced her hands on the table edge and swallowed a deep breath. "He's coming up the stairs right now. I almost trampled him getting here first, so I could warn you."

"Who are you talking about?" Molly couldn't remember inviting anyone who would generate a movie/rock star level of excitement in Cynthia, whose job was to collect tickets at the door.

"Him. The dude . . . you know . . . from last week."

Molly's eyes tracked the direction of Cynthia's waggling finger. Nick stood just inside the entrance of the room. He wore a dark pinstriped suit, white dress shirt, and red and blue striped tie. Drop dead gorgeous didn't begin to cover his appearance.

"Holy . . . " Molly caught herself and gulped down the S word, or at least half of it. Too late, unless Nick found something else amusing. It was enough to plaster a big grin across his face. He waggled his fingers in a brief wave, and her heart skidded against her ribs. His eyes stayed locked on hers. Then he shifted his attention toward a cluster of empty seats. He settled onto one. Molly tore her gaze away and fussed with the gavel and boxes of gift cards.

"Holy, my foot," Dominique whispered. "That's sin on the hoof if ever I saw it, and I think I see it now. I take it that's Mr. Condo."

"Shhh," Molly hissed. "He'll know you're talking about him."

"So what?"

"I sense trouble. That's what. Ignore him."

"I'm not sure I can, or if I even want to, but I'll certainly try."

"I wonder why he's here."

Dominique sucked in a deep breath and let it out in a murmured trill. "Lighting up the room, I'd say. Damn, but he's gorgeous."

Molly kept her eyes averted. Three nights ago, she'd almost amputated his toes when she practically ran over them with her car. Although certainly not on purpose. What did he expect, sneaking up and almost blinding her with a flashlight? She hadn't realized it was Nick and not the elusive rapist who preyed on lone women in the South of Market area. She'd acted like any sensible woman—she'd burned rubber. Now he was here and, in less than a minute, managed to totally shred her inner calm.

Molly leaned closer to Dominique and talked out of the side of her mouth. "Don't make it obvious. Can you see what he's doing?"

"He's browsing through the program. No, wait, now he's staring at you again."

"How does he look?"

"I already told you. H . . . O . . . T. and I don't need Ouija's confirmation. No wonder you let him kiss you."

"You did? Wow." Cynthia's smile stretched almost to her ears.

"No." Molly shook her head, and with perfect clarity, sketched a mental picture of herself glued to Nick in that shabby doorway. A ripple of heat glided up her neck. She grabbed a program off the table and swatted the air. Good luck. Only if she drifted on an Arctic ice floe could she hope to extinguish the embers that smoldered beneath her skin.

She turned to Dominique. "Does he look . . . annoyed by any chance?"

"You mean because of the near hit and run the other night?"

"Yes."

"If that's annoyed, I'll sign up for it any time. Aren't you going to return the wave?"

"No." Molly pressed her chin almost into her chest and snuck a glance at her watch. One minute to eight. Almost time to start. She pulled in her breath, held it, and let it out slowly. She waited for her heartbeat to return to something that resembled a normal rhythm. She adjusted the microphone.

"I'm ready to turn this thing on. So be quiet, both of you." She flipped the switch and gazed out at the crowd. She tried to keep her eyes from straying to Nick, but it was impossible to accomplish. Even more so than when she'd bought a box of See's candy and tried not to eat most of the chocolate-covered cherries on the way home. At least he'd quit staring at her. He paged through the program instead.

"Good evening." Molly rushed through her introduction in half the time it took when she practiced it. She blamed Nick for single-handedly destroying her nerves. "Shall we start?" She pulled a card out of the nearest box and read the notation at something just below warp speed. "The first item up for bid is a pair of seats on the aisle, center orchestra, to opening night at the opera." She paused and drew in a breath. "Included is an invitation to the gala dinner preceding the performance and the after-party." A low buzz wafted through the room. "We'll start the bidding at five hundred dollars."

She wondered how Nick felt about opera. She loved it and tried to attend at least one production a year, albeit perched high in the stratosphere. Anything by Puccini and Verdi. *Madame Butterfly* was her favorite. She almost never missed a performance.

A man seated in the first row raised his program.

"Do I hear five fifty?" Molly's gaze slid over to Nick. He sat with his hands on his knees and his mouth shut. Opera obviously wasn't one of his passions. Others in the audience appeared more receptive. A few minutes of heavy bidding ensued, after which a prominent high-powered attorney snagged the tickets for two thousand dollars.

Cynthia brought them over and collected his check.

The enthusiasm generated by the opera package encouraged Molly and she presented several other items, including a four-course dinner for two at one of the city's renowned restaurants. Less than an hour into the evening, her calculator showed a figure just shy of twenty thousand dollars. Nick still hadn't moved a hand. The gentleman who sat beside him bid eight hundred dollars and won two seats in the owners' box for the Giants' opening game the following season. She recalled Barbara telling her Nick never missed a Giants' opener. Suddenly he had no interest in baseball? What was that about? Okay, he passed on the opera. Lots of guys didn't appreciate it. But no interest in dinners at swanky restaurants, either? Maybe he liked abstract art. The painting was due to come up next.

"This is a wonderful representation of John Fuller's work." Molly hoped the artsy crowd wouldn't share her opinion that it resembled a frenzied romp executed by a bunch of baboons high on an illegal substance. A loud hum erupted from different sections of the room. It signaled promise.

"John's next showing is at the Golden State Gallery on Union Street next month. You are all invited to his open studio this Sunday, as well. Before you leave tonight, please pick up his business card at the podium downstairs in the restaurant." Those promotions were Molly's trade off with the artist. It was worth kissing his tush to snag one of his paintings. Rumor had it he was the next Jackson Pollack. "We'll open the bidding at five thousand dollars." She glanced at Nick. He gave a subtle shake of his head and grimaced. Molly bit back a smile.

Heated action from the moneyed crowd followed and promised a good haul. The painting sailed out the door for twenty-five thousand. That was abstract art, though. What Molly saw as chaos, someone else viewed as talent.

She brought the Hawaiian trip up for auction at the midpoint of the evening and didn't have to feign enthusiasm.

"Someone will spend a glorious week on the Island of Maui in a fabulous oceanfront home. The package includes two rounds of golf, a spa day, daily maid service, and use of a car." A burst of chatter filled the room. She waited for it to ebb. "My thanks to Helena Singleton who so generously offered her home for this fundraiser." Molly beamed a smile at the prolific author who sat in the front row. "The bidding will start at sixty-five hundred."

She glanced at Nick. Either he squeezed his tan out of a tube like she did or he ignored the dangers of too much sun and hit the beach. She figured him for the real thing, UV rays and all. An image of him stripped of his suit and everything else underneath popped into her head. Clear and sharp, there was nothing abstract about *that* picture. Molly's mouth went dry.

A man three rows back raised his hand. Quickly, the bidding escalated. Molly came out of her trance at eight thousand.

"Who'll bid nine?" Would Nick duke it out for a Hawaiian odyssey? Would he dare throw around such substantial money and then shortchange his tenants? He'd guarded his wallet all night. He'd never even raised an eyebrow before the case of champagne fell into someone's hands for twelve hundred dollars.

She guessed correctly about the Maui trip. The bidding climbed to nine thousand dollars in less time than it took her to apply a splash of color to her lips in the morning.

"Do I hear ninety-five hundred?"

The deputy mayor flicked his hand, the one that hadn't clutched the supermodel all night. What kind of salary did he earn to jump in at that level? Especially since the city was almost on the brink of bankruptcy. It didn't really matter. He dropped out before Molly banged down the gavel after the final bid of thirteen thousand.

The boxes were almost empty of donation cards when she

opened the bidding on a day trip to the wine country.

"I wish I could bid on this item myself. The package includes door-to-door limousine service, a hot air balloon ride over the Napa Valley, and a gourmet food basket. We've arranged for a table at Thistle Creek Cellars in their private dining room for after your flight. A bottle of vintage wine—either red or white—awaits you there. We'll start the bidding at five hundred dollars."

The room fell silent. Molly couldn't believe it. Gliding over the Napa Valley was one of life's pleasures she often promised herself but always put off. It usually had something to do with cost. A woman she recognized as the CEO of a large corporation headquartered in the city raised her program. Finally some action.

"Okay. I have five hundred. Do I hear five fifty?"

The room remained quiet except for the rustle of programs and people shifting in chairs.

"I guess some of you must have a height phobia. Would it help to smuggle the wine aboard before you leave the ground?" That garnered a few chuckles. With luck, now the logjam would break.

"Five fifty," a male voice called from a center row.

"That's the spirit. Who'll bid six hundred?"

The clock ticked and no one spoke.

"Seven hundred." A deep voice rolled forward from the back of the room. Nick's.

Seven? What happened to six? He must really want this package. Apparently, height didn't qualify as one of his fears.

"Okay." Encouraged by Nick overbidding, she called out, "Do I hear eight?"

Silence.

"You mean I'm going to have to let this go for seven hundred?" Nick rose to his feet just as she was about to throw in a plug for the clinic and its many good works.

"Okay, eight hundred."

Molly blinked. "Eight? You just bid seven." He looked and

sounded sober, but Molly had her doubts. Now it seemed he couldn't wait to give his money away.

"Yeah, but now I'm bidding eight." Nick nailed her with a sharp gaze.

"Well, all right . . . I guess. Your money's as green as anyone's." Perhaps even greener. "Is that the final bid?" Molly grabbed the gavel and her eyes searched the crowd. No other takers. She waited a few seconds anyway. It seemed Nick had a date to sail over the treetops. "Last chance. Going once . . . twice . . . "

"Hold on a minute." He stepped into the aisle.

"What?" He must have realized he overbid. Now would he insist on backtracking, maybe to the six hundred level?

"I'm not finished."

Oh, he'd nipped at something for sure. Not Pepsi. If she played along, maybe she could jack him up as high as nine hundred, even the thousand she'd hoped the package would garner.

"Did you want to change your bid?"

"Maybe."

"Oh."

"Unless someone else wants to jump in, my bid stands at eight hundred." He glanced around. No one seemed interested in upping him. "Okay, then, in that case, I'll go as high as twelve hundred, but that's only if Miss Molly up there comes along for the ride."

Chapter 12

A smattering of applause, a shrill whistle, and a male voice that croaked, "Go for it, buddy," greeted Nick's announcement.

Molly's chin dropped, and her mouth opened wide in perfect imitation of one of her favorite comic strip characters, Lio, when he either stepped into trouble or caused it. Her brows knit together. She couldn't have been more disconcerted if Nick climbed up on his chair and begun to perform a slow striptease.

"What are you talking about?"

"You heard me." Nick stood in the aisle, his jacket open, hands jammed in the pockets of his pinstriped pants. A black belt circled his waist and rode above narrow hips and the flattest stomach this side of a vegan convention. His legs looked as long as a carnival worker's who strode around fairgrounds on stilts. Molly could think of at least six women who'd kill to be trapped aloft with him beneath a hot air balloon. Was she one of them? Well, she wouldn't exactly *kill* for the privilege. Then again, it wasn't the worst proposition she'd ever had to juggle. It opened up too many problems, though. The warning "consorting with the enemy" came to mind. Having "consorted" once, she knew better than to repeat that mistake.

"I . . . um . . . unfortunately don't come as part of the package." She kept her tone light for the benefit of the audience, while she struggled against the undercurrent that pulled her toward and then away from Nick. "Since that's the case, perhaps you'd like to withdraw your bid."

"Uh-uh."

Molly's instincts told her to shut him down. "I have five fifty from the previous gentleman," she called out in a somewhat quavering tone. Then she cleared her throat. "Who'll make it six hundred?"

"Twelve fifty." Nick began to walk toward the stage.

"You can't raise your own bid."

Dominique snickered in her ear. "Says who?"

Nick paused halfway up the aisle. "You said you wished you could bid on the item."

"Well, yes, but . . . "

"There you are. You want to go, and I want to as well. So, why don't we go together?"

There seemed only one reason why he wanted to spend almost a whole day with her. If he were persuasive enough, his twelve hundred and fifty dollar investment could wind up saving him— she did a quick calculation—seven hundred fifty thousand if she got the tenants to agree to his original offer. He thought he could wear her down. Why wouldn't he after the way she'd let him do a lot more than she'd allowed her last date?

"Really, I can't accompany you." Ugh, she sounded like a school marm from a bygone era.

Dominique picked up the gavel and banged it on the table. "Really, she can. This item is herewith sold to the lucky gentleman standing in the aisle." She plucked the card with all the particulars out of Molly's hand and hurried over to Nick.

Someone gave a shrill whistle while a few others burst into applause.

"Gee, I wanted to bring him the card," Cynthia said. "He . . . is . . . so . . . hot."

Molly thought so, too.

Dominique spoke into his ear while he wrote the check. There was a height difference of several inches, and he had to cock his head to hear her. He laughed at something she said, and she laughed back. Molly tried to ignore them. However, her eyes kept flicking back as she auctioned the one-of-a-kind floor-standing vase another local artist had hand woven out of strips of colorful paper.

Nick passed Dominique his check and she said something that brought his head up and his gaze to Molly. What was going on with them? What mischief was her cousin up to? She didn't trust her as far as she could throw Aunt Vi's crystal ball. Molly lost track of the bids. When someone offered eleven hundred for the vase, she banged the gavel down and declared the bidding closed.

Cynthia plucked the card away from Molly and brought it to the winner. Then she scooted over to Nick and Dominique, who'd moved toward the back of the room. Her head bobbed as she spoke. She glanced back toward the stage and pointed at Molly. He listened, nodded, and shook her hand. Oh, sure, another introduction. Why should Cynthia be left out? Then both women seemed to talk at once. Nick smiled down at them. Between her cousin and her assistant, they had him almost purring.

Molly thanked everyone for their participation. The painting and vase and several other items were carted away, and the room began to clear. Then the author approached Nick. Though she was two decades older than him, with the surgical work she must have had done on her face, they looked close to being contemporaries. According to the *Chron*, she recently cut loose from her fifth husband. Maybe it was time to troll for another. She certainly hung onto Nick's hand long enough. Molly winced as a dart aimed by the Goddess of Jealousy pricked her skin.

She turned away and hurried over to the outlet in the back wall where she'd plugged in the microphone. She stooped and pulled the cord free. When she stood up, Nick was at her side. He fished the white card Dominique had given him out of his jacket pocket. It contained the information outlining the day's activities printed beneath a picture of a basket carried aloft by a colorful balloon.

"I've always wanted to go up in one of these things, but I never seemed to have the time. I couldn't pass it up."

"What happened to your sister?" Molly wondered if Barbara had colluded with her brother or had been bribed or pressured into giving up her seat at the auction. Maybe she envisioned Cupid nailing Molly and Nick with his little arrow while they floated above the grapevines. Maybe the family really couldn't wait to hustle him to the altar. Well, they had a big surprise coming if they expected her to become the next Mrs. Mancini.

"Hmm, she couldn't make it." Nick gave no further explanation.

Molly wound the microphone cord into a coil. "Look, you don't have to go through with this. I can withdraw the item."

"Why would you withdraw it? Anyway, it's too late now. We have a date."

Date?

Molly returned to the table and repackaged the microphone and gavel.

"The card says any Saturday for the next month. The prediction is for the low eighties this weekend. Sounds like perfect flying weather to me."

Molly had always subscribed to the theory nothing in life was perfect. The body occupying the space about two feet from her and fueled by high octane testosterone Mother Nature rarely dispensed came pretty close, though. Could she handle a few hours alone with him in a venue *Travel Magazine* voted one of the most romantic in the country? She thought so. She couldn't imagine any situation cropping up that would allow him to maneuver her into another faux marriage.

"The clinic could certainly use the money."

"That's exactly what I thought. It would have been a shame to let this trip go for five fifty. The clinic performs a much-needed service down there in SoMa. I'm glad I had a chance to do my share to keep it in operation."

His coming across like Dr. Albert Schweitzer, the long-gone champion of the sick and needy, didn't fool Molly. He had an ulterior motive: saving himself a suitcase full of money.

"So, how about this Saturday?"

She couldn't see any purpose in putting off the inevitable. "Sure, Saturday's fine. Give me the card and I'll make the necessary arrangements."

"Uh-uh. We're going on my dime, so I'll take care of it. I'll pick you up at home. That's not a problem anymore, is it? Or do you still consider me a stranger?"

Well, an intimate stranger if such a thing existed.

"No, it's not a problem." She took the card and wrote her address on the back. They agreed he'd come by for her at eleven o'clock on Saturday.

Molly put the box containing the microphone she'd borrowed from City Hall into a shopping bag. She flattened the two empty boxes and added them to the bag too. Nick leaned back against the table and folded his arms across his chest.

"I'm sorry I startled you Monday night." He seemed truly apologetic, not like a man who'd almost had his toes pancaked.

Molly grimaced. "I had no idea it was you. Not until it was too late."

"I'm sure you didn't." His tone lacked conviction. Still, there was no reproach in his eyes in spite of her quick get-away.

She waited for him to pump her about the association meeting.

"How often do the tenants get together?"

Molly shrugged. "I don't know. They're pretty secretive."

"Are the meetings always held on Monday nights?"

"As far as I know they've only had two." She couldn't remember when the group first met. She wasn't included.

"Let me know when they hold the next one. I'd like to attend."

Molly recalled the great "secrets to the enemy" speech delivered by the Attila the Hun wannabe, Duncan Serk. "I don't think that will happen any time soon."

"Why not?"

"I suggested it, but they voted it down."

He didn't respond right away. "Okay, we'll leave it for now. Thanks for being honest."

She wanted to tell him his "for now" was more likely to turn into forever. Not unless he had a way to hijack the seven more easily intimidated souls and perform a Duncan Serk on them.

"Oh, and thanks for the cookies."

Bewilderment clouded her brain. "What cookies?"

"I had a visit Wednesday morning from Mrs. Zamoulian, along with a couple from my building. She brought me a plate of home-baked cookies."

"Really?"

"Yeah. She picked a nice variety—peanut butter, chocolate chip, and coconut. I guess she wanted to make sure she hit at least one of my favorites. She did, and then some. In baseball parlance, that's called batting a triple. They went down great with my morning coffee." He grinned, adding to the wattage from the overhead lights. "I won't need a jolt of sugar for the next year. She said it was your idea."

Molly had no recollection of ordering up an overload of sweets. Then she remembered the thug, Duncan Serk who spouted something about cookies, but not in a friendly manner.

"I think the suggestion came from one of your tenants. Do you remember Mr. Serk?"

He nodded. "Oh, sure. Serk the jerk. You'd need to undergo a lobotomy to forget him."

Molly thought the description less than fitting. The man could be dangerous.

"That doesn't sound like anything he'd propose. In fact the opposite."

"I don't believe he meant it in the way Mrs. Z understood it." She told him about Serk's threat.

Nick shrugged and didn't seem worried about having his nose mashed courtesy of his tenant's fists. Nick was taller, leaner, and came across like he kept himself in really good shape. She guessed he could deck Serk even before the man had a chance to fully curl his stubby fingers into anything potentially lethal.

"It was a nice gesture from her, anyway," Molly said.

"She wanted to negotiate. I wonder who that idea came from."

"It's a common practice."

Nick unfolded his arms and rested his palms against the edge of the table and leaned back. "She said you taught them about give and take."

"Perhaps something along those lines came up."

"The negotiating team didn't say anything about giving, however. It was mostly taking. Except for the cookies, I didn't see a whole lot of goodwill on their part."

"They don't have your experience."

"True. They've never had to negotiate union contracts." He shook his head. "Sometimes I think my tenants are harder to deal with than a bunch of hardhats."

"If you made the first move . . . "

"And upped the ante, you mean?"

"That seems like a good start."

He moved away from the table. Two steps brought him close enough to Molly for her to get a good whiff of his aftershave. It hinted of sandalwood blended with a touch of juniper. His dark hair was tousled enough to give her heart a bump. She knew he didn't need extra padding to fill out the shoulders of his suit jacket. Every bone, muscle, and sinew beneath it was built with expert precision.

"I said I'd go to thirty."

"You did?"

"That's pretty much my top offer. You might pass that along to them. While you're at it, remind them that, if I go up, they need to come down."

"You mean to ninety-five."

He shook his head. "Uh-uh. They're going to have to make a bigger adjustment than that."

"Well, you'd better negotiate it. I'm not putting myself in the middle."

"You already are."

"I can't bargain with you. Is that what you planned for Saturday? To trap me up in a balloon and hammer away over money?"

He didn't answer right away, which seemed to prove her point. The twelve fifty he'd bid was a future investment against a million dollar loss. Okay. She'd give him several hundred thousand dollars' worth of opinion the second he brought up money.

"Not at all. On Saturday we'll just be two people out to have some fun." He touched the tip of her chin with his bent finger, like he did the first time in her office. Now he kept it there longer. "You know how to have fun, Ms. Molly, don't you?"

She'd have liked to ask the same question of him but suspected she'd get that drowsy, sated, rolling around in the wild, king of the beasts look from him again. She kept her response to a simple yes. Which was just as well. The moment his finger made contact with her skin, her heartbeat went into quickstep.

When he took his finger away, she didn't have to ask herself if she liked it when he touched her. She did.

"Okay. So we're on for Saturday."

"You won't bring up the situation with your tenants?"

"Not even once. Let's put anything that approaches finances off limits. Why ruin what may turn out to be a perfect day by dragging along any problems? Agreed?"

"That will take an awful lot of restraint. Personally, I don't think you can do it." She'd bet her next ten paychecks on finances becoming the center of conversation. Why else would he want to corner her in a floating basket two hundred feet above the ground? At the very least, he'd try to use her as a go-between. What other interest could he have in her?

He placed his hands on her shoulders. "I'll make a deal with you. If I mention anything along those lines, I'll add a couple thousand dollars to the thirty I offered."

Restraint, to which she was no stranger, kept her mouth from doing another Lio imitation. Could she have been wrong about his motive when he outbid himself? Perhaps he just wanted to end the contention that seemed to grow between them. Should she trust that he spoke the truth? Hmmm.

"I'm going to take that as a challenge."

He smiled. "I'm up for it."

"What if I broach it?" Or, just as importantly, the clinic. What better time to get a straight answer? While they admired the scenery, she could slip in a question as to whether or not he had any further expansion plans. Technically, it could be considered breaking his "no finance, no problems" rule, since the purchase of property involved money and the loss of the clinic would create a huge problem. Somehow, she'd find a way to skirt around the restriction.

"Will you?"

"I don't . . . ah . . . expect to. If something slips out, though, what will you do, nick a couple thousand off the thirty?"

He took another step forward. He moved with a rolling gait that brought her eyes to his hips, a spark of heat to her cheeks, and a stab of guilty pleasure into her heart. She dragged her gaze up to his.

"There's a word for people who promise something then back down. When I give my word, it's solid."

"If I do. Slip, I mean. What then?"

This time, he didn't bother with a finger under her chin. He put his hands on either side of her face. "Trust me." She smelled minty toothpaste on his breath. "I'll find a way to puncture that balloon—and I don't mean the one we'll be drifting under—the second it lifts off the ground. Understand what I'm talking about?" His lids dipped and his lips remained parted. For a moment, she thought he might kiss her again and show her exactly what he was talking about.

A brushfire claimed the skin under his hands and leaped down Molly's throat and into her chest. She figured he'd have no trouble deflating whatever balloon she was foolish enough to launch. So it became vital for her to remember to use subtlety while giving the impression she held up her end of their bargain. Either she did it right or somewhere, as they floated over the treetops, her subconscious was liable to collide with his thought transference. She wouldn't need Ouija to predict the outcome.

Chapter 13

Confident he knew every major thoroughfare and back street in San Francisco better than most other natives, Nick easily found Molly's address. The house climbed three stories above a small neatly trimmed lawn that bordered a tree-shaded sidewalk and was painted pale blue, with raspberry and white trim under the eaves and around the windows. Spindled railings flanked the eight or so steps that led to a front door set back under a pediment. The Victorian features—slim columns bracketing windows, latticework, and the intricately carved open designs set into the upper corners of a small second floor porch—whizzed straight to his builder's heart. One day he wouldn't mind owning one like it. He priced the house easily at a couple of mil.

Molly's Chevy hugged the curb in front. He found a spot three doors down with barely enough room to fit his hybrid. He cut the motor but stayed behind the wheel.

He'd arrived ten minutes early despite taking the time to rip into the box of corn flakes and carton of milk his mother had brought over the previous evening, along with a basket that bulged with fruit. The fruit would stay in the refrigerator until the next time she dropped over. He'd been healthy all his life in spite of shunning fruit and vegetables, even as a kid. You'd think by now his mother would have given up. Fruit didn't come anywhere close to what he needed. What he needed was something his mother couldn't provide. He thought of Molly. Was he pumped? Sure. Molly was attractive and bright—and his for the day. She had plenty of sex appeal, too, made even more potent since she seemed unaware of it. Embers smoldered under a controlled outer shell. He'd brought them close to the surface once and wouldn't mind trying for a full-fledged conflagration. Would she let him? He looked forward to finding out.

When he'd talked with her after the auction, he'd gotten the impression she might have started to weaken. She'd warned him about Serk and encouraged the tenants to negotiate with him. A small step but at least it headed in the right direction and didn't cost him anything. Maybe the hundred thou wasn't chiseled in stone. Maybe she'd taken a harder look at his side of the problem and understood it better. For all he knew, she was one of those bleeding hearts out to save the world. Maybe he could bring her around to wanting to save him.

The apartment house wasn't the first time he had to deal with tenants. He'd faced the same situation three years ago in the Outer Mission. Forget twenty-five thousand. He'd offered fifteen and the tenants had grabbed it and were out in a week. He'd expected the same thing this time. He'd never considered himself naïve. Anything but. Savvy, informed, and well aware of what was happening around him was a more accurate assessment.

Now he regretted that he'd volunteered to put the impasse with his tenants off limits. All morning, he'd asked himself the same question: Why had he decided to take the high road? When she'd asked if he intended to hammer away at her during the balloon ride, he'd thought *shit yes*, then quickly denied it. The truth wouldn't have gotten him in the same county with her, no less in a floating basket. He wanted her ear—and, okay, a little more—maybe a lot more—but why kill his best opportunity? Yeah, that wasn't his smartest move. He needed Molly to convince his tenants to come down out of the stratosphere and onto solid ground. Even if they roasted an ox for him in the space alongside his trailer, he couldn't move up much further than the thirty K. She could persuade them to accept his offer. Today would have been perfect to work a little magic on her.

But a deal was a deal. He couldn't go back on his word. He'd have to use a little creativity.

He snapped off his seat belt and flexed his arm muscles. When he moved his head in a circular motion, he heard the joints crack. He hadn't slept well. Last night he'd spent several hours parked in the spot where the surveillance guy should have been watching the condos. Except, he'd fired him on Monday.

Nothing had happened at the construction site to cause him concern, so at two in the morning, he'd dragged his tired body home and crawled into bed. But he couldn't fall asleep. As soon as he hit the sheets, he'd started to think about Molly. He pictured her long legs and then slowly dragged his tired eyes up from there. Although near exhaustion, he'd had no trouble when he mentally peeled her clothes off and ran his hands over every part of her. Touching her in places he knew she'd never let him. The problem with that was, his body had started giving him a message: either jerk off or go to sleep. Solo sex had never appealed to him so he'd chosen the latter. Now his body gave the impression he'd been on a two-day binge. Being less than one hundred percent could shoot his creativity all to hell.

He shook his head in hopes it would revive him. Then he climbed out of the car, shoved the keys into a front pocket of his jeans, and walked the short distance to her house. It was one of the better examples of Victorians in the city. It commanded his attention again, and he paused a few more moments to admire it.

A wrought iron gate met him at the foot of the stairs. He fumbled with the lever, pulled the gate open, and climbed up to the small front porch. A brass plate built into a side wall held two doorbells alongside an equal number of name slots. Hewitt was printed on the top one and the name Grandy below it. Probably the aunt occupied two floors.

The door swung open before he had a chance to ring Molly's bell. A woman dressed in a yellow halter top, knee-length pink shorts, and cowboy boots stood in the filtered light. Two long gray-flecked braids hung from her head like thick ropes rubber-banded above frayed edges. Willie Nelson in drag came to mind.

"Hi, you must be Nick. I'm Molly's Aunt Vi. Come on inside. She's running late."

He pulled off his sunglasses and hooked them on the neck of his T-shirt. Then he followed her into a foyer where an oak combination coat rack and metal umbrella stand occupied one wall. Even to his untrained eye, the piece looked like an expensive antique. A staircase led to the second floor. He followed Molly's aunt and entered what he assumed was the downstairs part of her living quarters.

Apparently, she was a huge fern fan. They dangled in beaded slings from every corner of the living room. A couple more hung in muted sunlight that spread in through a pair of windows. A huge macramé owl, perched on a yard-long branch, took up most of the opposite wall. Enough candles to set the neighborhood on fire, if anyone was crazy enough to light them all at once, occupied a coffee table. Another table held a hookah and a crystal ball.

Holy shit. This was the woman who raised Molly.

"Have a seat." She pointed to a brown overstuffed sofa that looked as if it could swallow a small person. He sank down into it and wondered if he'd need a lifeline to haul himself back up.

"Let me find you something to drink."

She spun out of the room before he had a chance to forestall her and returned a minute later with two glasses of something yellow. He hoped it was only lemonade. Probably a tree half the height of the house grew in the backyard and provided Molly and her aunt with enough vitamin C to ward of any forthcoming plagues. The two of them should get together with his mother sometime. On second thought, maybe not. She handed him a glass.

"Do you live in the city?" Vi eased into a plump companion chair.

"Yes, I do."

"You rent, correct?"

"Yeah." His gaze strayed to the crystal ball. Nah.

"Do you play poker?"

"Excuse me?" He put his free hand on his knee and leaned forward.

"Do you play cards?"

"Not too often." Occasionally, he played gin rummy with his father. He took a sip of his drink and his lips puckered. Apparently, he was in a sugar-free zone. An organic garden probably flourished behind the house as well.

"That's the reason Molly's late this morning. She overslept. We had one heck of a poker game here last night. It didn't break up until midnight. Molly was the big winner. She cleaned my daughter and me out."

Yeah, he already knew she was pretty skillful at relieving people of their money. "How much did she win?"

"Plenty. The last pot had a buck forty in it. She won it with a straight flush. Drew an inside card, too."

"That was luck." Chunky ice cubes, the kind produced by metal trays, filled his glass. His hand began to freeze. He looked around for a place to set down his drink.

"Partly luck. It also took some skill."

No wonder Molly was so good at stonewalling. What was she, some sort of card shark? He did a quick recalculation on how long it might take him to lure her away from his tenants and onto his team. Did he have that much time?

"Of course, she snagged three of the four wild cards. When that happens, no one else has a chance."

Wild cards. He smiled.

"Hi, Nick."

Molly stood in the open doorway and held a cellophane-wrapped food basket cradled in her arms. Her hair fluffed out from her head in a mass of soft, copper curls. She wore a yellow, orange, and white flowered sundress with narrow shoulder straps and red buttons down the front. Her toenails were painted the same cherry red that matched the shade on her lips and fingernails.

It showed off well with her flat-heeled sandals. The little white jacket she carried didn't seem like it would do much to keep her warm two hundred feet above the ground. Maybe if she shivered from the chill, she'd let him hold her in his arms. Then maybe he'd get lucky and find out if her lipstick tasted like cherries. Just imagining it signaled an anatomical wakeup call. *Jeez, and in front of the aunt. What the hell am I thinking?*

"Hello, Molly."

He had only one chance to haul himself out of the sofa or come across like an incompetent ass. It occurred to him to knock off a few candles and park his drink on the coffee table. Instead, he flexed his leg muscles, tightened his grip on the glass, and put enough energy into his movement to propel himself up and out of the beast's embrace.

Molly stepped into the room.

"Very good." She grinned. "You didn't spill a drop. It takes most people at least three tries to spring up out of that thing."

"It's all in the legs." He tried not to sound smug as if he performed an Olympic feat.

A few steps brought him close enough to touch her, which he had the sense not to do. She smelled faintly of apricots. He breathed in the scent. Then he remembered he was supposed to be a gentleman and not out to seduce her.

"Here, let me hold that." He took the food basket out of her arms.

Her aunt stood up with no trouble, but then he figured she had years of practice extricating herself from the furniture. As she relieved him of his glass, she gave her niece a tiny nod. Molly frowned. He assumed all the facial maneuvering had something to do with him.

Chapter 14

"My aunt's a bit eccentric," Molly said once they reached the sidewalk.

"Yeah, I noticed. It doesn't seem to have rubbed off on you, though. Or maybe you have your own crystal ball."

"That's only for show."

Nick put his hand on her lower back and started to steer her toward his car. "And the hookah?"

"Oh, that. She claims she hasn't smoked anything illegal since the Summer of Love." Molly looked out at the street in both directions. Then she spotted the N MAN 1 license plate. "Where's the limo?"

"I canceled it. I hope you don't mind." Nick fished his car keys out of his pocket.

"Not in the least. I'm not into limos. Actually, I don't go in for most kinds of formal stuff."

"Yeah, neither do I. I didn't think you did, either. So I took a chance." He popped the trunk and set the food basket inside.

Once in the car with the motor running and the cool air flowing, he turned toward her. "I'm pretty casual. So we have at least two things in common."

"Two?" She hadn't thought they had *anything* in common.

He put his hand on the edge of her seat back. "The other is something I'm not allowed to mention."

"Wha . . ." Then she got it. "Oh. You mean the ten . . . But we're on opposite sides."

"Not really."

"How do you figure that?"

"Well . . ." He paused and then shook his head. "No, we made a deal. I had to remind myself all morning not to head there. I woke up a few times last night and wondered if I'd be a few thousand dollars poorer at the end of the day." He shrugged.

"It was on your mind all night?"

"Along with one or two other things that were a lot more pleasant."

"It's not worth losing sleep over." He did seem a bit less animated than usual. "I mean, if you should happen to sort of unconsciously mention . . . *you know what* . . . well, I don't want you to spend the whole day worrying." *Especially since I intend to somehow find a way to mention my own you know what.*

"No, I made the rule. As far as I'm concerned, it's ironclad." He twirled a few strands of her hair around his finger. "Sometimes I wonder if any of the other stuff is worth it, though."

"Other stuff?" His thumb touched her earlobe, and she felt a pleasant buzz slide all the way down her body and into her toes. "What other stuff?"

"Hey, we're out for fun." He smoothed the lock of hair behind her ear. "So let's get on with it. We're liable to hit traffic heading toward the bridge." He put on his sunglasses—the Sexiest Man Alive ones—and pulled the car away from the curb. "If you'd like, I'll answer your question later."

"Well, sure. I suppose. I do have another one, though." Here came the perfect opportunity to grill him. Sooner than she'd hoped.

"Shoot."

"Do you think there's any further interest in . . . ah . . . building on our block in SoMa?" She was careful not to mention right away her suspicion the interest might come from him.

"I think it's possible. No, probable. It's a prime target for urban renewal. Someone's bound to put together the necessary financing."

"Like . . . who?"

He shrugged.

She angled her body so she half faced him. "Like you, for instance?"

"When I finish my condos and sell them . . . wait a minute, I'm not allowed to mention anything about the . . . you know."

"I'll give you a one-time dispensation."

He laughed. "Okay, I might have . . ."

"Might have what?"

"Some interest, but it depends . . . wait a minute. I think I used up my dispensation."

"I can't lose the clinic." Molly's worry and frustration poured out in her tone. Right now, she didn't care about rules or penalties for breaking them.

"It shouldn't be too hard to relocate down there in SoMa."

"Any street would be impossible. We don't pay rent."

"Sweet."

"Is that all you have to say?"

He gave her a quick glance. "You're in tight with the mayor. Maybe he could help you out. I read plans are afoot to clean up Sixth Street. I'm sure the clinic would be a welcome addition. You can write another grant. Anyway, let's put all this on hold for now. I thought we already agreed on that." His full attention shifted to the road as he wiggled through traffic.

Oh, he was interested all right. The way he cut her off proved it. He was a man who knew what he wanted and knew how to make it happen. Molly's shoulders slumped.

The usual sea of autos met them as they headed into Golden Gate Park. Sunlight bounced off the shiny black hood of Nick's car, and Molly fished her sunglasses out of her shoulder bag. Then she settled back against her seat. The balmy weather brought out the walkers, and people had already set up picnics on the lawns and tables in the park meadows. Dogs ran loose. Kids chased Frisbees while bicyclists clogged some of the paths. It was a glorious San Francisco day. Since there weren't all that many of them, she put her concerns on hold and made up her mind to enjoy the next few hours. She glanced out the side window. It seemed there were more than the usual number of joggers. Maybe that was how Nick kept in such good shape. Some people went to extremes running up and down the steepest hills in the city.

"Do you jog?"

"I never got into jogging." He glanced at her then turned his attention back to the road. "Do you?"

"No. I tried it a few times. It's too much like punishment."

"That's how I see it."

Hmm. More common ground?

"How do you keep in shape?" Maybe he lifted weights or did karate. Or kickboxing. That could come in handy if he had to defend himself against Duncan Serk.

"I eat junk food."

"Stop." The way his jeans fit him left little to the imagination. No bulges anywhere except where her eyes had no business to stray.

"No, I'm serious. I eat it all the time."

She screwed up her mouth and scrunched her eyebrows then threw him one of her "don't try to kid me" expressions, but he watched the road ahead. If he ate junk food, could that mean he didn't have a steady girlfriend? Of course, a lot of women these days didn't hang out in the kitchen. There were all the times every month she brought home a dinner salad or something hot and already prepared from Whole Foods. If *she* dated him, she'd cook up enough of a storm to put a sizeable dent in the supermarket chain's pre-cooked food profits.

"I eat mostly take out. I know a place in the Mission that makes the best enchiladas this side of Tijuana. If you request it, they'll pile on extra cheese."

Extra cheese. She thought about the food basket in the trunk of the car. She'd picked it up the previous afternoon from the caterers. Some of the food it contained seemed far from ordinary, such as smoked eel. Would anything that exotic appeal to a man who thrilled to a cheesy enchilada? She was pretty sure the caterers hadn't included anything with a south-of-the-border taste. She hoped that wouldn't be a problem.

They passed through the Presidio, the former army base, then onto the Golden Gate Bridge. Crowds of pedestrians, some with cameras dangling around their necks, some pushing baby carriages, thronged the walkway along with bicycle riders and roller skaters. The bridge was probably the hottest tourist attraction in San Francisco, but locals took advantage of it, too. Walking the span was something Molly often talked about but never earnestly pursued. Dozens of sailboats dotted the bay and circled Alcatraz Island. The sun was a golden splash on a pale blue canvas. She looked forward to the balloon ride and the picnic later with Nick.

"I owned a boat once. Well, a tenth of a boat. I chipped in with a bunch of other guys. It was right after I graduated from college."

"You went in with nine others? How big was the boat?"

"Not too big. I didn't have the time to use it enough. I sold my share a couple of years later."

"What made you go in on it?"

"We all thought it would be a great way to attract women. It worked for a few of the guys." He shrugged.

What a waste of money. He could have invested in a skateboard and, with that body and those looks, gotten the same results. Maybe he'd arrived at the same conclusion.

Traffic thinned as they passed through Marin County and onto the two lanes that headed toward Napa. Neat rows of grapevines covered the gently rolling hills and stretched for miles. Tiny silver streamers anchored amid the vines, meant to discourage the birds from eating the grapes, fluttered in the breeze. The valley was one of Molly's favorite places. Only about an hour north of San Francisco, it lured locals as well as tourists for wine tasting, shopping, and fine dining. She didn't know of any restaurants in the area where you could order an enchilada with extra cheese, though.

She glanced over at Nick. "When's the last time you were up here?"

"Two weeks ago."

"Really? Yet you bid on the balloon ride. You must like it here.

I mean, to come back so soon."

"I own a house in Napa."

"Oh." That took big bucks. "I thought only movie stars and tech wizards could afford this area." Her tone said, *Explain that!*

"Well, for now it's only part of a house."

"Don't tell me. You're partners in it with nine other guys."

He laughed. "No, I'm the only one who'll live there, eventually. I hope."

Talk about ways to reel in women. A house anywhere in the Napa Valley would draw them like mosquitoes to standing water.

"Why did you refer to it as being only part of a house?"

"It's nowhere near finished. There's not much more than a roof and four walls. I've barely made a dent inside."

"It sounds like you're building it by yourself."

"I work on it every chance I get, but not often enough." He glanced at her, then brought his concentration back to the highway. "Maybe I could show it to you later if there's time. It's really the spectacular view that makes it special."

"I'd love to see it." She wondered if the offer was spontaneous or part of some master plan he'd hatched during his sleepless night. Maybe it coincided with whatever had prompted him to bid on the package. At the moment she didn't much care.

Nick followed the directions on a posted sign and turned onto a narrow dirt road. It ended at a field where a yellow and red striped balloon floated above a passenger basket. Two other couples were already onboard. He parked the car under a shade tree.

"How much of my twelve hundred fifty dollar bid is paying for the ride?" he asked as they walked toward the basket.

"None of it is. Like all the other items in the auction, it was donated."

"That's very generous. Is the owner a relative or something?"

"No. We saved his life at the clinic last year. He just happened to be half a block away when he had a heart attack. Someone drove him over, and Dr. Ed worked on him while we waited for an ambulance. Thank goodness it turned out to be a mild attack. He said to call him if there was ever anything he could do to repay us. So that's why we're here today."

Nick put his arm around Molly's back. "You people are full of good deeds, aren't you?"

She wondered if that was a compliment or a subtle reminder about her connection to his tenants. She let it drop. Whatever his intentions, she'd made up her mind not to let anything ruin the day's excursion.

Molly introduced Nick to the owner/operator. They chatted for a few moments about the mechanics of becoming airborne. When, finally, the last of the riders climbed aboard, the owner fired the jets, and they lifted off with a gentle sway. The sun spread a carpet of heat over the valley, and Molly slipped into her jacket. Why spoil the day with a sunburn? Trees dotted the ground on either side of the field and merged in the distance. The balloon hovered well above the earth. They rose higher over the leafy canopies, and the whole valley spread out below them. The air was crisp and clear. Molly spotted the skyscrapers in downtown San Francisco. The bay sparkled under a brilliant sun, giving the illusion of buildings floating on water.

She kept a grip on the basket's wicker rim and lifted her face to the breeze as it swept over her. It sifted through her hair like gentle fingers. She hoped it wouldn't undo all the hard work she'd gone through for at least half an hour that morning to tame it. She'd used tons of conditioner, then had to rinse almost forever, which had made her late.

Nick stood close behind her. When the basket brushed a leafy branch and gave a little bump, he clasped her shoulders presumably to steady her. Except she only swayed a tiny bit. It was nice to feel a man's strong touch. Nick's touch, if she wanted to admit it. It excited her. Everything about him excited her. She'd have to be hooked up to life support not to feel the tingle that caused goose bumps to sprout on her skin.

He kept his hands on her shoulders, even after the basket steadied. It wasn't hard to figure out that he liked being close to her. Chemistry seemed to build between them and it was useless to deny her attraction to him. It grew stronger in spite of everything. It defied the odds. She tried to project into the hours ahead, after the ride ended and they were alone again. Would their molecules mesh or combust? She had a premonition that before the day ended, she'd have her answer.

Chapter 15

"I have an idea," Nick said once they were back on land and inside his car. "Why don't we have our picnic at my house in Napa? It's not very far, about twenty minutes or so. I'd like to show it to you. That is, if you don't have to rush right back to the city."

"That sounds like fun." No equivocating, no pretending she had another commitment, like a Saturday night date. He probably didn't have one, either, unless he planned to hurry her in and out. A quick peek at her watch confirmed it was close to two thirty. By the time they drove to his house and he showed her the spectacular view and whatever else, ate their lunch—leisurely, she hoped—then drove back to San Francisco in the Saturday evening traffic, it should be too late for him to spruce up for a big blowout on the town. At least, that's how she imagined it, how she wanted to imagine it.

She remembered the heat from his hands when he'd held her shoulders. It had flared right through her jacket as if he'd branded her. She didn't foresee putting up a whole lot of resistance if he wanted physical contact again. After wandering for almost a year in the dating desert, she'd more than earned a wallow at the waterhole. It didn't mean she'd fall madly in love with him. She shrugged out of her jacket and tossed it onto the rear seat.

Nick headed toward the highway. Beams of sunlight intensified the car's bright black finish; cool air began to circulate inside. He rummaged in the storage compartment between their seats and fished out a CD. "Do you like Tony Bennett?"

"Hmm."

He inserted the disc, and the tenor's voice filled the car with a low, silky growl. Contentment spread through Molly as if she were on a real date with a desirable man. At least she had the desirable part right. She glanced at Nick. His index finger tapped the steering wheel in time to the music. He even hummed a couple of bars. His body language hinted he was relaxed and enjoying himself. Nothing about him seemed to suggest he had an agenda. If he did, like he planned to get in her face and break his rule about not mentioning finances, she couldn't see it.

When they reached Route 29, the four-lane highway that bisected the valley, he headed north. Several wineries dotted the land on either side of the road. They were set amid seemingly endless acres of grapevines. Most of the properties stretched toward the gently sloping hills. If the cars in the parking lots were any indication, plenty of people took advantage of the winery tours and the picnic areas that sprouted on some of the grounds. It occurred to Molly the bottle of wine included in the item he bid on waited for them at Thistle Creek.

She reminded Nick. "They promised me a great vintage. Not that I'd know the difference. If you want, we could stop by there and pick it up."

"It doesn't matter to me. I'll leave it up to you."

"Maybe not. Everyone's probably busy in the tasting room. I just thought because you paid for it."

"I'm sure I have some wine at the house. I know there's beer in the fridge. That's what I usually drink."

"I'd better phone the winery to let them know we won't stop by," she said and called them on her cell. She was glad Nick had suggested they picnic at his house. The private room at Thistle Creek was beautifully appointed with redwood beams and acres of glass walls that let in the view of the grapevines and rolling hills, but it was in the midst of a very public area. Today she wanted privacy. If Nick's place were half as nice as it sounded, it would provide the perfect ambiance.

They cruised along the main highway for a few minutes before he turned onto a secondary road. From there he headed north along the

Silverado Trail. They drove by wineries whose names she recognized. Some of those labels ran well into the high two figures and even three. Special pressings cost even more. No connoisseur, she usually stuck to whatever brand of wine her supermarket put on sale.

Thickly canopied trees cast dappled shade onto the narrow road. Houses, some mansion-sized, perched on the hills. She wondered if one of them belonged to Nick.

Minutes later, he maneuvered onto another two-lane road. As they came around a bend, a high stone wall appeared. He pulled up in front of the tall wrought iron gate blocking their path. He lowered the car window, reached out, and punched a code into a metal keypad set into the stone. The gate swung open and they proceeded through. Grapevines staked in even rows bordered the drive and covered the ground as far as Molly could see.

"Do you own a winery?"

"No. This spread belongs to a friend. He sold me a half acre."

Nick followed the twisting drive over a rise. When it branched in two directions, he took the one that veered toward a low rectangular stone building. His house, she presumed. He parked in front and cut the motor.

"This is what's taken up so much of my time and . . . ." He rubbed three fingers together in the international sign for money. "Someday, I hope to finish it. The building is the original winery. The first vines were planted here over a hundred years ago. Todd, the guy who owns this property, built a state-of-the-art complex about a quarter mile down the road. This just sat vacant, and when he offered to sell it to me, I jumped at it."

He disengaged the locks, and Molly stepped out of the car. Nick joined her.

"How long have you owned your half acre?"

"A little under three years."

"I would have picked your house out right away."

"How's that?"

She pointed to the roof. "The solar panels. Greening the environment. Isn't that your passion?"

"Yeah." A grin played around the corners of his mouth. "It's one of them, anyway."

He didn't have to explain. His tone and the deep pitch of his voice said it for him. He was no stranger to passion. She wondered how many women he'd invited here and what he did with them once he hustled them inside his stone bunker. She also wondered what he planned to do with her, if anything. A pleasant shiver skipped down her spine.

"Those panels took eight months to install. I had to replace the original roof. Before we go inside, I want to show you the view."

He placed his hand against her back and led her around to the other side of the house. She felt something possessive in those long fingers that seemed more to caress than guide her. Or maybe it was her imagination. They walked across an ill-tended lawn—apparently, no time or money to sod it—toward where the ground sloped away leaving an unobstructed view of San Francisco Bay in the distance. The tall buildings that delineated the downtown area seemed to poke at the sky through the hazy light.

"It's awesome." He must have paid plenty for part of an acre. If he sold it, would the money be enough to placate his tenants? Then one look at his face killed the thought. Passion—the kind that had nothing to do with the seduction of women—again etched into every muscle, pore, and sexy crease. In order for him to surrender this little bit of paradise, someone would have to yank the deed from his stiff, dead hands.

"Someday I'd like to sink a hot tub, just about where we're standing."

She had a sudden vision of being cradled in a gush of steamy bubbles as she sipped wine and enjoyed the bay and city views. She almost felt the soothing water as it lapped against her breasts. Then she pictured Nick sitting beside her, his dark hair damp and mussed. He tipped a beer bottle up to his mouth. Foamy water sluiced off his tanned shoulders. Her bare cleavage suggested she was naked.

" . . . a swimming pool over there."

And, of course, if *she* were naked . . . an image of him reclining against the rim of the tub, his long legs outstretched, hit her with the force of a Muni bus.

"Molly?"

His voice shredded her fantasy.

"Sorry."

"Are you okay?"

Noooo. Not with the squirmy feeling that had crept up her thighs. "Oh, sure. What did you say?"

"It would be great to have a swimming pool someday."

He sounded uncertain but probably not about the pool as much as her having left planet Earth for a moment.

"That's a few years from now . . . if at all." He put his hand on her shoulder. "Come on. I'll show you inside the house. It's really unfinished, so don't expect too much."

He had her full attention now. Hot tubs, pools, solar panels—there seemed no end to his spendthrift ways.

Unfinished turned out to be an understatement. Once through the front door, it became obvious the house contained nothing more than a big empty space. Almost three years and all he had to show for it was a new roof. If he had gobs of money, wouldn't he at least have put in a bathroom? It would be a necessity if he worked to make the house livable every chance he got. Maybe he didn't have pots of money to throw around after all.

"The bathroom's in here if you'd like to use it." He opened a door and exposed an area spacious enough to host a wine tasting. A gleaming black porcelain tub—more than adequate for two and featuring Jacuzzi jets—was nestled into the far corner. The gray slate floor, plump charcoal towels, and pricey chrome fixtures made her blink. Spotless, it looked as if a herd of maids had recently galloped through the room. The only thing missing was a crystal chandelier dropping like a starburst from the ceiling.

Instead, he'd installed recessed lighting.

On second thought . . . about those pots of money . . . just let him cry poverty even once.

"Uh, maybe later."

"I put that in first, for obvious reasons. The rest will fall into place eventually. I'll stick a couple of bedrooms and another bath over there."

He waved toward the far end of the room where a pair of matching stained glass windows, reminiscent of Tiffany, were cut into the stone wall. Vivid shades of indigo and lavender in the grape clusters set off the different hues that composed the surrounding green leaves.

"Hopefully it'll happen in my lifetime, barring . . . umm . . . circumstances . . . and before someone carts me off to a rest home."

Circumstances? Cute. His pitch was so subtle she couldn't come right out and accuse him of breaking his rule.

"I've given myself another couple of years to complete everything. As you can see, it will take a lot of work."

Molly scanned the main living area. A scuffed stone floor supported a pair of sawhorses. A blueprint, tacked down at the corners, lay open on them. She walked over and glanced at it. Although she was unfamiliar with architectural drawings, the convergence of lines seemed to indicate different rooms. She assumed it was the plan for his house. "Is this the 'other stuff' you mentioned earlier? You said it could turn out not to be worth all the trouble."

He nodded. "I planned to finish everything a year ago. That was the initial goal I set. Obviously, I had to retrench. I just can't spare the kind of time needed. Or, for that matter, the expense right now."

That was the second time he slipped in money. Talk about continually breaking a rule, without actually *breaking* it. He was good.

Her synapses still fired, too. "If you don't see any way to complete the work, why don't you sell the property?"

"It's crossed my mind, given my current problems." He held up his hands in a defensive gesture. "Don't worry. I won't go there." An expression that rivaled the most angelic altar boy's suffused his face.

"Be honest, you just can't bring yourself to part with it."

"That's not entirely true. Granted, I'd let it go only as a last resort. I could survive if I absolutely had to sell and there was a way to do it."

"Don't you think that down the road you absolutely might have to find a way?" She held up her hands. "That wasn't a reference to you-know-what. Without the time and money to finish this project—and I can see how it would break your heart to abandon it . . ." *Oh, yes, I can really feel his pain. Ha!* "Yet, it might be best to let it go anyway, regardless of other . . . matters that shall remain unmentioned. It seems to bring you more guilt than pleasure."

He laughed. "That's okay. I know what you think. I've got a couple of other problems. One, I carry a mortgage on this place. Second, when I bought the property, it was with the stipulation that if I ever decided to sell, it had to be back to Todd. He doesn't want a succession of strangers living here, who could blame him? We kicked the idea around a couple of months ago. He's strapped with the new expansion. So even if it became an absolute necessity, I have no choice. Selling right now is not an option."

Molly had to smile. He was better than good. Way, way better. She wondered if he'd ever thought about running for public office. He'd be right out front bamboozling the voters. Probably, she was supposed to pass the information on to his tenants. Like Duncan Serk would care Nick had a slight problem with his weekend retreat in Napa. Still, Nick did offer to sell or, at least, claimed he did. Since she didn't figure him for a liar, she decided to believe him. Heck, she wanted to believe him.

"The only way to finish this house in the near future would be to unload the San Francisco property where my future condos and tenants are located. The man I bought the three parcels from approached me recently and made a serious offer."

"Have you considered it?"

"Not at present."

"It sounds like if you sold, it would solve your problems."

"If all I cared about was money, yes. This is the kind of guy who would invite the sheriff in the front door and run the tenants out the back. Without a buyout, either. Count on it. I heard a few stories about how stingy he was with the heat, how the plumbing often quit for days, and how he was impossible to get a hold of to make necessary repairs."

"In other words, you're the only thing standing between your tenants and the street."

"I guess you could look at it that way."

Was he putting her on? Who was *he* channeling, Robin Hood?

"Don't sell." She laid her hand lightly on his arm. Her eyes pleaded with him.

"I won't as long as there's a chance my tenants do an about face and decide to become reasonable. I haven't given up hope yet. Anyway, this conversation probably cost me a couple of grand. So, before I'm out any more, why don't I rescue our food basket from the car? What will eventually become a kitchen is that way. I'll only be a minute."

Molly headed in the direction he indicated. An opening in the only wall that didn't feature exposed stone led to a room that contained a relic of a refrigerator and another pair of saw horses. They supported two long stout planks that together formed a surface deep enough to serve as a table for their picnic. Maybe he had a couple of folding chairs stashed somewhere. A sheaf of blueprints lay stacked at one end of the planks. Molly only had time to peruse the top print when Nick entered the kitchen with the basket. He also carried a plaid blanket.

"Are these for your construction project?" She replaced the prints. "There seem to be too many for a single house. Don't worry. It won't cost you a cent to answer."

"Yeah." He spread the blanket on the planks and set the basket on it. He began to remove the cellophane. "I've kept those extra copies up here ever since someone broke into the trailer and trashed my office."

"Really? Do you know who was responsible?"

His expression implied the answer didn't require Einstein's brain.

"You think it was one of your tenants?" A picture of Duncan Serk wielding a crowbar came to mind.

He shrugged. "I won't know anything unless the police come up with an answer. I'm not counting on it, though. Still, there's no way the frequent vandalism is going to halt the construction."

She guessed he expected her to pass that on, too.

"It's a pretty ambitious project for such a downtrodden area."

"Maybe I'll start a trend after all."

Not a single vestige of the apartment house appeared in the blueprint she scanned. On paper, it was already obliterated.

"You mean inspire other builders to follow suit like you suggested earlier." Molly hoped not.

"Is that such a bad idea? Last time I heard, it was called urban renewal or beautification or just turning a crappy area into someplace habitable." He wadded up the cellophane and pitched it into a nearby bucket. "Come on, Molly, admit it. There are areas South of Market desperately in need of improvement. Don't tell me you were against all the new construction that blossomed downtown and around the Giants' new ballpark in China Basin."

"No . . . not exactly."

"I'm going to take that as a definite no. So, we're in agreement there. See, we do think alike." He removed two small jars from the basket, one that contained mustard and the other chutney, and set them aside. "Why don't we eat?"

Molly removed a couple of small ice packs she'd wedged down among the food items to keep them fresh.

"I think there should be a few things in here for a starving man."

"I'm sorry I don't have any furniture. That doesn't mean we can't sit."

He placed his hands around her waist. Strong hands, yet with a suppleness in the fingers that made her want him to stake a claim on that particular piece of territory and stay for a while. A long while. Her sundress served as the slimmest barrier between her skin and his. She might as well have worn a sheet of saran wrap. She held her breath and stifled the purr that throbbed deep in her throat.

He lifted her up and sat her on the blanket. "I'm starved," he said in an almost hushed tone. His eyes stayed on hers; his fingers probed her sides.

She tried not to read anything suggestive in any of it. Not when her synapses twanged like guitar strings and the word "willing" flashed in giant neon letters through her addled brain.

He blew air out through his mouth. "I think we need something to drink."

Molly swallowed hard and nodded her agreement.

He removed his hands.

A wine rack atop the refrigerator held three bottles of red. He selected one, brought it over to Molly and offered it for her inspection as if he were a Sommelier.

"Would madam care for Cabernet or something cold from the refrigerator?"

"Do you have Chardonnay?" It surprised her that her voice sounded normal and not like she just survived a bungee jump off the Transamerica Pyramid.

"No. I meant beer. Sorry."

"Hmm. I'll take the Cabernet. Not that I don't ever drink beer, but that's usually at an outdoor barbeque, in the heat." It was pleasantly cool inside the house with all the stone.

He retrieved an opener and stemmed glass from the top of the refrigerator. She assumed he kept the wineglass for visitors since he preferred beer. Possibly—no, probably—he came up here plenty of times with women over the course of three years. A twinge of jealousy pricked Molly's skin. The opener was the two-pronged kind that Molly had never mastered. Naturally, he extracted the cork with no effort. He filled her glass halfway and handed it to her. Then he fetched a beer from the fridge and joined her on the blanket with the basket between them.

"Okay. Let's see what we have in here." He retrieved two black handled knives, forks, and spoons from the basket and laid them aside. A pair of linen napkins along with two small china plates followed. He passed one of each to Molly. She set them on her lap. Next he produced crackers, cheese, and a link of summer sausage. "Oh, good. I was afraid we were going to be stuck with girly food. Why don't we start with these?" He used a knife to load a hunk of brie onto a cracker and handed it to her.

She figured he wasn't much of an hors d'oeuvre man.

He cut off a thick slice of sausage and put it on her plate. He added another slice to a cracker and bit into it. Crumbs scattered and he caught most of them with his free hand. He brushed the others off his lap.

He gave her a sheepish smile. "I guess I'm not very good at this. Usually, when I eat a cracker, I push the whole thing in my mouth."

Molly bet he probably managed it without looking like Gordo the Gastronomic Glutton, too.

"Go for it." She fished out a tin of caviar. She held it toward him.

He pulled the edges of his lips down so far the tendons in his neck corded. "I'm not into exotic foods."

"I forgot. You prefer junk."

He smiled. "There's a lot to be said for it."

"Okay. Then, I guess we can scratch the jellied eel."

He tilted his head toward her. "Absolutely, unless the big quake hits pronto and that's all we have left to eat. How about you?"

She shuddered and wrinkled her nose. "Not even then."

He laughed and lightly tapped her cheek with his knuckle.

She felt another surge of heat.

He rummaged around in the basket. "What's this?" He held up a plastic container of pasta salad with pesto. He removed the lid and sniffed. "Hmm. I'll bet this tastes good."

Man food. Green, too. No wonder it appealed to him. They ate quietly for a while. Molly discovered a jar of olives, along with smoked salmon pate (her favorite), chips and salsa (his), dried fruit, which they both passed on, and chocolate fudge shortbread cookies, which they devoured.

"I'm glad I bid on the Napa package." He dusted the last of the crumbs off his hands. "I had a really good time today."

"So did I."

He stood and took her plate and glass from her and put them aside with his. He set the basket on the floor. "I'm glad, too, that I got to know you a little better."

"Why is that?"

"I found out more about what you're like. We're pretty similar in a lot of ways."

"You mean the jellied eel."

He moved in front of her. "I mean in important ways."

She perched several feet above the floor and sat close to the edge of the plank. Her knees bumped his hard abs just above the waistband of his jeans. Her shins brushed his fly.

"Really, like what?" She debated whether to move her legs. In case he hadn't noticed, she decided to keep them in a holding pattern. Why direct his attention *there*?

He rested his hands on the blanket, one on either side of her. His thumbs lightly stroked her fingers. "Oh . . . I think we proved today we're both pretty easy to get along with. We're considerate and caring. We're both serious about our work. Come to think of it, too, we know how to get down and dirty and have a good time."

She nodded, although she wasn't sure about the "down and

dirty" part. She might have questioned one or two other points as well. Right now, though, he was proving a lot more than easy to get along with. As for her, she was nano-seconds away from feeling just plain easy.

"This was fun."

"I'm glad you think so. You spent plenty of money on today's outing."

"It was worth every dollar."

He placed his hands around her waist. His thumbs pressed into soft flesh as his fingers spread along her lower back. A shiver prickled her skin and spiraled into her toes and scalp. Her abdominal muscles tensed. She wondered if the "down and dirty" part was about to begin. She looked into his eyes and saw her desire reflected back at her. She laid her palms against his chest and touched lightly, her fingers rigid, making up her mind as to just how "dirty" she wanted to get with him.

His forehead rubbed the spot above one of her eyebrows. The edge of his nose touched the tip of hers. A corner of his lips grazed her cheek. Then his mouth moved over hers. Any thought of pushing him away evaporated under a seductive power that turned her hands to marshmallow fluff. The warmth from his mouth sent her body heat into a zone she'd never experienced. The kiss deepened and her heart pumped so fast it thumped inside her chest. The temperature in the room shot from cool to warm to something close to a tropical burn. Her lips parted, and he slid his tongue inside her mouth. A moan echoed from deep inside her throat, like the ocean's roar in her ears. Her Aunt Vi's warning flicked along the edges of her mind: "Either ride him until he's spent or prepare to be gored." How prophetic. He edged back just about the time she thought she'd need resuscitation from a posse of EMTs.

It took a few moments before she remembered how to breathe like a normal woman.

"You taste like chocolate cookies," he said.

"Is that good?"

His hands moved up her back. "So good, I'd like more."

"Are you going to kiss me again?"

"That's sounds like a plan." He smiled. "Do you want me to?"

Did she? Sure, she did, although it probably wasn't a smart idea. He looked more than ready. So why didn't he just do it? She didn't recall him negotiating with her either of the other two times.

"Well, do you?" His finger traced a slow S curve down her spine.

"I . . . think so . . . " Why couldn't she just come right out and say yes? Maybe because warning bells were already . . . if not clanging, at least pinging.

His nostrils twitched.

"Though maybe you shouldn't." If she kissed him again now, would she wind up looking like a fool later if he bulldozed the clinic right out from under her desk chair?

"That's what I like, a woman who knows her mind. You're not a tease, are you?"

"Certainly not."

The tips of his fingers played with the moist flesh at the back of her neck. "Then let's start from the beginning. Do you want me to kiss you again?"

"Yes. But . . . "

"Screw *but*."

He took hold of her head with both hands and angled his body between her knees. His mouth teased hers for a moment then came down with a possession that cramped her toes and brought her arms around his back. The muscles in his shoulders tensed where she pressed her fingers. His thumbs circled along the outer ridge of her earlobes and her skin tingled as if he tickled her with a thousand silky threads. Fiery heat pooled deep inside her, confirming her strong attraction to him.

He dragged his mouth away from hers and kissed her throat. His tongue flicked her skin, hot and wet and demanding. She pulled in her breath. The tips of her fingers pressed deeper into his muscles. Her nipples grew stiff and pushed against his chest. He hooked his thumbs under the slender straps of her sundress and peeled them off her shoulders. His mouth and tongue followed their descent while he began to undo the buttons at the front of her dress. He slid his hands beneath the fabric and stroked her breasts.

"No bra," he whispered against her ear.

"I was . . . in a hurry." She breathed rather than spoke the words. "The straps . . . show, too."

His fingers brushed her nipples, stiffening them further until they felt as hard as two perfectly matched stones. "We definitely can't have that."

Her knees clamped against his hips.

"Hmm. You feel good."

The tingle that started in her breasts curled into the deepest part of her body. She squirmed under his feathery touch. She brought her hands to his chest and rubbed her palms against hard pectoral muscles. She kissed his neck.

He peeled off the top of her dress. With one hand, he cupped her breast and brought it to his mouth. His other hand moved lightly up her thigh. His thumb stroked the flesh on the inner side and paused for a moment at the elastic band that edged her panties. She groaned and her body swayed; the muscles in her abdomen tightened. She rubbed her chin along his shoulder. He raised her knees higher up onto his hips then slid his thumb inside her panties and caressed her hot, slick flesh, sliding inside her, up as far as he could reach. She yelped and shuddered as he pushed his finger in and out of her. It was like nothing she'd ever experienced before. It was . . . hellacious. "You feel better than good." He licked the aureole that circled her nipple.

She reached down and worked open the button on his jeans and pulled his shirt out of the waistband. She slid her hand over his hard abdomen then followed the trail of soft hair that led beneath the band of his underwear. She bet something felt better than good down there, too.

"Nick . . . Nick?"

Had she, in a moment of passion, called his name? If so, she didn't recognize her voice. Who could blame her with what was happening to her body? Damn if she didn't feel the beginnings of an orgasm. Another few moments and it would tear through her like a scythe slashing through a poppy field.

"Hey, buddy . . . you in there?"

That was definitely not her voice. Nor was she in a position to knock on the front door.

"Holy shit."

No trouble recognizing that voice as Nick's.

He didn't move for a moment. Then he shook his head as if he'd just come out of a dream. "Holy shit on a stick." His hands, so busy giving her the most mind-blowing pleasure one minute, stilled and then withdrew. He unlocked her legs from around his hips and took a few tentative steps back. Cool air rushed at her naked skin.

"Hey, bud. It's Todd. I saw your car out front. You okay in there?" The sound of knuckles rapping on glass carried into the kitchen.

"Yeah. Give me a minute."

Her eyes locked with Nick's. He looked dazed. Exactly the way she felt. Then he retreated farther and zipped his jeans. From his pained expression, Molly couldn't tell if he was still hard or just sorry for the interruption. As soon as he turned away, she gathered the front of her dress and buttoned it in record time. Her hands shook like she'd just been dumped into an ice bath.

The front door opened and closed, then there was silence, except for the soft tone of Nick's voice and then Todd's. She straightened her dress and smoothed down her skirt. Her body still tingled everywhere Nick had touched her. She had to figure that meant only one thing: she'd gone from pissed to bliss in such a short time it probably hadn't even registered on the clock. It wouldn't take more than another session with him for her to stare the L word in the face. Not such a good idea. To fall in love with Nick Mancini was as dangerous as walking down a dark street infested with gangbangers and paying no attention to the danger. Too late, though—she was halfway there already.

Chapter 16

Although the game between the Giants and Mets had turned into a real cliffhanger—bottom of the seventh, the Giants behind one nothing with bases loaded and two outs—Nick couldn't concentrate on the action. He stood in the doorway of his parents' family room, where his father and brother—the newlywed—and his nephew and two brothers-in-law sat. It might as well have tuned into a tiddlywinks tournament. No matter who came up to bat, all he could picture was Molly half naked with her hand down his pants.

He didn't want to dwell on it, given the spontaneous reaction liable to burst forth behind his zipper. Was there a better way to ruin a Sunday lunch with the family? He had considered begging off, but the only excuse his mother would accept was he'd suffered a heart attack and taken up residency in a hospital. Maybe not even that would have worked since this Sunday lunch honored the recently returned honeymoon couple. Ever since his mother had steered three of her children to the altar, she'd rushed at him faster than an Amtrak Express.

Earlier, she'd spouted more than a few words on the subject of matrimony and all the advantages he was missing out on by not following his younger brother's example. "Younger" being the key word, as if, at Nick's age, he didn't hurry, his interests could turn to housing cats instead of a wife. That had provided the perfect segue into when he planned to bring Molly around again. Why hadn't he invited her to this shindig? He'd mumbled something along the lines of, "Give it up, Mom," a declaration she'd chosen to ignore. No surprise there.

Although having spent a total of ten minutes with Molly, his mother had anointed her "the perfect companion" for him. *Companion*, like he had one foot in a retirement home. She'd continued on to suggest he should "find a way to become closer to her." She would have had an apoplectic fit if she saw how close he'd gotten to her in his sorry excuse for a kitchen the day before.

"I don't know why they pay a guy who hits two forty a few million dollars," his father lamented. "The best he can do in a clutch is a pop-up. I can't believe they won the World Series."

Nick took a slug of beer and watched the Giants stream off the field. They'd tied the score but couldn't bring home the extra run. Any other time, he would have been right in there close to the action and added his own expletive-deleted commentary. He loved baseball like some men loved their Harleys. Not today. Today he couldn't keep his mind off Molly and how she'd felt and tasted. Her skin was so creamy soft it was like stroking butter. Every one of his senses still thrummed at the memory of her. Even now he couldn't figure out what in hell had made him act like a mongrel in heat.

He couldn't decide whether or not he'd dodged a bullet when Todd had showed up at his door the previous afternoon. He had halfway hit a home run with Molly, which wasn't anything he'd consciously planned when he suggested they share the picnic at his Napa house. Sure, he needed her on his team, but he envisioned luring her there with subtlety. He used to be good at finessing a situation. Instead, he'd let his hands rule his head. At least he'd gotten across the message about being financially strapped, that it wasn't fiction he concocted on the spur of the moment. She'd seemed to believe he'd made overtures to Todd about buying back the Napa property and would have sold it if possible, which was the truth. He gave himself credit for introducing his financial woes without hitting her over the head with a wine bottle. On second thought, the way he'd slipped it in smacked of the old Mancini finesse. So the day wasn't a complete loss.

He'd never consciously planned to maneuver Molly into bed or jump her bones on a cold, stone floor. That said something for his motive. He hadn't even had a sleeping bag on hand, no less a bed. Or a condom. Jeez, where was his mind? Having sex with her might have—no, forget might—*would* have doomed any chance he had to win her over. This morning, she would have concluded he'd used her and deserved to morph into a creature with a curly tail and a snout. She'd lead the tenants like a rioting mob and hang him in effigy from a light pole. Shit. He'd dodged a bullet, all right. He took a long slug from the beer bottle that had turned warm in his hand.

Long before he met Molly, he'd concluded there were only three reasons to make love to a woman. One: You're horny and she's willing and available, you know from the get-go you'll never see her again and you don't care. Two: You're horny, she's willing, and you sign on for the short term. Then there's number three: The big enchilada. Horny becomes desire, her willingness turns to passion, and there are no more thoughts of the short term. You're in a relationship and somewhere along the way, it becomes a lifelong commitment. That's the kind of man Molly deserved, man number three. However, at his stage in life, he was still stuck at number two.

That was probably why he'd felt like a heel all day. Not just a heel. A shit heel. A rat, a flea-bitten cur. She wasn't the kind of woman who slept around, who took sex as casually as she trolled the supermarket for organic vegetables. She ran a clinic. She knew better than anyone about the dangers of unprotected sex, just as he understood the possible consequences of leaving home without a condom. Was he willing to take such a risk with her? Yesterday, he'd wanted her more than he could remember ever wanting another woman. Would she have taken the risk with him? At least, thanks to Todd, the decision had become moot. However, there was one positive: She'd engaged in that little escapade with him in his kitchen. That put her halfway onto his team. Where he wanted her. Where he needed her. So why did it make him feel like such a snake?

"Hey, Nick, since when don't you return phone calls?"

His sister's voice blew at him. He looked up at Barbara bearing down on him with purpose written across her face.

"Well?" She parked herself beside him in the doorway. "I left you two messages yesterday. Don't you check your voice mail?"

He dangled the beer bottle in his hands and tried to look contrite. "I've been busy. Sorry. I meant to get back to you, but I . . . ah . . . got busy." A tableau of him and Molly groping each other swam before his eyes.

"Are you working on weekends again? You need to quit that and get a social life."

Sometimes, when her motherly instinct kicked in, his sister had a tendency to treat him like a son instead of a brother. He gave an appeasing nod, which he hoped would kill the subject, and took another pull off the bottle.

His eyes wandered toward the TV screen, but all he could think about was what had happened with Molly. That, coupled with Barbara butting into his life, made him feel jumpy and irritated.

"I thought you'd bring Molly with you today." Barbara's elbow brushed against his forearm.

"What gave you that idea?" He drained his beer and thought this would be a good time to escape into the kitchen for another one.

"I heard it from Mom."

"Scratch anything Mom says on the subject of Molly."

"Why?"

"Mom's delusional."

"Really? She seems sane to me."

"Tell her she's wasting her time butting into my life."

"You can tell her."

"Why bother? She never listens."

"She would if, for once, you told her something she wanted to hear."

This conversation really needed to end. "Here's something you can pass on to Mom. I have no plans to bring Molly around for lunch or dinner or anything else." He executed a chopping motion with his hand to emphasize the fact. It was bad enough having one woman trying to run his life. He didn't need two. While he was at it, he threw in Serena/Sabrina who'd stalked him all week. So that made three.

Should he move out of the doorway and go over to where the men were hunkered down in front of the set? He stared at the screen. What the hell was happening on the field? Who were the Giants even playing?

"I . . . we . . . Mom and I thought you might be dating her. Emily, who for once showed up on time, agrees. We brought her up to speed in the kitchen. Beth, too."

Fortunately, the TV sound was turned up to accommodate his father's diminished hearing. He didn't need the male members of his family to rag on him if they overheard his and Barbara's conversation. Usually they stayed out of his business, but lately everything in his life had turned upside down.

"You all thought wrong."

"Then why did you practically get on your knees and beg me to let you take my place at Molly's auction and promise to babysit Joey for a weekend so Sean and I could spend some private time together? We thought it was because of . . . ."

" . . . leverage." He rolled the empty bottle in his hands. He'd never needed another beer more in his life.

"Leverage? What's that supposed to mean?"

"You majored in English. Figure it out."

"Very funny."

The loud crack of a bat brought his attention back to the TV. His brother was on his feet yelling and pumping his fist. The Giants must have gotten a hit, maybe even brought in a run while his sister conducted her inquisition. He took a few steps into the family room, feigning interest in a game he'd long since lost track of.

Barbara followed him. "Okay, I get the point. At least tell me if it worked."

"Yeah, I think it did."

Before his sister could pepper him with another battery of questions, he made his move. Not into the kitchen. Go in there and he'd be quadruple-teamed for sure. No, the empty chair beside his father beckoned. Quickly, he headed for the safety of men.

Chapter 17

Molly couldn't remember the last time she'd spent such a sleepless night. Probably the summer after she'd turned twelve and her dad sent her to boarding camp for two weeks. The adjustment had been difficult, and she'd stumbled around like a sleep-deprived zombie for the first couple of days. Then, wham, as if someone had wound her up like a mechanical Barbie, she'd jumped into every activity and even brought home a swimming trophy.

Since then, she'd shed a few tears over a broken romance and spent an occasional restless night. Nothing like she'd experienced since she'd tossed the dice in Nick's kitchen. That wasn't all she'd tossed. Her common sense had flown right out his front door. Even a second glass of Chardonnay after she'd arrived home didn't ensure a restful night. If all Nick intended was to seduce her so she'd ditch his tenants and switch sides, then she'd rolled snake eyes for sure.

It would help ease her guilt if she had some idea how he felt about her. He'd acted as if he were attracted. It hadn't taken a whole lot of words from him to convince her. Heck, if she remembered correctly, he'd been pretty economical with those. What he did say had made her all squishy inside, along with the way he'd kissed and touched her. Could she have mistaken his interest? They definitely meshed. Chemistry ruled in his rustic kitchen. His hands were gentle, like a lover's. No slam-bang bam, I'll get my rocks off and the heck with you. There was caring in his kiss, in his touch. At her age, she'd had enough experience to recognize the difference.

She slumped down in her kitchen chair and leaned her elbows on the table. She clasped her hands, rested her chin on her bent fingers, and tried to rouse her listless body and confused brain.

She woke at 5:00 a.m. in a tangle of sheets.

A half hour later, she abandoned sleep.

After she prowled around the apartment for a couple of hours and cleaned up a week's worth of mess, she fell back into bed and dozed fitfully.

Up again at 9:00, she dragged her body downstairs and fetched the Sunday *Chronicle* off the doorstep. She concentrated on the entertainment section. This was no morning to overload her brain with bad news.

Nothing caught her interest. She would have used the time to work on her next fund-raiser, but no interesting ideas surfaced. Instead, she spent an hour trying to reconcile her growing feelings for Nick. Her body got hot and tingly when she thought about him. Only one thing could put that to rest. Unfortunately, it was attached to his groin, and he was miles away. He probably slept like he'd downed a double dose of sleeping pills.

Maybe she was just suffering from a serious case of lust. She was as entitled to it as a man. Lust was a whole lot easier to recover from than unrequited love. She wasn't ready for love, unrequited or otherwise. Certainly not with Nick, not unless he lived up to his own sterling PR and proved he really was one of the good guys. Yesterday, he'd all but promised not to leave his tenants vulnerable. That required money. Did he have it stashed somewhere? He claimed not to, and she wanted to believe him. So what choice did he have? Either he evicted his tenants and forced them to take his latest offer of thirty thousand—which in about five years would turn into a dried-up sinkhole—or he'd have to halt construction on his project. Where would that put him financially? Maybe into bankruptcy.

Still, how could she urge the tenants to accept his offer? She couldn't turn traitor and sell them out. There was the clinic, too. What if they had to relocate? What if Nick forced it to close? He didn't have to act immediately. Once his condos sold, the additional properties might look attractive to him. Dominique had said as much. He could anchor the block with condos. He might even buy almost everything in between.

So what did her feelings about him matter? She could drop them on a BART track and wait for the 8:49 to thunder over them.

The ceiling light hurt her eyes. She closed them and an image of the good-guy Nick popped up behind her lids. If men were ice cream sundaes, he was a double scoop of butter pecan nestled in a well of hot fudge and topped with whipped cream, chocolate sprinkles, and a plump cherry. She rolled her tongue around her mouth. Where would she begin to lick him?

Her phone rang before she dug any deeper into her fantasy. Nick? She checked the caller ID. It was her Aunt Vi. Crap. Earlier in the week, they'd made a date to go to the Farmer's Market at the Ferry Building.

Molly eyed the vintage clock shaped like a big green teacup that her aunt had given her on one of her last birthdays. Twelve twenty-two. She'd prowled around for hours and accomplished zip. Unless she counted printing the word Nick on her pad three times in big block letters. She'd drawn a halo over one and a pair of horns above another. Since she sensed he fell somewhere between an angel and a devil, she left the third blank.

She grabbed the phone before voice mail activated.

"Hi, Aunt Vi." Her deeper than usual voice warned of a scratchy throat. Terrific. This was no time to come down with a cold. Not when she needed a clear head. Something told her a showdown between Nick and his tenants couldn't be too far off. She pulled her limp body out of the chair, ran some water, and carried a glassful back to the table.

"I heard you walking around up there. Are you ready to go to the market?"

Molly stifled a groan. "Oh, sure. I just need time to shower and dress."

"You're taking your time today. You must have had fun up in Napa."

"Oh, yes. It was . . . nice." Molly almost bit her tongue.

"Have you eaten lunch?"

"Not yet."

"When you're ready, come down and we'll grab a quick cup of tea and some fruit and one of those yummy alfalfa scones Trudie baked yesterday. I have some interesting news from her. It might not mean much, but then you never can tell."

The mole. Molly braced herself for disaster. Her aunt hung up before she could inquire.

Molly pushed herself out of her chair and tore off the sheet of paper. She stared at it for a moment. What were the chances Nick had spent a sleepless night and paced the floor as she had, all lustful and unfulfilled? What fantasy, if any, might he have played out about her? Would she see him again and not just on a drive-by? He'd been pretty quiet on the return to San Francisco. When he did chat, he'd steered clear of their friendly little tussle. Maybe he'd already forgotten he'd touched her in a very intimate place and that she'd touched him back. Or at least, she'd been about to when his friend shattered the spell.

She hesitated to ball up the sheet of paper. That would be like disposing of Nick, plucking him out of her heart and mind. She wasn't ready yet. How could she keep it lying around, though? What if her aunt or cousin found it? NICK, NICK, NICK. Like she'd erected a stupid shrine. Now her aunt waited to grill her about the balloon ride and its aftermath.

Molly folded the paper carefully and carried it into her bedroom. She slipped it into her underwear drawer between the lacy bra and bikini panties she'd purchased the previous month. An impulse buy, they'd cost more than she could afford. Why had she splurged on them? At the time, there hadn't even been a hint of a hot relationship. So maybe she was ready for one, ready for someone like Nick—but without needy tenants or any other kind of baggage—to shake up her life. He'd rocked her foundation yesterday. Would he try for a repeat? She doubted it. Instead of lamenting the loss, she should be grateful. A repeat clearly spelled trouble in letters a hundred times larger than the ones in which she'd printed his name.

She showered, dressed in cut-off khakis, a raspberry T-shirt, and sandals and by twelve-thirty sat in her aunt's kitchen. She sipped a cup of tea and choked down one of Trudie's alfalfa scones.

"I didn't hear you come in last night." Vi gathered a pair of wicker baskets from a utility closet and lay them on the floor beside the table.

"Oh?" Molly had never employed such stealth. When she'd arrived home, she'd removed her shoes and climbed up to her apartment on tiptoes. "Did you go to bed early?"

"No earlier than usual. Maybe I became too engrossed in the new cooking show on cable. It's called *Eat And Purge Your Way To Better Health*. Next weekend I'll try the oat bran waffles. You break open a few capsules of Vitamin E and add that to a pinch of desiccated cod and pulverized seaweed for the topping. I'll bring you up a batch. Supposedly, they freeze well."

"That sounds yummy." Maybe next weekend Molly would check if the Russians still booked flights to their space station.

"So, how did the balloon thing go?" Vi asked.

On the way downstairs, Molly had prepared herself for the question. "It went well."

"Good. No mishaps? I burned an incense stick to be on the safe side."

"I'm sure that helped."

"Did Nick enjoy himself?"

A thousand tingly pinpricks invaded Molly's chest and danced south. *Oh, yes.* "He seemed to."

"So, what do you think?"

"What do I think about . . . ?"

Vi made a horizontal wavy motion with her hands. "About you and Nick getting together again?"

"You mean on a real date?"

"You've thought along those lines, haven't you? Good. I like him. The way he looked at you, kiddo, he's very interested."

Molly finished her tea and carried the cup over to the sink. "He thinks I can convince his tenants to lower their demands. I can't. He claims to have their welfare at heart. Does he? I don't know for sure. He also claims to be practically broke. Is he? I don't know that, either. It's too complicated. So don't expect him to ring this bell again anytime soon."

"I'll burn more incense."

"Don't bother. There isn't enough of it on the planet to change things. Anyway, it isn't like I'm in love with him or even gaga over him." Well, she was sort of gaga, at least, if her heart and body were any indication. It was best, however, not to confess that to her aunt. Not unless she wanted an overload of incense clogging her nasal passages for the next year. "He's handsome, sexy, forceful, bright, and probably has ten more positive attributes I haven't even discovered. Even with all those pluses, he's not for me."

Vi rose, picked up the wicker baskets, and handed one to Molly. "Wanna bet?"

"No."

Molly slung her purse over her shoulder and followed her aunt out the front door.

"You're sure this isn't too early? Did I rush you out before you finished your scone?" They walked toward her aunt's truck.

The remains of the scone, wrapped in a paper napkin, resided in Molly's purse. "Tell Trudie she's a genius."

Dappled sun spread through the leafy trees and warmed Molly's skin. She hoped her energy would soon return. She'd hate to spend the rest of the day moping.

"Another reason I wanted to get to the market and back before three is I need to work on my costume for the upcoming Love Parade."

Last year, against her protestations, her aunt and Trudie had dragged Molly along with them. A fistfight had broken out midway through the festivities and the police had swarmed the area. The hem of her aunt's gown—she'd recreated Mother Earth with a "living" hat—had fallen victim to a horde of marauding gender-bending pixies and they'd had to fight to keep the gown from being ripped off her body.

They settled in the truck.

"Trudie knows just about everyone who has a connection to a city agency," Vi said. "She should since she's worked at the Hall of Records for forty years."

"You mean snooped."

"I guess you could say that."

"I would and worse." Molly grabbed the armrest as the truck swerved around a bicyclist who'd wandered too close to traffic.

"Anyway, she's friendly with a gal who works for the Department of Buildings. It seems Nick isn't the only one who's staked a claim to that particular area of SoMa."

"Someone else is building condos?"

"The Blackthorn Group. They bought up a whole chunk of city real estate across the street from Nick's project. At least half the block. The plans are drawn and the permits issued. It's still hush-hush right now. Trudie said their project is mixed use. The plans call for a commercial high-rise almost as tall as the Trans America Pyramid and a hotel. The remainder is slated for residential. A small park in the middle with trees and benches will create a tranquil space. The ground floor of the commercial building will house restaurants and shops, the top floors condos. Trudie said it sounds swanky. Whoever builds nearby is going to make a killing. Nick included."

Molly, who'd slumped in her seat, jolted up and faced her aunt. "What do you mean by 'a killing?'"

"Whatever Nick expected to price his lofts at, he can easily ask more. That half of the block will turn into a showplace. Trudie's friend says to expect builders to swarm down there."

Nick had never mentioned the Blackthorn project. If he knew

about it, would he let thirteen people stand in the way of his making "a killing?" All that money would just about ensure his interest in expanding down the street. Angel or devil? Molly still wasn't certain. This latest news ensured something was about to happen, maybe quickly. Mentally, she pictured Nick beneath a halo and hoped for the best.

Chapter 18

Molly hadn't thought it was possible: two sleepless nights in a row. That had to speak to something deeper than lust, something that kept a woman tossing in her bed at night. *Don't let it be love.* The word lurked in her brain like a serial intruder, and she skirted around it for two days. She didn't want to fall in love with Nick. Not when the whole relocation thing with his tenants and the vulnerability of the clinic floated above her head like a dark cloud ready to dump buckets of acid rain down.

Molly tapped her pencil against her desk. Since she couldn't sleep, she'd decided she might as well come to work early. Maybe she could squeeze out all thoughts of Nick if she focused on planning her next event. Sure, like if she bought a pair of hiking boots she could conquer Mount Everest. She glanced at the yellow lined page in front of her. All she'd managed were a few doodles across the top. At least it wasn't filled with a dozen variations of his name. Her heart wanted to follow the already trod route, but her brain resisted and won. A small victory, although probably the first of many future battles.

She leaned back in her chair, closed her eyes, and sighed. Maybe she could catch a quick nap. It might help her come up with a spectacular idea later for her next fundraiser.

A loud rap against the front door snapped her eyes open. It sounded like someone struck the metal with something hard, like a mallet. It could be a street person or, more than likely, someone with a medical problem. Dr. Ed wasn't even in yet. She went to the door and squinted through the peephole. Mrs. Zamoulian. Molly quickly worked the three locks and opened the door.

"Molly, you need to come." Mrs. Zamoulian flapped inside, visibly agitated, if a flushed face and flyaway bun were any indication.

She dragged along a rectangular sheet of cardboard mounted to a yard-long piece of wood. Writing, thick and black and probably made with a felt tip pen, ran across the cardboard in a downward slope. Two words had an X slashed through the middle. Whatever its purpose, the message was sure to attract attention.

"Mrs. Z." Molly took the sign and led the woman into her office. "Is something wrong?"

"It's that Serk. He says my spelling is shit . . . Excuse me, I didn't mean to offend . . . and that *he* is in charge of all the words. This is what he told me to print."

Molly took a closer look at the sign and read the uneven lettering. GREDY NOOKELHEAD BILDER. STAY OUT OF HER.

"Ah . . . Mrs. Z, what's going on?"

"It's a picket." The small, frail woman pulled her shoulders back and seemed to grow at least three inches.

"Picket?"

"We use your idea."

"Mine?"

"You know. Quiet but firm. We take your advice."

"My advice." Then Molly remembered the night of the association meeting. Ideas floated as to what constituted a silent protest. *Her* ideas, one of which she borrowed—no—*stole* from Nick. Of course, he hadn't been serious when he suggested they were ramping up to picket his condo project. Now it seemed the tenants had thrust the idea into action. "How many of you are involved in this . . . picket?"

"Everyone. I need you to fix my words."

Molly laid the sign on her desk. No amount of fixing was going to make sense out of this jumble of letters, but she couldn't tell that to Mrs. Z. They'd have to start over with a fresh piece of cardboard. She glanced around her office. Nothing useful.

"I think you should redo this. Do you have any other materials at home?"

"He does." Mrs. Z's eyes narrowed, and her nostrils flared. "Mr. Serk?"

"He says he will make sign. I say no way, Mr. Bully. Then I think of an idea. I tell him Molly will do it. Yes?"

Molly agreed, too tired to search her brain for an escape route out of the impending hell of confronting Duncan Serk. She grabbed her purse, the sign, and Mrs. Z's arm. She locked the door and headed for the apartment house. The tenants shambled in a line that stretched across the sidewalk in front of their building. Apparently, Mr. Serk had been busy. A glance confirmed he had a much better command of the language than Mrs. Z. Except for a couple of double negatives and misplaced commas, he managed to get his message across. Everyone carried picket signs. The demands started and ended with money—and lots of it. There were also a few brickbats aimed at Nick. When she helped Mrs. Z redo her contribution, she'd try to steer her away from "gredy" and especially "nookelhead" and onto something that might make her landlord more supportive.

Molly spotted extra cardboard, pens, and a staple gun. Should she ask permission or just collect what she required and get busy? One look at Duncan Serk stomping along the curb, and she opted for her second choice. She grabbed the necessary items and led Mrs. Z to a corner of the building farthest from the association scourge. It was only steps from Nick's construction site. Only two members of his work crew had arrived so far, but one held a cell phone in his hand. Suspicion gnawed at her that Nick already knew about the rebel movement that had sprung up outside his property. She propped the cardboard against the scarred wood of the building's façade.

"Okay, let's think of something that gets your point across. *Gredy*, I mean greedy, is thought provoking but, perhaps, not as positive as another approach. You want to state your position clearly without creating ill will. Remember, as you once said, you don't need a gun to catch bees. Just honey." Actually, Molly thought it was flies, but what difference did it make? Nick was going to be madder than ten hives full of stingers when he saw this rag-tag gang picketing his site.

"It was his idea." Mrs. Z pointed to Serk. "He's the nookelhead. I try to tell him what I want to say. He does not listen."

"I will. Tell me what message you'd like on your sign and I'll print it."

Mrs. Z patted Molly's arm. "You're a good girl. Smart, too. You I trust."

Molly smiled, touched by Mrs. Z's confidence in her. "Okay, let's compose something in your words, something you'd like to tell Mr. Mancini. Let it come from your heart."

Mrs. Z thought for a moment. "I want to tell him I need a roof on my head. This is my home. Do not take away."

A thin film of moisture blurred Molly's vision, and she blinked back the beginnings of a tear. She gave Mrs. Z a quick hug and began to work on the roof idea.

She penciled in a few words in large block letters. When the cardboard was filled, she stepped back to assess the impact of the message.

MY HOME

IS UNDER THIS ROOF

DO NOT TAKE IT AWAY

She read it aloud to Mrs. Z. "Is that closer to what you wanted to say?"

"You are such a clever girl. You told that Mr. Builder exactly how I feel. The others, they can show him the ill will."

Molly grabbed a black felt tip pen, propped the sign against the building façade and began to trace over the penciled letters. The jagged, uneven wall made it difficult to hold the cardboard steady. Mrs. Z had wandered over to help one of the other women just when Molly needed another hand.

The pen hit a particularly rough spot, creating a squiggle. "Oh, crap." Molly began to trace a straight line over the squiggly one.

"Do you need help?"

The hand that extended from the cuff of a pale blue shirt sleeve took up a position beside Molly's. She glanced over her shoulder and up into Nick's eyes. The vibrant amber had deepened to rusty mud.

"Hello, Nick." The last time she'd gazed into those eyes, they'd been heavy with sexual desire. Now they looked mad, sad, and anything but glad to see her. A quick glance at her watch showed the time at 7:31. He'd lost little time hurrying to the site.

"This is your idea, I suppose."

He spoke close to her ear.

"No. Well, sort of no, if you consider I'm not the original source. I'm helping Mrs. Z with spelling and penmanship."

"Is that your source over there?" He thrust his chin in Duncan Serk's direction.

"Actually, it's a lot closer than him."

"Someone ought to tell him he misspelled *doofus*. I think it has only one 's'."

Nick stood close enough for Molly to see his hair was still damp. It looked furrowed, as if he'd raked his fingers through it, like he jumped out of the shower and into his clothes and raced to the site. A thick lock fell toward one eye. Her stomach flip-flopped at the mere thought of brushing it back.

He took the pen from her, capped it, and put it in his pocket. Then he moved her hand and the sign slid down the wood façade to her feet.

"The idea came from you, Nick."

He frowned. "Try something more original."

He held her hand, the ring finger and pinky, anyway. Did that mean, in spite of the picketing, he still wanted to touch some part of her? More likely, he was afraid she'd bolt before he finished blaming her for everything from the housing crunch to global warming.

"Do you recall the morning you charged into my office? You said you were surprised your tenants weren't picketing you."

"So . . ."

She told him that at the association meeting someone, *possibly* her . . . mentioned a silent protest could, under the right conditions, be more effective than a bunch of people shouting. Picketing seemed like a good example. "I would never have thought of this on my own."

He shook his head and the frown melted. "You were supposed to stay out of it."

"I am out."

He nudged the picket sign with the toe of his shoe. "You keep digging in deeper."

"Is that what Saturday was all about? *Programming* me to turn my back on these people?"

"What? Hell no. Is that what you think?"

She shrugged. "It occurred to me."

"So that's why you're here making picket signs?" His thumb rubbed her pinky. Disappointment colored his tone, his expression turned hurt as if his best friend had abandoned him.

"Only one sign."

"When this is resolved, you and I are going to sit down and thrash this whole thing through."

"By then, one of us might not be talking to the other."

"Then let's go somewhere right now." He moved a few inches closer.

"Don't step over this line." She pointed to the thin ribbon of chipped concrete that outlined the sidewalk squares.

He frowned. "Why not?"

"It's a boundary line, like at a demilitarized zone."

"What have you people geared up for here, World War Three?"

She shook her head. "Mrs. Z said the tenants agreed to stay on their side of the line and not cross onto your property." Molly glanced over his shoulder to where a trio of workmen loitered near the construction site.

"Even Serk?"

"Well, I understand he was resistant. But only at first."

"That's city turf they're on."

"They have a right."

"Uh-oh." Nick dropped her hand. The muscles in his face tightened. He'd gone from abandoned to pissed off in less than a minute.

She glanced behind her. Duncan Serk, whose sign read DIRTY STINKIN, GREEDY, DOOFUSS, TALK AIN'T NO GOOD NO MORE stalked their way, one hand balled into a fist.

"Go back to work, Molly." Nick lifted her a few inches off the sidewalk and put her down on his side of the line. "Now."

The construction workers fingered their tool belts and moved closer to Nick. He waved them off and walked toward Serk. Molly stood her ground.

"Do you have a permit?" Nick asked Serk in a calm tone.

"Huh?"

"You're congregating on city property. You need a permit for that."

Serk frowned. His features compressed into tight lines around his ferret-like eyes. His mouth opened, but no sound came out.

"If you check with the police department, you'll find that no more than three people can be out here at one time." He fingered the cell phone clipped to his belt. "If you'd like, I can call the local police station and get clarification."

Molly had never heard of such a rule except for parades and demonstrations that involved large numbers of unruly people. Or gatherings in countries run by brutal dictators.

"While I do that, I'll have the cops investigate those studs you've stapled your signs to. If those are materials stolen from my worksite, you'll have to explain that, as well."

"Huh?"

Apparently, Duncan Serk was a man of single words when confronted by someone who stood up to him.

"It's illegal for this many people to gather. Unless you want the women arrested along with you, they should clear off the street. The men can continue picketing in front of the building. Just don't cross that line over there." Nick pointed to what Molly had referred to as the demilitarized zone.

Four or five additional construction workers arrived and stood clustered near Molly.

One of the other male tenants headed over to Nick. "We don't want any trouble. Right, Serk?"

"Yeah. Yeah, sure. We don't want no trouble, but we're stickin' to our demands."

Serk turned away without waiting for a reply from Nick. The women had already cleared off the sidewalk, except for Mrs. Z who seemed reluctant until Molly caught her eye and motioned for her to follow the others inside.

Only four men remained in front of the building. Nick walked back to Molly.

"Hey, boss. Nice goin'." One of the construction workers pumped his fist. Another slapped Nick on the back.

"Okay, it's over. If anyone comes onto this property when I'm not at the site, call me. Don't get into any hassles with them."

"Those guys ain't gonna cause trouble. You took care of that, boss."

"All right, it's over. Let's get busy."

The workers drifted onto the construction site.

Molly asked Nick, "Did they really need a permit?"

He shrugged. "I have no idea."

"You told them they did."

"It saved a lot of potential trouble. Good thing the real doofus isn't as stubborn as you."

She let that pass but only because she admired the way Nick had dealt with the situation.

"Serk's a bully. When you show a bully you're not afraid of him, he backs down."

"Well, that one certainly did." She cast a glance at Serk. He leaned against the building and puffed on a cigarette, his sign propped beside him. He seemed to have lost most of his aggression.

"That was nice of you to allow the men to continue picketing the apartment house. You could have made a huge issue when you discovered they'd helped themselves to your wood."

"Helped themselves? They stole it."

"Well, whatever. Anyway, you defused the situation. You seem pretty good at that."

His grin told her he was pleased with the way everything turned out. "Yeah, I've always had a knack for handling people."

"So I see."

He nodded and his grin widened. "Just so you know."

"Should I consider that fair warning?"

"Uh-huh."

"Really? How do you plan to handle me?"

He touched the tip of her nose with his finger. "That's easy. Now that I know what you like."

"Huh?" Damn, was that the best she could manage? Now she sounded like she'd just channeled Duncan Serk.

Chapter 19

Molly spent the remainder of the morning trying not to imitate a narcolepsy victim. By ten o'clock, the burst of energy that had carried her through the earlier hours at the picket line had dissipated and left her limp and fatigued. A glance at her calendar reminded her she needed to work on the budget. She'd already ruined two spreadsheets and cursed at her computer. The source of the problem wasn't technical. It was her. Cynthia supplied seemingly endless mugs of hot, strong coffee, but even the caffeine rush hadn't jolted Molly into a livelier mood.

She made a concerted effort to focus on all things mathematical. Still, her thoughts wandered back to Nick and how he'd accused Duncan Serk of breaking the law and cowed the bully. As if she had a tiny video recorder lodged in her brain, she freeze-framed his face and got hot and mushy and all but melted into her office chair. Was that any way to plan a budget? Not with her recent numerical ineptitude.

Something else had wrapped itself around her mind: Nick's cryptic pronouncement of "Now I know what you like." What did that mean? He'd discovered she enjoyed chocolate cookies, the Napa Valley, living in San Francisco, and—who would have guessed—*getting down and dirty* along with a whole lot of other things that were basically inconsequential. On the important side, he'd found out what made her squirm and moan and come close to having an orgasm without actually *doing* it. The past two nights she relived *that* exact moment. Would it happen again in real time? She wanted it to but, in a burst of self-preservation, she kicked it to the bottom of her wish list. Either that or turn herself into a fire eater because what she'd played with in Napa had the explosive power of a neutron bomb.

A light drizzle gave some much needed sparkle to the otherwise dingy sidewalk. Once inside her car, Molly got the motor started and the windshield wipers in motion. Then, without conscious thought, she whipped a U-turn, which pointed her in the opposite direction of her usual route home. She slowed the car and waited for her brain to figure out what was up. Uh-oh. She was headed straight toward Nick's construction site. Hmm. Now what would Dominique make of that? Probably the desire to be in proximity to Nick, or at least his workplace. Had it lurked all day in Molly's subconscious? Was that why she acted on it? That was crazy. Then again, so was everything that happened to her in the past week and a half. She hoped it didn't mean her head lost the battle with her heart. Wouldn't that be great? She could forever cruise the streets where Nick slapped up condos or whatever else he intended to build.

She was almost halfway there, so she decided to continue. Once she passed the corner of the site, she'd angle up to Market and then hook onto Castro. Probably more traffic that way, but she didn't feel like making another U-turn. Cars parked on both sides narrowed the street, and dusk edged closer to darkness. Also, the drizzle turned into rain.

She eased up on the gas as she approached the construction site. Alongside it, light spilled from the rain-streaked windows that fronted Mrs. Z's apartment. Most of the other units appeared dark. Molly slowed then stopped when she came abreast of Nick's temporary office. It showed no signs of life. She pushed on the accelerator but had only advanced a few feet when she spotted his car parked across from the site. He was possibly—no *probably*—inside the apartment building. Mrs. Z hadn't mentioned another association meeting. Still, he could be negotiating with his tenants. Then, again, he could be passing out eviction notices.

Molly waited for a break in traffic then whipped a U-turn at the corner and pulled in behind Nick's hybrid. Just as she killed her lights, did she see a vague outline of a person in the rear seat, leaning back against the curbside door? She edged forward against the steering wheel and squinted. On a clearer night, the streetlamp would have given more illumination. Tonight, mist and fog shrouded its glow. Her windows began to steam and she rubbed at the windshield.

Rain streaked his back window. Still, she was now certain someone hunkered down inside his car. Whoever it was glanced toward hers, waited a few moments, then turned back toward the building site. Nick? Why would he sit out here in the dark? Or it could be a homeless person. Once she'd forgotten to lock one of her doors and found an inebriated man sprawled across her backseat. It had taken her and Dr. Jake close to a half hour to coax him out.

Common sense told her to head straight home. But when, lately, had she used common sense?

She shut down the motor, palmed her keys, and climbed out of the car. She checked the street for traffic then dashed around the front of the vehicle to his curbside window. She bent down and peered through the steamy, moisture-streaked glass to the back of a man's head and compiled an inventory: dark hair stylishly cut, shoulders that only the gods could have chiseled, and a lower arm resting on the front seat back and advertising muscles upon muscles. It was Nick. Should she check to see if he was okay? She tapped on the glass.

The window rolled down a few inches.

"Molly?" He pushed open the door. "What the hell?" He reached out and grabbed her arm. "Get in here." He moved across to the middle of the seat and pulled her in beside him. He closed the door and slid the window up before any more rain slanted in.

The cool air inside his car, along with her damp blouse, chilled her. She pushed her keys into her pocket and crossed her arms over her chest and rubbed her shoulders.

"What are you doing here?" He brushed a damp, springy curl off her forehead. "Your hair is wet."

"I was on my way home." She blotted some of the moisture off her cheeks with the back of her hand.

"Shouldn't you have been heading north? You're going in the opposite direction."

Yes, but I was obeying this crazy impulse . . .

"I got turned around in the rain." At least it sounded plausible.

"I'm glad." His smile lifted the night gloom. "I'm sorry you got wet on my account."

"I spotted your car and wondered if maybe you were inside the apartment building."

"Why would I be in there?"

"Uh . . . " Should she ruin their cozy chat and confess her earlier suspicion he might have nudged his tenants toward a quick exit date? "I thought maybe you had . . . uh . . . reinforced the rules with Mr. Serk."

"He left an hour ago."

Steam smudged the windows. Sitting so close to Nick dissipated the coolness inside the car. They nestled in the quiet gloom, with their thighs and shoulders close enough to touch. A lick of heat burnt through Molly's clothes. Why did she have to feel so damn comfortable with him? So comfortable, she could have spent the rest of the night there and rubbed body parts with him while he waited for . . . what? Who?

"Are you expecting someone?" God, what if it was a date? But then, wouldn't he have stayed inside his trailer? Maybe not. A woman could hop from her car into his and not get too wet. Just like she had.

"You might say that." He checked his watch, one with a large glow-in-the-dark face and a batch of dials. An awkward sensation settled in Molly's chest and sent her comfort zone into a downward spiral. After she barged in on him, she could wind up looking like a fool. Those nasty impulses were bound to cause her all kinds of trouble. "I'm keeping you from something." *Someone?* "I guess I should head home." She reached for the door handle.

"Don't leave yet." He covered her hand with his. "Though, if I'm going to keep an eye out over there, we have to switch positions."

Positions? The last one with Nick had subsequently turned her brain to goo.

"The security I hired to keep tabs on the site after dark didn't work out. I've had to do my own surveillance off and on for the past week."

"You're still having problems?"

"Yeah."

Molly peered across Nick to the construction site. "Do you think it's Serk?"

"It's possible. But whoever it is can't delay the construction indefinitely. It'll take something really big to shut it down."

"How big?"

"Like a major collapse or a fire gutting the place."

"If Serk's responsible, shutting down your project almost guarantees he'll keep his apartment."

"Not forever. I'd rebuild and post more security down here."

Molly smiled. "I'll bet about . . . eighty thousand a unit could solve everyone's problems." She gave a vigorous nod as if she expected him to jump at her proposal. "I wondered if maybe you were inside negotiating with them."

"Eighty thou?" He laughed. "I love the way you squander money I don't have."

"Well, admit it, it has almost as nice a ring as a hundred. I'll bet they'd come down off their original demand if you proposed eighty."

He shook his head. "They and *you* have to show a lot more flexibility than that."

"I think they could be flexible."

"Serk, too?"

"Well, maybe not him. But he's only one vote."

"How about you?" He fingered the collar of her blouse. The pulse at the base of her throat began to throb even though he hadn't made contact with her bare skin.

"Me?" She tried for a laugh but instead gave a good impression of a woman being strangled.

"Yeah, you." He took his hand away and rested it on the seatback.

It took a few moments for her heart rate to settle down. "Oh, no question."

"Okay, then. How does forty sound?"

"Forty?"

"Tell them I'm willing to go that high."

Molly frowned. "Haven't we been through this before? You can tell them. If you think that's a way to get your project built . . . "

"The project will happen, Molly. Believe it."

Oh, she did. Like she believed the heat that spread along her thigh had everything to do with its proximity to his.

"I'll be as fair as possible." He glanced across the street. "If I'm going to catch someone monkeying around in there tonight, I have to face the other direction."

"I'm in the way. Maybe I should go." The "maybe," spoken halfheartedly, said she didn't want to leave and hoped he didn't want her to.

"No, don't go. At least not yet. We just have to change positions."

She couldn't remember the last time she'd gotten so close and chummy in the backseat of a car. In spite of the rain, warmth and contentment spread through her body. Because of Nick. She gave a quiet, blissful sigh.

"Molly?"

"Yes?"

"Are we going to flip-flop, or what?"

She gave her head a mental shake. "Sorry."

"Okay, then. Are you ready?"

Rain, heavier than before, pelted the car roof.

"You'll get wet out there when you come around to this side."

"Who's talking about leaving the car?" He put one arm around her back and his free hand on her hip. "Here, climb over me." He opened his legs.

Chapter 20

Molly's eyes glommed onto his crotch as if he had a brand new car registration with her name on it stashed in there.

"Climb . . . ?"

"Put your left knee between my legs." He started to lift her up out of the seat.

He wore tight jeans, and even in the semi-gloom, she made out a telltale bulge. He was either the most trusting man in the world or he'd performed this maneuver many times.

"Just stay between my knees, sweetie, and you'll do fine."

Molly put her hands on his shoulders. Then, as he guided her, she lifted her rear end up off the seat and placed her left knee where it belonged. Her skirt rode up a few inches as he brought her around to face him. Her lips hovered inches from his. Any closer and her ability to function would drop to something akin to a blow-up doll. His breath warmed her cheek.

Her right knee followed her left and she straddled his leg. Poised above him, she forgot how simple it was to breathe, so she didn't. When he put his hand on the back of her leg, she figured she'd probably never draw a breath again.

However he managed it, he rolled her across his lap. Then he changed places with her. Once again, he leaned against the rear passenger door, with her now in the middle of the seat. He placed his left arm around her and slid her toward him. They pretty much occupied one space. Cozy. Molly had no complaints.

"Now that I can look over your shoulder, I'm in a better position to spy." During all the maneuvering, he angled his left leg and shoulder against the seat back. His right leg, also bent at the knee, held her in the crook of his lower body. There were positions, and then there were *positions*. She snuggled closer and leaned back against his chest. He cupped her shoulder in his right hand. Why had he ever wondered if she could be flexible?

Spy talk reminded Molly of "the mole." She told Nick about the information Trudie passed on—that a good portion of the block across the street and at Nick's end was earmarked for a multi-gazillion dollar property. "Are you familiar with the Blackthorn Group?"

"Yeah, they're into major projects. They built a couple of those new residential high-rises on the Embarcadero. They'd have the money and the clout to build something similar down here."

"Trudie, my aunt's friend, seems to think everyone with a stake in this area will make a killing." She turned her face and looked up at Nick. "That includes you."

He remained quiet. Molly wondered if his mental calculator had already racked up the kinds of figures that could entice a self-proclaimed fair-minded man to veer toward greed. A financial killing could prove a powerful incentive.

His thumb moved lightly back and forth along her upper arm. "Do you remember I mentioned the guy who sold me the three parcels—the warehouse, apartment building, and vacant lot—I'm building on?"

"You said he offered you a buy-back."

"He sold initially to raise cash to invest in a project in the Mission District. He was one of several partners. I understand they had everything in place—building permits, approval from the Board of Supervisors, neighborhood cooperation. It was a go. Now, it's a no-go. It all fell through for some reason."

"So he wants back in on your site."

Nick shifted slightly. "He must have found out something about the buildings planned for across the street. That's why he made me the offer. It didn't make sense at the time. Now, with Blackthorn in the mix, I have my suspicions. I'd like to find out what he knows about Blackthorn's plans for their project."

Molly followed his line of thinking. Along with Duncan Serk, there was now another man—the one who'd evict the tenants without so much as a good-bye—with good reason to delay work on Nick's condos. Neither he nor Serk sounded like candidates for the Citizen of the Year award.

Behind her, Nick stiffened and sat up straight.

"Did you hear something?" He dropped his right foot to the floor and leaned forward. "It sounded like metal striking metal."

Except for the rain, which had slackened, an almost vacuum-like silence shrouded the area, odd for a city that usually throbbed with life. Molly listened for traffic. Maybe there had been a fender bender.

She shook her head. "I don't hear anything. Can you tell where the sound came from?"

"My guess is from across the street."

The rain slid in narrow streaks down the car windows. Another light glowed inside the apartment house. The construction site remained dark.

"I'd better take a look over there." Nick slid his left leg around and over the front seat. He opened the glove compartment and fished out a flashlight. He flicked it on and then off. "Lock the door and don't open it unless you know it's me." He slipped out of the car before she could suggest he arm himself with a tire iron or something equally lethal.

By the time Molly scooted over to the far side window and cleared away some of the evaporation, Nick had crossed the street. He paused for several moments at the construction fence. The beam from the flashlight swung in an erratic arc. Then he rolled the gate aside and entered the site. She listened for any noise that might emanate from that area, but the only sounds were her quickened breath and the soft patter of rain on the car roof. Maybe he'd been mistaken about the scrape of metal. Molly clenched her teeth.

A car cruised by. The whoosh of tires as they spun over the wet street cracked the silence. Then it passed and quiet returned. A beam of light swung from one end of the construction site to another. Nick's flashlight? Or someone else's? Stress poked at a spot between Molly's shoulder blades. Nick had been gone way too long. She squinted at her watch. No luck. Not without a luminous dial, and she didn't want to turn on the interior light.

She couldn't wait any longer. Her imagination pictured him knocked unconscious or worse. The hybrid became claustrophobic, as if somehow shrunk to the size of a Smart car. She needed air, needed to get outside, needed reassurance and to find Nick. Or to call the police. There was a station two blocks from the clinic. But her cell phone was in her purse, which was locked in her car.

She disregarded Nick's warning and slid out onto the slick sidewalk. She ran to her car, grabbed her purse, and fumbled inside for her phone. Other women kept theirs in a side pocket for easy access. She'd developed the bad habit of just tossing hers in. Now she had to wade past her wallet, a notepad, tissues, a comb, a mirror, a granola bar, and two loose lipsticks. Finally, she had her hands on the phone. She backed up and hit something solid. Her heart leaped and she swung around and almost stumbled over Nick.

"Jeez, don't you ever listen?" He reached in and unlocked the rear door, then grabbed Molly's arm and pushed her onto the seat. After he secured the front, he climbed in after her. This time he didn't have to bother with optimum positions. He pulled closed the rear door.

"I thought you were in trouble. You were gone for an hour, at least." She fluffed his wet shirt as if that would dry the rain spots.

He shook his head. "It took five minutes, tops. I wasted half the time dealing with the gate lock. I had to hold the flashlight under my arm while I worked the combination. Good thing I kept it simple—two right, four left, two right. That way, none of the guys would have trouble remembering it."

He didn't sound concerned. It was just about the longest five minutes of Molly's life. Her heart still pumped out extra beats.

"Did you find anyone?" She flipped closed her phone and slipped it into her skirt pocket.

"No, but I caught a glimpse of someone. He climbed the rear fence and hopped over it. He'd slashed the windscreen on the street side to get a toehold in the chain link. No matter how secure a fence, a determined person will find a way onto a construction site. By the time I reached the spot, he was gone."

"I'll bet it was Serk."

Nick shrugged. "Maybe. The guy looked about the same size. I didn't catch a good enough look."

"I almost phoned the police."

His soft laugh filled the car. She guessed he wasn't annoyed at her any more.

"You should stay out of the rain. You got all wet." He wrapped one arm around her shoulders and brushed damp hair off her face.

"So did you." She straightened his shirt collar.

He rubbed her bare arm, the one that wasn't pressed against his chest. "You must be cold."

Cold? *Au contraire.*

"Let me warm you up. It's the least I can do, considering you were ready to send for the rescue squad."

His hand moved off her shoulder. His fingers spread through her hair and he tipped her head close to his. The hand that had rubbed her arm now massaged her hip, then her thigh. She shivered when it touched her bare knee.

"Are you still cold?" He slipped his hand beneath her skirt hem. Heat as intense as a solar flare scored the flesh beneath his fingers. He touched the hollow in her throat with the tip of his tongue.

Molly swallowed a moan. Her body temperature shot into a zone elevated enough to further endanger the polar ice caps. His lips branded her cheek, then her throat again. A familiar tingle cramped her toes and fingers. She slid one arm around his back and the other onto his shoulder. If his shirt was still damp, she couldn't feel it. She touched the side of his face. The heat that came off his body enveloped her.

His kiss, when it came, was soft at first. Then it deepened as she parted her lips. She wrapped her other arm around his neck and draped a leg over his thigh. Another impulse. Each one harder to resist than the last. Should she have quashed it? Probably. She pushed his forty thousand dollar offer to the darkest corner of her mind. Tomorrow, she'd wonder if that was behind all this kanoodling. Right now, her body craved being close to his. Heat pooled in her abdomen. She sucked his tongue and a groan came from deep inside his throat. Then he broke the kiss.

"It's been a long time since I fooled around in the backseat of a car." He kissed her ear.

"Me, too."

"I sure as hell want to fool around with you, Miss Molly. Not here, though."

While his thoughts ran to just fooling around, hers had taken an entirely different route—love. That introduced just about the worst complication into an already very complicated relationship. She didn't have to look across the street to where his tenants hunkered down in their little fortress for a reminder.

"Come home with me." He tipped her head back.

He gazed at her with passion and desire, if not love. He wanted her as much as she wanted him. Could desire substitute for love? Not in her experience. In his, perhaps. Could she let Nick make love to her and then walk away with no expectations? How casual would sex be with him? After they "fooled around," then what? She didn't want a one-night stand. Not with any man and definitely not with Nick. There was no way to explain she wanted more than lust, not without total honesty. How could she tell him she wanted more than just casual sex, wanted something deeper that lasted beyond a few nights? She removed her arms from around his neck, pulled back her leg and sat up.

"I think . . . " She cleared her throat.

"Don't." His finger glided across her cheek.

"One of us has to."

"Okay. Then I'll be the one. *I* think it's about time you came home with me." He kissed the tip of her nose. "No, wait, I take that back. I know it's time."

"Are you always so sure of everything?"

"No. But I am about you and me."

You and me. Since when was there a you and me? An us?

It wouldn't take too much more for her to weaken. Her body had already shot love darts into her brain. "I wish I was. Sure . . . I mean."

He rubbed his cheek against hers. His beard had grown in enough to feel bristly but not too rough. She touched his face and almost caved right then.

"We both know it will happen eventually. We're both ready."

Ready? For what? Just plain old lust? She fell back on her old argument. "Why make life any more complicated?"

"Molly, any life without some complications would be damn boring."

"Maybe."

"Absolutely."

"I suppose." She let out a sigh.

"Look, I'm not going to push you. I won't go home all hurt if you decide tonight isn't right."

He'd given her an out, the kind designed to not make her come across like a pris. Why did he always have to be so damn . . . insightful?

"It will always be your decision."

Her relationship with Nick was like a wild ride down a rapids-choked river. Either you expertly maneuvered around boulders or suffered the consequences. She was a grown woman and not sixteen anymore. So why cling to virtue? Back then, that was important. Now she clung to self-protection. Where did she head with him, other than bed? If she was this conflicted, what kind of sexual partner would she make? She beat down the strong impulse to find out.

"I can't go home with you tonight."

He grimaced and put his hand over his heart. "I'm wounded."

If he'd put his hand anywhere near her heart, this conversation would have ended two minutes ago.

"I'm sorry."

He reached into his jeans pocket for his wallet.

"Do you have a pen?"

She leaned over the front seat and rummaged in her purse until she found one.

He took out a business card and wrote on the back.

"This is my home phone and address." He put the card in her hand. "Just in case you change your mind."

"I won't." She tried to sound forceful, more to convince herself than him. Instead, dejection crept into her tone.

"Okay. Just remember what Confucius said on the subject."

"Said about what subject?"

He handed her the pen, opened the car door, and put one foot outside. "About what happens to a man who goes home without a desirable woman."

A couple of thoughts flashed through her mind, neither of which she could repeat to him.

He bent to clear the roof of the car and backed out onto the sidewalk. "Good night, Molly."

"You're not going to tell me?"

"Tell you what?"

"About what Confucius said."

He closed the door, crouched down, and mouthed something unintelligible through the side window. Then he blew her a kiss and walked to his car.

Chapter 21

The moment Nick entered his darkened apartment, a hollowness slammed into his chest. It hit him like a sucker punch that caught him on his blind side. He didn't have to overwork his brain to figure it out. For the first time in his life, he'd become acquainted with loneliness. He realized now the long hours he usually worked had masked the emptiness in his life. Could he continue on like that? He didn't think so. Not since he met Molly.

He didn't bother with the switch that controlled the living room lights. The dimness, except for the muted glow from the streetlamp, framed his mood. He walked down the short hallway toward the kitchen, opened his shirt, and pulled it off. The subtle scent of apricots clung to the collar. He clenched his teeth against the image of holding Molly in his arms. Then the hollowness spread, and he had no clue how to stop it. Maybe a beer might help. Didn't lonely people drown their sorrow in alcohol?

He went into the kitchen, dumped his shirt on the counter, and yanked open the refrigerator door. An assortment of fruit—apples, pears, peaches, and a couple of fuzzy brown things—cluttered the bottom shelf. A loaf of bread, encrusted in some kind of tiny, black pellets, rubbed up against a carton of eggs, a forest of celery, and a bag of sissy carrots. Three kinds of juice in half gallon-size bottles took up most of the top shelf. His mother had dropped by. Why must it be the wrong woman? He groaned.

When he'd given his father an extra key—in case of an emergency, like he got cold cocked by a steel beam—he hadn't anticipated his mother using it to steer him toward a vitamin-packed diet. It reminded him he hadn't eaten since he'd wolfed down a slice of pizza around three that afternoon. If he could possibly choke anything down, he'd send out for a couple of burritos. However, his stomach had slammed the door on the idea of food.

He reached in behind the juice and extracted a bottle of beer. He popped the cap, took a couple of giant slugs, and waited for relief. But it would take something stronger than beer to numb his mind to Molly. For once, he wished he saw the virtue in guzzling gin. He finished the beer and left the bottle on the counter. Before he started on a second, he needed a long, hot shower. If that headed him in the wrong direction, a long cold one. He unzipped his jeans and walked into the bathroom.

It took almost a full minute before the pipes spurted enough hot water. He shucked his pants and stepped under the spray. For all his body knew, the showerhead could have spit bullets at him. That's how empty he felt. He soaped up, shampooed his hair, and cursed himself for letting Molly off the hook. All she needed was a little persuasion. Didn't he used to be *the man* when it came to that? So why hadn't he used it? Ego? Nah. He was afraid to scare her away altogether. Especially if what he envisioned as a night of bliss turned into a Titanic-sized mistake for her.

The shower did nothing to mitigate the disappointment of coming home solo. He wrapped a towel around his hips, shuffled back into the kitchen, and popped another beer. One sip and he pushed it aside. The shallow breaths he sucked in only brought on lightheadedness, as if he spun around on a carnival ride. Maybe he needed food after all. Nothing packaged in Styrofoam would satisfy his hunger, though. For any kind of satisfaction he needed Molly. He leaned against the counter and tried to remember a time, not too long ago, when he'd skated on the upside of life. He was in the process of squeezing his brain for a couple of highlights when the phone rang.

*

Molly kept her foot on the brake, one hand on the steering wheel, and the other clutched around her cell phone. Even with the interior light, it was hard to read the numbers on the back of Nick's card. With each ring, she became convinced she dialed the wrong number or that he'd taken a detour and hadn't reached home yet. She was pretty sure she had the right building—a modern four story above an underground garage and fronted in redwood and expansive windows. A pair of glass doors scrolled with brass led to a compact lobby. It was the kind of place she envisioned Nick living in. Lights blazed from a first and third floor unit. She wondered if he hunkered down in one of those. If not, maybe he'd decided to indulge in a super-sized taco at his favorite hole-in-the-wall restaurant out in the Mission.

The thought of food turned her stomach into a pit of tangled nerves. Her palm had sprouted so much sweat, it was a wonder the phone didn't slide out of her hand. Four rings and still no answer. Two more and she'd put the Chevy to the test and find out if it could do zero to sixty in ten seconds. Every reason to come this far started to sound like psychotic babble. Maybe she was just plain crazy and not just crazy in love with Nick. She let an extra ring go by. Then it cut off, and he came on the line.

"Nick here."

Her heart took a detour into her throat, muting her.

"Hello?"

She squeezed her eyes shut, then opened them wide. "Hi, Nick. It's me."

"Molly." Almost a whisper. "Where are you?" he said in a stronger tone.

"I'm double parked outside your building. I drove around the block twice and across the avenue and couldn't find any place to park. Someone pulled a truck up onto the sidewalk in front of the building next door. If I do it, too, I'm afraid I'll get a ticket or towed or whatever they do in this part of town." She couldn't stop babbling.

"Don't go anywhere."

By the time she reached the point of telling him she'd try the next block once more in case someone left to go on a late date or to work the night shift—babble, babble—he had charged out the front door of his building. Shirtless, his jeans were open at least a couple of inches below the waist. She sucked in her breath.

"Oh," she exhaled into the phone. "You're here." She reached over and unlocked the door.

He slid into the seat beside her. A shock of dark hair fell across his forehead and curled close to his ear. Damp. Not from the rain. That had stopped while she'd sat in her car in SoMa for twenty minutes and debated whether or not to follow him home. Finally, the self that controlled her heart won over the measured one that programmed her head. He didn't touch her. Maybe he feared he'd frighten her off, which was silly. Now he was so close, only the gear shift kept her from leaping into his lap. Her nerves had settled; she'd made the right decision.

"There's no place to park."

"The stall next to mine is empty. My neighbor drove down to LA and won't be back for a few days. Back up and pull all the way into the driveway in front of the grate. I'll raise it from inside the garage." He slid halfway out of the car, then ducked his head back in. "Don't go anywhere."

She smiled.

Once outside, he sprinted back into his building. Anxious? A moment later, he reappeared in the underground parking area. He engaged something on the side wall, and the security gate rose. She pulled ahead, and he climbed back inside the car and guided her into an empty slot.

He didn't touch her until he helped her out of the driver's seat. As they walked toward an elevator, he held her hand. Then he put his arm around her while they ascended. She leaned against him. Neither spoke. She had no trouble figuring out his apartment when they reached his floor. It was the one with the wide open door.

"Someone was in a hurry." She stepped inside.

He pulled the door closed, then took her in his arms and held her. His heart thumped against her chest. Now that she was calm, he seemed nervous.

"I'm glad you changed your mind." Then he kissed her slowly, gently, as if she were made of fine porcelain and liable to shatter if he pressed too hard. Hmm. She liked that he hadn't backed her up against a wall and started groping her private parts. He understood something she thought important about a sexual encounter, at least the first one. Don't morph into Cro-Magnon Man.

When the kiss ended, Nick took her hand and led her into the living room. Although dim, furniture shapes stood out—sofa, club chair, coffee table. Only one picture hung on the wall—the Golden Gate Bridge lit at night. No clutter. Not even a beer bottle or program guide on the coffee table.

"You're pretty neat."

"I don't spend much time here."

Out on the prowl a lot? She stopped before she almost blurted it. Why remind him about other women in his life? Even if it turned out she wasn't destined to be *the* one.

"Is that the kitchen?" A light burned behind a glass panel above the stove.

"Yeah. Are you hungry?"

"Hmm." Now that her stomach had settled and her nerves were behaving like good little children, she could eat a twenty-ounce T-bone steak. Wasn't a craving for food supposed to happen *after* sex? "Are you?"

"I guess so. I could order something in if you don't mind waiting." He sounded as enthusiastic as a man stuck out in the open in a lightning storm.

"Isn't there anything in the refrigerator?"

"Well, yeah, but nothing fit to eat."

She smiled and gave him a quick hug. "I could go for some junk."

She headed for the kitchen before he could stop her. He followed a step behind. She dropped her purse on the table. He hung up the phone, grabbed his shirt off the counter, and threw it over the back of a chair.

"Let's see." She opened the refrigerator door and took a quick inventory. She gathered a few pieces of fruit and laid them on the counter. "Oh, good, I love kiwi."

He frowned. "Stuff like that will make your hair fall out."

"We'll see." She rinsed off a waxy red apple. "Do you have any knives?"

He opened a drawer and handed her one. She sliced up half the apple. "Here." She offered him a couple of thin wedges.

"If that's what it takes." He pushed the apple slices into his mouth. "How come all the healthy food?"

"My mother is on a crusade."

"She worries about you."

He shook his head.

Molly smiled. "Try this." She held up a peach. He eyed it as if it might explode on contact with his mouth. "Come on. You survived the apple." She brushed at the wayward lock on his forehead. "You still have your hair."

He took the peach and bit into it. Then he handed the rest to her. She consumed everything, even the bits that clung to the core, which she dropped into the sink.

She skinned half of the kiwi, sliced off a section and put it in his hand.

"Is this the penalty phase?"

"Have you done anything to warrant a penalty?"

He brushed her cheek with his thumb. "Not yet."

She bit down along the side edge of her bottom lip.

"I won't play rough, Miss Molly."

She almost cut her finger as she skimmed off another piece of kiwi.

He swallowed the fruit and grimaced.

"Do you want any more?"

"Uh-uh."

Moist green particles clung to her fingers. "Do you have something I can put this in?"

"Yeah." He took what was left of the kiwi and tossed it in the sink. The knife followed. Then he took her hand and sucked her fingers one at a time. He went about it with slow, erotic deliberation, as if enjoying the taste of the fruit this time. He kept his eyes on hers, eyes that had darkened with need and wanting.

That triggered a hot, tingly sensation that never made it to Molly's toes. It pit-stopped right at her deepest core, and she got all twitchy. She'd been with men before, well, three, anyway, and this feeling had never hit so fast or so hard. She hadn't been in love with any of those others. She was in love with Nick.

When he finished tasting her fingers, he kissed her palm. She wanted him to start on all her other body parts, but she didn't want to rush him. He put his hand on the back of her neck and drew her in close. The fragrance of fresh fruit mingled in the air with the scent of manly soap that clung to him. She laid the back of her hand against his bare chest. Hair tickled her skin. The dark swirl trailed down his chest, over hard muscles, and into the partial opening of his jeans. She squashed the impulse to follow its path. Tonight, sex in his kitchen held no place on her menu.

His fingers threaded through her hair. His mouth came down on hers with a passion that stilled her breath. Whatever had pumped up his heartbeat earlier had apparently quieted, and he was back in full command. His mouth tasted like fruit salad, and Molly wanted to eat her way through every last speck of it. His tongue did a circuit inside her mouth, and he pulled her in so close she felt his ribs against the undersides of her arms.

Finally, he let her go. "I guess that's one way to get your vitamins."

She looked at him and grinned. "And I practically had to force you."

"Not anymore."

He lifted her onto her toes. She pressed her fingertips into his broad shoulders and tried to climb onto his hips. Her skirt scotched the attempt.

She didn't have to give him instructions. He released the button, opened the zipper and drew the skirt down her legs. She stepped out of it, and he tossed it in the direction of a chair and caught the seat.

"Well, you fixed that problem."

He nipped the tip of her ear. "That's me. Mr. Helpful. No job too big or too small."

She was left wearing shoes, panties, her bra, and a blouse. He rubbed his hands up the backs of her thighs, and her muscles rippled.

"Want to try that last maneuver again?"

"You bet."

He put his hands on her butt and lifted her up onto his hips. She wrapped her legs around his waist and twined her arms around his neck. Her heart beat in quick-step time. She pressed close against his bare skin and the toned muscles beneath it. Her pulse ricocheted when he kissed her throat. His fingers slipped beneath her blouse. Goose bumps that must have equaled robin's eggs popped up across her back.

"Another thing," he said.

"What's that?"

"Your bra is too tight."

"I suppose Mr. Helpful can do something about that, too."

"Quicker than you can say, 'Open sesame.'"

He undid the buttons on her blouse as well. A minute later, she was down to shoes and panties. God, the slow pace drove her crazy. Maybe he waited for her to pick it up. She didn't know his preference—did he like aggressive women or did he prefer to take the lead? When it came to sex, she'd never been a take-charge kind of woman. The anticipation of being with him changed that. Now she couldn't wait for him to get right to it. Her body slid a few inches down his. He was rock hard. How long could he last?

"Let's continue this in the bedroom."

"Mind reader," she whispered in his ear.

Seconds later, she was in a room where slanted blinds let in diffused light. The bed was king-sized and covered with a white top sheet. A large mirror hung above a double dresser. She watched herself and Nick in it as he set her down on the foot of the bed and knelt to take off her shoes.

"You're not going to need these."

That left her skimpy bikini panties.

She hoped this was another "open sesame" moment, because she was ready for him to get her naked and himself, too. She was really, really ready for that. The other times she'd touched him, he'd been dressed. In retrospect, she might have thought overly so. She thought exactly that now, even though she was certain he wasn't wearing Calvin Klein briefs under those jeans. A man in a hurry. She wanted to see every part of him, not just the broad back she stared at in the mirror. She wanted to touch him all over.

When he stood, she reached for his zipper. "I can't think of a single reason why you should need these."

Noting the bulge behind his zipper, she took care not to emasculate him and slid it down slowly. He popped right out, in perfect proportion. Like all the other parts of his body. Did size matter? That was one problem she wouldn't have to worry about. She had to remind herself not to come right then, but it was a struggle. She couldn't look away, but she couldn't seem to do anything but look.

He sunk his fingers into her hair and kissed the top of her head. "You'd better finish what you started." His tone was ragged, and his breath came fast and rough.

She slipped her hands under the waistband of his jeans and slid them down over his buttocks and long muscular legs. He kicked off his Docksiders then his jeans. Her mouth opened as she pulled in her breath. A really aggressive woman would have put that mouth to better use. She decided to hold hers in reserve for another night, if he invited her back. Instead, she took him in her hand and lightly stroked the long rock-solid shaft with her thumb nail. A groan ripped from deep inside his throat. After a while, he took her hand away.

"Maybe we'd better save that for later."

She looked up into his eyes. "I thought you could leap tall buildings in a single bound."

He kissed her palm, the one that had been wrapped around his engorged penis. "I learned a lot on the way to becoming a man. One of the most important things I remember was never to come in a woman's hand. I don't want to come until I'm inside you. Then not for a long while, either."

Her abdominal muscles bunched in anticipation.

He picked her up, carried her to the side of the bed, and dropped her right in the middle. He knelt back on his heels beside her, got his thumbs under the waistband of her panties and slipped them down and off. A delicious shiver followed their path down her legs then rebounded into her chest. They disappeared over the side of the bed. Now her clothes were in two different rooms, and she was in no hurry to collect them.

He gazed down at her sprawled naked on the sheet. "Gooooood golly . . . Miss . . . " He half sang the intro then stopped. "How often must you have heard that one."

"Pretty often, but never quite that way." She grinned.

He leaned down and over her and started at her throat with wet, hot kisses, then moved slowly down to the soft ridge between her collarbones. She stroked one side of his face with the tips of her fingers. The skin felt almost emery board rough now. A shudder slid from her head to her feet and she imagined the feel of it against the rest of her body. He cupped one breast and took it in his mouth and licked and sucked the nipple. That sent a spasm into the V where her thighs converged: Could he have got her any hotter or wetter?

He cupped both her breasts in his hands and rubbed his chin lightly against her nipples, barely grazing them. She gave a little yelp as a streak of pleasure surged through her. She sank her hands in his hair and pulled his head up. He gave her a deep, hungry kiss that went on so long she wondered if she'd ever breathe again. When he slid his mouth away, she touched her lips with her fingers. No one had ever kissed her like that. She could still feel the residual buzz of current that spread across her mouth.

He kissed her throat and the cleft between her breasts, then worked his way down her abdomen with the tip of his tongue. He ended at her navel where he circled the indentation. His hand glided up the inside of her thigh, and she squirmed and opened her legs further. He stroked her with his thumb, unhurried, and touched the spot between her legs that made her gasp with pleasure. Was this good? Oh, yes, better than good. So much better she couldn't find a fitting word for it. Hellaciously fantastic was as close as she could come. Come. God, don't let her do that. Still, she felt herself edging closer.

"Nick." A ragged sound rasped from her throat. She watched in the mirror as he touched and tormented her. She reached down and dug her hands through the hair at the sides of his head. "I think you should . . . you know . . . "

He dragged his mouth up her body until it almost touched her parted lips. "Get down to more serious business?"

"Hmm, yes, more . . . "

He leaned across the bed, opened a drawer in the nightstand and took out two foil packets. He left one on the stand, ripped the other open, and slid on the condom.

"Take fair warning. Once will not be enough tonight."

She certainly hoped not.

Chapter 22

He settled between her legs and stroked her for a moment, then pushed inside her. For a moment, he stayed perfectly still, poised above her, his hands braced alongside her body. Then he withdrew almost completely before he plunged part way in again.

"Is this serious enough for you?"

"Mmm."

"Do you want more?" He slid in deeper.

"Yes, more . . ."

He plunged farther and began to stroke gently. "Like this?"

"Yes." The feel of him inside her made her pull in her breath and hold it until she was almost dizzy.

He pumped harder and faster. "Like this?"

Oh God, if she didn't already love him.

His mouth came down over hers. His tongue entered her mouth and he thrust his engorged penis deeper inside her. The more she squirmed and moaned, the harder he thrust. She wrapped her legs around his waist and he wove his fingers through her hair and held her as he rammed deep and hard. She clutched his shoulders and rocked in unison to his body's rhythm. Pleasure hit her in rolling waves that pushed her to the edge of climax. She held on, waiting for him, and wondered just how many buildings he could leap in just one bound. Every thrust told her his erection was still rock hard. Her body had reached the point where it could no longer stop the orgasms that racked her limbs and pulled everything tight inside her.

"Molly," he gasped and buried his face against her neck and shuddered to a climax. He lay still for a while. His breath came in rapid spurts. Then he withdrew from her. She unwound her legs from across his back. The sheet felt sticky hot under her feet, just like her body.

"Don't move." He got up off the bed and went into the bathroom. When he came back, he lay down beside her and brushed a thick lock of curly hair off her forehead. "This is all I've thought about these past days."

She stroked his cheek with the back of her hand. He needed a shave, but that only made him more handsome, better than any of the guys in magazine ads or hot movie stars. "You mean even when you poked around in the dark earlier and searched for some bad guy?"

"No." He rolled onto his back. "From that first day in your office."

"You thought about making love to me when you were so mad?"

He brushed her bottom lip with his thumb. "I wasn't really that mad, especially after I saw you."

"Yes, you were."

"Okay, I was pissed, but I still wondered what it would be like, if it would be good."

As she snuggled against him, she laid her arm across his chest. "Was it?"

"It was fantastic. I came close to confirming that in Napa."

"What was bidding on that trip really about, anyway?"

"At first, it was about getting you alone and winning you over to my side. But then it became all about enjoying the day with you. What Cynthia and Dominique told me about you at the auction proved true. You're warm and bright and funny. Everything about that day felt right."

"It did for me, too."

"I was right about something else, also."

"What?"

"Your hair."

She sat partway up and looked down into in his eyes. "What about it?"

"I wondered if it would stick out all over like heating coils after hot sex."

"Oh my God." She shot all the way up and stared into the mirror. "I look freaky." She clapped her hands against the curls that stuck out in almost every direction.

Nick laughed and pulled her back down beside him. "You look beautiful. Just imagine how I would have felt if I hadn't curled your hair."

"Is that some sort of a test with you?"

"No."

She lay against him, so happy, and yet it wasn't a complete happiness. Complete happiness is saying, "I love you," after sex. She couldn't say anything approaching that to him. Maybe she'd never say it. Maybe tonight was all there would ever be for him and her. That sucked.

She had a perfect view of them in the mirror. He had his arm around her and her head rested against his chest. They looked like a contented couple who'd just had great sex. Tonight, she wanted to give in to the fantasy that they were a couple in a committed relationship. Only he controlled the kind she wanted . . . needed. He controlled everything, even beyond the sex. She might eventually come to think of this as the million-dollar relationship, all in the debit column. A relationship that, inadvertently, she'd somehow instigated. Thanks to her blithely offered *opinions*, his tenants held out for a big payoff—and rightly so—one he swore he couldn't afford. Now she was cemented in the middle. It was as if a bus bore down on her from one end and a sixteen-wheeler truck from the other. She didn't dare think about the clinic and its possible demise under his bulldozer. Not tonight, when she was so happy.

He wound a curl around his finger and kissed her lightly on the lips.

"What are you thinking about?"

How could she answer his question? Certainly not with the truth. Maybe if she didn't answer, he'd go back to whatever thoughts had occupied him.

"Molly?"

"Hmm."

"Don't you want to tell me?"

"Is it important?"

"It is to me." He sounded serious.

That's when she decided on a half-truth. "I was thinking . . . I'm glad I came over tonight." Ooh. That sounded like they'd just had a hot game of Scrabble instead of the hottest sex on the planet.

"That's close enough."

"Close enough to what?"

"To what I thought. That I'm one lucky guy that you changed your mind."

He followed the curve of her body until his hand rested on her hip. Then he tipped her head back and kissed her with the same depth of desire and need as before. He stroked her thigh, then trailed the back of his hand up her body to her breast. Deliciously hot tingles poked at her skin everywhere he touched. Then he reached for the other packet he left on the nightstand and took out the condom.

"Okay, Miss Molly, show me what else you've got."

She reached up, threw her arms around his neck, dragged him down on top of her, and showed him more than he'd probably ever expected.

*

Molly awoke from a sound sleep and gazed around the unfamiliar room. For a moment, she couldn't figure out where she was or how she got there. Then her gaze settled on Nick. He lay on his back, one arm bent at the elbow and resting above his head on the pillow. He was naked and so was she. It didn't take her aunt's crystal ball to figure out why.

She sat up and glanced at the clock on the nightstand. The luminous dial showed 5:19. Yikes. She hadn't been home in almost twenty-four hours.

Maybe she'd better not wake him. She slipped quietly from the bed. By last count, they'd made love three times. She remembered every moment, enough at least to plaster a smug, self-satisfied grin on her face. Was three times ever enough? Right now didn't seem like the optimal moment to find out.

Her last recollection of her shoes and panties was they'd landed somewhere on the carpet at the foot of the bed. She began to hunt. Eventually, she found them and slipped them on. The rest of her clothing resided somewhere in the kitchen. Nick had left the stove light on, and she stumbled in that direction without a mishap.

She had her bra fastened and her skirt halfway zipped up when he appeared in the doorway. He raked his hands through his hair and walked into the kitchen. His jeans were on but only partially zipped. Serious stubble shadowed his face.

"What are you doing?"

"I'm getting dressed." She reached for her blouse, which lay in a heap on the kitchen counter.

"Why?"

"I have to go home."

He frowned. "What for?"

"I have to shower and change my clothes."

"I have a bathroom with plenty of running water."

She slipped on her blouse. "There are things in my bathroom I need."

"Like what?"

"Well, my toothbrush, for one."

"Oh." He frowned, then his expression brightened. "We can share mine."

She smiled. At least he hadn't offered her a brand new unopened one, like he kept a supply on hand in case of an unplanned sleepover.

"It's a generous offer, but I have to decline." This didn't seem the right time to mention that after shampooing her hair, she'd require whole gobs of conditioner to tame it. He probably didn't need any.

"I thought we'd have breakfast. I know a place that serves the best burrito within a hundred miles. I want to take you there."

Did a quick bite in a hole-in-the-wall Mexican joint qualify as a real date? She liked to think so. The only other time they'd shared food, he'd won her in an auction. She glanced down at her skirt and blouse.

"I can't go anywhere like this except home. My clothes are all wrinkled." That would give the burrito crowd something to gossip about.

"I could probably round up an iron from somewhere."

She almost laughed but swallowed it in case he'd take any levity as a sign she might weaken.

"Your neighbors might not appreciate being awakened at this hour." She buttoned her blouse and tucked it into her skirt. Her mouth felt like it had sprouted cat fur and her body ached for a hot water-logging, skin-shriveling shower.

He held up his hands, palms facing her. Disappointment etched his facial muscles. "Okay, I suppose there are a bunch of girly things you have to do. I'll drive you home."

"My car is in your garage. I don't need a ride."

"It's five thirty in the morning. I'm not going to let you drive home alone."

She glanced at the wall clock. "It's almost twenty of six. By the time I hit the street, it will start to become light."

He came over to her and put his hands on her shoulders. "Did I remember to tell you you're one of the most stubborn people I know?"

She almost said, "Yes, along with your tenants," but decided it best to stay away from the T word. Not after she'd had the most mind-blowing night of her life and wanted another.

"I'm a grownup. I can handle the streets at dawn. Lots of people will be on their way to work. I won't be the only one out there." Pale light had started to filter into the apartment through the balcony doors.

"Okay, I'll concede round one. Round two is mine. I'm taking you down to the garage." He fished his shirt off a chair and jammed his arms into the sleeves. While he worked on the buttons with one hand, he placed the other on her shoulder. She grabbed her purse. He led her to the front door.

He put his arm around her in the elevator. When they reached her car, she fished out her keys and pushed them into the lock. Nick opened the door, and she slid onto the seat.

"Promise me one thing," he said.

"What's that?"

"Next time, you'll stay the night and have breakfast with me."

Next time. "Sure."

He closed the car door, and she pulled out of the slot. She headed up the ramp that led to the street and watched for traffic but mostly watched him. He stood in the opening of the garage, his hands on his hips. Her heart squeezed in her chest. Maybe it wasn't hopeless after all. He'd said "next time." He knew she wouldn't turn traitor on his tenants. So maybe he had a plan. After all, he'd admitted he'd thought about her ever since that first day. He'd had almost two weeks to come up with a solution.

Maybe he felt more for her than he showed on the surface. Tonight must have told him something about her strong attraction to him. Would he equate that for love and return it? She smiled as she drove toward home, confident she was heading toward something good with him.

*

When her taillights disappeared, Nick closed the security gate and rode the elevator back up to his apartment. He usually never paid attention to the emptiness, but now that he'd admitted to it, without Molly there, it hit him even harder.

He shucked his shirt and pants and went into the bathroom and ran the shower. As he stepped under the spray, his mind turned into a movie factory that produced flickering images of him and Molly making love. It went on long enough for the bathroom to fill with steam and the water to turn cool. He remembered all the places he'd touched her and it turned him on, setting off fireworks in his head. No woman had ever excited him like that before. From that first day in her office, he'd thought about getting her naked. When it finally happened, he'd just let his body do all the thinking for him.

He toweled off and headed for the bedroom. He wondered if this thing he had going with her would turn into a documentary short or a full-length feature. There were a couple of Olympic-sized hurdles he still had to jump over—no, not jump, vault. Whether their movie lasted for ten minutes or two hours, he'd thread the first reel tonight after he took her someplace special for dinner. He'd walk over to her office later and set up the date.

He dressed in slacks, a dress shirt, and a tie, and was about to head for his favorite Mexican restaurant when his phone rang. His first thought was of Molly. He couldn't think of anyone else who'd call him at six thirty on that particular morning. He took the call in the kitchen and almost said, "Good morning, sweetheart." Good thing he held back. It wasn't Molly on the other end of the line but a man who introduced himself as Detective Larsen.

Chapter 23

Molly spent a longer time than usual doing damage control to her hair. Then, dressed in a crisp white blouse and the new navy blue linen suit she'd recently splurged on at Nordstrom's, she maneuvered her car through the Tuesday morning commuter traffic.

Two SUVs cut her off, and she realized she'd better pay more attention before she wound up in an accident. That meant she had to stop thinking about Nick. She'd done nothing else ever since she'd pulled away from his garage. She relived every moment, held tight each memory. Images flooded her mind and along with them came questions. Would she see him today? Would he ask her out on a date? When, if ever, would they make love again? She stayed away from the most important questions—would he reach an equitable settlement with his tenants and in the future build somewhere far away from the clinic? If both didn't happen, there could be no relationship. And if not, how could she live the rest of her life without him?

The traffic thinned as she drove into the South of Market area. She picked up more speed as she neared the construction site. A quick glance at the dashboard clock told her it was almost eight thirty. Nick should be around by now. Her heart did a little flip-flop in anticipation. She didn't want to interrupt him—just look. Okay, stare shamelessly. That should be enough to get her through the morning.

But when she went to make the turn onto his end of the street, a police car blocked it and a patrolman waved away rubberneckers. She slowed to a crawl. Several vehicles, including squad cars, a fire engine and an ambulance, jammed the street. The far end of the block where the clinic stood was cordoned off as well. She searched for Nick through the throng of policemen that crowded the sidewalk. Her mind raced with every possible disaster—"something big" that closed down the site, a fire had torn through the apartment building, a tenant had suffered a heart attack. Maybe Duncan Serk had discovered a more lethal way, other than a picket line, to shove his point home.

The cop approached her. "Move it, lady."

She braked, leaned over, and lowered the passenger side window. "What happened?"

"Did you hear me? I said get going." The cop signaled with his thumb. He gripped the handle of the baton attached to his belt with his other hand. His pinched face and dark glaring eyes invited no further questions.

"Yes, officer." Molly crossed the intersection and hunted for a place to park. She spotted a loading zone midway down the avenue and decided to chance it. She squeezed in behind a linen service van, locked up, and hiked back in her three-inch wedge heels. When she reached the corner, the same policemen intercepted her.

"You again. You can't go down there."

All the vehicles were parked haphazardly in the street directly in front of the apartment house. She thought she spotted Mrs. Z and a couple of the tenants.

She pointed to the building. "I know the people who live in those apartments. I need to speak with them."

"You want to get arrested?" The patrolman reached behind his back to where she thought he might keep his handcuffs.

"Well, no . . . "

"Then beat it."

Several cars had stopped at the intersection and blocked traffic. A crowd gathered at the corner. The patrolman blew his whistle and signaled for the drivers to move on. Molly scooted down the street the moment he averted his eyes. When a gravelly voice called, "Hey, you, get back here," she broke into a somewhat wobbly sprint as if the moment called for her to warm up for next year's Bay to Breakers race. She slowed down only when she reached the apartment/construction site.

The gate in the security fence that protected the corner site was rolled aside to reveal a gaping hole that had been gouged into the side of the apartment house at ground level. A heavy steel beam protruded from it. Long jagged splints of wood littered the empty space between the condo site and the occupied building. Three streamers of yellow police tape cordoned off the hole and the front door as well. Wooden sawhorses closed off the sidewalk. An emergency medical technician administered oxygen to one of the tenants, the arthritic lady. Another woman sat at the curb, dazed. Duncan Serk paced in the street and puffed on a cigarette. Other tenants milled around near Nick's trailer. He stood by a squad car talking to a couple of policemen.

As Molly slipped around the sawhorses, Mrs. Z rushed toward her.

"Molly," she panted. "They said not to go back inside. The whole place can crash down on our heads. Didn't I once tell you?"

"What happened?"

Mrs. Z pulled Molly closer to the construction site. "You see that." She pointed to the steel beam that poked into the building. "It flew from somewhere in there where they make the condos. The gas, you should have smelled it. Some people are still dizzy."

"When did it happen?"

"I was asleep. It was dark. I only had time to throw on some clothes." She smoothed the skirt of a faded purple and black print cotton housedress. "Mr. Sanchez helped me get out. Someone called the police, and all these people came."

"Are you all right?" Molly put her arm around Mrs. Z. "Did you speak with the medical technicians?"

"I had the oxygen. I told them I don't need it, but . . ." She waved her hand as if swatting away a mosquito. "I took a sniff to make them happy."

Molly stared at the jagged hole in the apartment house wall. Apparently, as the beam had crashed through the wooden siding, it ruptured the gas line. Although she figured a PG&E crew had capped it by now, the air still smelled faintly gaseous. She didn't need a blueprint to figure out how it happened. A rough wooden floor had been laid across two thirds of the condo's second story. Steel, probably meant for use on an upper portion of the structure, was stacked there. Several other beams were visible from the street. Somehow, one of them slid loose—or was dragged to the lip of the floor and given a push. It then flipped down over the edge and crashed into the apartment building. A sick feeling settled in Molly's stomach at the thought that it could have killed someone.

While she comforted Mrs. Z, she glanced at Duncan Serk. He leaned against a police car and clutched an ever-present cigarette in his paw. She'd never really taken a good look at his hands before. They appeared beefy and strong enough to lift heavy objects. His arms—the size of small tree trunks—bulged with muscles visible where he'd chopped the sleeves off his T-shirt. He could wrestle with a steel beam, especially if he had help. Was he responsible? It left him momentarily homeless, but she supposed someone like Serk wouldn't think that far. Maybe he thought if he destabilized the building, it'd fast track a payout from his landlord. He didn't have the smarts to follow his actions past the initial idea. Nick could have the building condemned and—voila—no more tenants. Yes, Serk was stupid and disgruntled enough to cause serious damage.

Then there was the mystery man, the one Nick had chased the previous night. Then, too, there was Nick. He came out a winner. God, she hated herself for even thinking it. Still, he wouldn't be human if he didn't feel some relief if the building wound up condemned.

"We can't live here anymore," Mrs. Z said. "It isn't safe. You talk to that Mr. Builder. You tell him we need our money now."

Molly glanced over at Nick. Stress dug deep furrows into his brow and pulled his clenched jaw into a tight line. She couldn't think of a single reason why he should listen to her. A night of great sex only bought you so much influence. The building was off limits, and the tenants would soon be dispersed. He no longer had to concern himself with pickets, leaflets, and demands for money. Who was going to make him dig deep into his wallet? Duncan Serk? He could threaten all he wanted. Nick could probably have him arrested for harassment.

"Now we have to move—to what and where I don't know," Mrs. Z moaned.

Two women, who Molly recognized from social services, spoke with several of the tenants. They'd make temporary arrangements and perhaps use the Good Samaritan occupancy law, the one recently enacted by the mayor. Its purpose was to find temporary housing at the same rental rate for tenants whose homes became uninhabitable after a disaster. Since occupancy was limited to twelve months, Mrs. Z and the others would eventually have to locate permanent housing. Even those temporary arrangements would take time. Social workers needed to be assigned and rental units made available. None of it would happen quickly. She hated to think any of them might have to spend even a few nights in a shelter. When Molly had worked in social services, the long line of people who were waiting for the city to find them affordable apartments had seemed endless.

Molly suggested Mrs. Z talk to the women from the city's services. "They'll help you get settled."

"You'll talk to him?" Mrs. Z pointed to Nick.

"Yes, I will." Although she could promise nothing.

Molly stood alone on the sidewalk and watched the surreal scene. How long would she have to wait until Nick was free? One thing was certain: She refused to leave until they spoke. He'd glanced at her a couple of times, but looked detached, as if they hadn't just shared a night of intimacy. Finally, when the policemen dispersed, he walked over to her.

"Molly." He put his hand on her arm, then let it drop to his side. He looked wrung out, as if he'd just speed-climbed Half Dome in Yosemite. Of course, he hadn't slept much last night, either. His eyes lacked their usual spark. His voice rasped. She wanted to ease the lines that chiseled his brow.

"Hello." Last night, he'd touched every part of her body. He'd brought her to heights she'd never experienced before or ever expected to reach. This morning, he seemed like a stranger.

He gestured toward the building. "I never imagined anything like this could happen. Not when the construction site was the target."

"What do the police think?"

He shrugged. "They wrote it up as an accident. No one was hurt. It's a low priority."

"Not for your tenants."

"The police are aware of that. I'm aware of it, too."

"Do you have any ideas how it happened . . . who could have . . . ?"

He glanced toward Duncan Serk, who'd resumed pacing and sucking on yet another cigarette. "I have one or two."

"You think it was him?" Serk's eyes had folded into slits. A scowl furrowed the loose, jowly skin on his face. He looked as volatile as a lit fuse.

"Let's say he's a candidate."

"Then why damage the building? Why would anyone do something to make themself homeless?"

"Maybe he didn't expect the beam to land where it did. He could have levered it to crash down through the ground floor and take most of it into the foundation. That would destabilize the walls. We would have to rebuild almost from scratch. The angle was off, though. It flipped over the side and through the apartment house wall. That wall is nothing but flimsy wood. A man couldn't have done it alone."

"No."

"I know how you must feel."

"What about you?" What better time to broach the subject of compensation? The only circumstance that could make such a disaster worse was if a section of the building had collapsed and seriously hurt someone. "What do you plan to do about your tenants?"

He frowned. "I can't answer your question right now. I'll need time to work it out. It's a hell of a mess."

Molly nodded. "It is for them. I guess you got lucky, though."

"What are you talking about?"

"This is what you wanted all along. They're out. Now you can tear down this old wreck and finish your project." Anger mixed with accusation in her tone. She was tired and upset and needed to rail at someone. Last night she'd felt like a lottery winner and this morning, like she'd lost the winning ticket.

"Is that what you think? I'm happy about this situation?"

She let a few seconds pass. "I'm not sure how you feel about it."

"I feel like shit." He raked his hand through his hair. "What are you saying, Molly? You think I'm responsible?"

Tears built behind her eyes and she blinked furiously to keep them from spilling over. Her imperfect little single-night love affair was about to combust.

It was as if he'd taken her hesitation for consent. "Do you think that after you pulled out of my garage, I jumped into my car, tore down here, and shot a steel beam into the building?"

In the time it took him to hurl the accusation at her, she managed to get better control of her emotions.

"I'm not blaming you. What does it matter? Unless they have family or friends who can take them in, your tenants will probably end up in shelters until they can be placed in temporary housing. Or, *if* there are any vacancies, some will be lucky to move into a single-room occupancy building. Do you know what it costs to rent a room that's about half the size of your trailer? Six hundred to a thousand dollars a month. That's without a kitchen or a private bath. You can't squeeze in much more than a bed, a chair and someplace to hang a few clothes. They're infested with roaches and mice . . . "

"I know about SRO buildings."

"Have you ever been inside of one?"

"No."

"Then you have no idea how really awful they are." When she'd worked in social services, it had sickened her every time she'd had to direct someone there.

"Molly . . ." He brought his hands up and she thought he was going to touch her.

She backed away. Any contact was out of bounds if she was going to hold him responsible for his tenants' welfare. Her willpower wasn't forged from iron, after all, and she obviously didn't have much of it when it came to Nick. She'd never felt so vulnerable.

"Look, somehow I'll make it right."

Today, "somehow" didn't work for her. "How . . . when?"

He rubbed the back of his neck. "I can't do anything right now, but I'll do whatever I can as soon as I can. Only I can't put a million bucks on the table. You need to understand that. It's not by choice. It's through necessity. I won't promise what I can't deliver."

"I'm not asking you to."

"Fine, we're in agreement there."

"You have to figure something out."

He glanced around at the remaining squad cars and emergency vehicles. "This isn't a good time to talk. A city housing inspector is on the way. They should have condemned this building a long time ago. It was never earthquake proof. It's too late now. It has to come down. I'll call you . . . "

"There's nothing to talk about. We've stomped this into the ground how many times? Your tenants need you to rescue them. Now more than ever." Her strong passion for justice superseded her anger. "You told me once you were one of the good guys."

"I am. How often do I have to prove it?"

He'd already proved he could take her safe little world and crash it down on her head.

"You don't have very much faith in me."

Her emotions were so raw it would take very little for her to lose control. Couldn't he see anything from her point of view? Her backing his tenants didn't mean a lack of faith in him. He stepped back and started to turn away from her.

"I do, Nick. I trust you." Her voice came out weak and shaky, without the conviction she felt.

He turned to face her. His expression held a mixture of hurt and disappointment. "No, you don't. Why should you?"

Why should she?

"Because I . . . love you." She had only mouthed the words, didn't dare voice them.

Except for the twitch in his lower lip, he stood perfectly still.

A shock wave tore through Molly. Was she crazy to admit something so important to a man who, aside from taking her to bed, had in no serious way returned the sentiment? Seconds ticked by, but he still hadn't moved or worse, spoken. Okay, to be fair, she'd taken him by surprise. How much time did he need to tell her he shared her feelings? He remained mute. She shook her head. "Forget about what you think I said."

"Forget it?"

She nodded so vigorously, her neck snapped.

"Yes."

He gave a low, strained laugh, as if it were all a big joke. "Whatever you want."

She felt worse than a fool. One more confession and someone might come along and cart her off to Napa. Not to Nick's house, but to the state hospital where they housed people who proved they couldn't think straight.

"I have to go." Last night she'd stuck to him like a Velcro strip. Now she wanted the sidewalk to open up and suck her down to Hades.

"Sure." Nick looked resigned to their parting. Did she sense a little relief there, too? "I'll be in touch, or you can call me. Whatever." He turned and walked over to where his crew waited.

I'll be in touch. The kiss of death for a woman, trumped only by *I'm very fond of you.* Would he call? Why should he when she'd just told him there was nothing to talk about?

Molly clenched her jaw and ran as fast as her wedge heels allowed back to her car. At least she'd dodged a ticket, probably the only good news she'd have for the rest of the year. She yanked open the door and slumped behind the wheel. From the start, a chasm separated her and Nick. It had eroded into a Grand Canyon-sized space now. She loved him, and he didn't love her back. What he felt for her was a sexual urge and nothing more. Sure, he wanted her, and because she wanted him so much, she'd broken her rule on casual sex. Only, for her, there was nothing casual about the sex with Nick or her feelings for him. They were the real deal.

She pulled out into traffic and another thought jammed her brain. Had last night been part of a plan, about more than just the desire to take her to bed? Had he used her, as well? What better way to get her to back off from his tenants than a night of incredible sex and a promise for more? Maybe it built from the day in Napa when she'd let him touch her just about everywhere. She'd bet her knock-off Jimmy Choo wedge heels he had an infallible instinct about women. He *knew* she wanted him. He *knew* the sex would be more than casual for her. He *knew* she'd want a lot more. Maybe the only way for her to stay in his orbit was to convince his tenants to accept his offer. She banged her fist on the steering wheel.

Tears welled in her eyes. This time she didn't hold them back. If he'd planned that all along, he'd wasted his time. Thanks to the mystery saboteur, he'd been handed exactly what he wanted: a vacant building. And it hadn't cost anywhere near a million dollars to accomplish, either.

Chapter 24

As soon as everyone left the scene, Nick headed for his trailer. He yanked off his tie and tossed it onto his desk, then rolled up his shirtsleeves. He needed to drag his body and mind onto a plateau where he didn't feel like he'd just barreled over a cliff. The take-out coffee he'd grabbed at a Peet's on Market Street had turned sour in his stomach, and his head throbbed like hell as if he'd walked face first into a utility pole. The disaster at the apartment building had a lot to do with that, along with Molly, who'd opened her heart to him and then just as quickly slammed it shut.

Throwing something like that at him, hands down, at the worst moment of his life—had pole-axed him. His benumbed brain had barely processed her words. His mental capacity had now at least nudged beyond the fifty percent point. Still the question remained as to how much to believe of her declaration. The way she'd mouthed it was one hell of a way to convince a man she trusted him. Did she mean it? Did he want her to?

Right now he had neither the time nor the inclination to fall in love. Especially with Molly. Of all the women he'd ever known, he considered her by far the most unpredictable. Also, the most stubborn, infuriating, and unreasonable. Then again, when she turned those big sparkling brown eyes on him, he wanted to draw her close and hold her until the next millennium. As well as kiss her and touch her. So, yeah, he questioned if they could go the distance. To all her better qualities, of which he made mental notes, he added loyalty and caring. At least she proved as much with his tenants, if not to him.

He sank down in his chair and propped his feet on his desk. He had to stop thinking about her. He needed to move forward. Fast.

His project was behind schedule. He had to focus on business unless he wanted to join Serk and the others in an SRO hotel. He didn't have the luxury of slacking off. It was already close to late September. He'd anticipated having at least a third of the lofts completed and a sales office open by now. There was a high demand for housing in the city—he'd expected to sell most of the units off the blueprints by this point.

First, though, he had to deal with the apartment building. It needed everything inside cleared out and everyone's personal effects stored. Until then, his crew couldn't start the demolition. He needed to keep in touch with the Department of Social Services and stay current on the situation with his tenants. He needed promos of each new unit's layout to show prospective buyers. The printer should have had them a week ago. And he had to deal with the sabotage. He'd move out of his apartment and onto the construction site in order to stop it.

Heat built inside the trailer, and he hauled himself out of the chair and flipped on the floor fan. His crew had removed the steel beam from the apartment building side wall. Now hammering sounds were coming from the site. He hoped the guys could make more than the usual progress today. He'd have to go into overtime with them. Another expense he hadn't counted on. He pulled a set of tracings out of the storage bin and laid them on the desk. Another big decision loomed: how much to price each loft unit.

He'd been hoping for a small miracle before the million dollar demands and recent declarations of love walloped him—to realize enough of a profit to pay off his bank loans and settle with his tenants at twenty-five Gs a pop. Had he been living in a bubble? A month ago, he'd thought he'd raise enough money from the sale of the condos to make an offer on a property he'd been eying—a rarely used and run-down alley close to the Old Mint. Most people avoided it but he considered it a hidden gem.

But that was before his tenants, backed by Molly, had made an impossible demand. Now they had no leverage with the building condemned. He could offer the original twenty-five grand, and they'd have to take it. Hell, he was in a position to offer them nada. That was the upside of the whole mess. Still, he'd never back off on his word. He'd made them an offer and he damn well expected to stick to it. He'd have to say *hasta la vista* to a future with Molly, though, once they accepted the twenty-five thousand. That was a downside he wasn't sure he cared to risk.

He braced his hands on the desk and leaned over it. Yeah, pretty soon he'd have to make a decision on how strongly he felt about Molly Hewitt.

*

Molly hooked onto the freeway. She hadn't taken a day off in months. Now she wanted to put as many miles between herself and the morning's disaster as possible. Tokyo sounded about right, although a budget buster, so she decided on home. She fished her cell phone out of her purse. Should the street reopen, she left a message for Cynthia with the excuse she came down with the flu. She needed something vile in case she decided to take off an extra day.

Her tears had dried by the time she reached home. Yet she still felt as numb as if she'd stumbled down a dark hole and only just clawed her way back up. Her energy level was at its lowest ebb. It took every effort to place one foot ahead of the other. She just wanted to fall onto her bed and stay there for a year.

She opened the front door. The muted whine of a flute drifted from her aunt's apartment. For as long as she could remember, her aunt had faithfully practiced Yoga. Molly did, too, but intermittently. Mostly when stress at the clinic caused her shoulders and neck muscles to cramp. She could use a whole lot of wellness right about now. Something that would raise her consciousness to a higher plane where she wouldn't have to confront anything negative. Only her body had other ideas. Bed beckoned.

"Molly? Is that you?"

The only sound she'd made was the key turning in the lock. Unfortunately, her Aunt Vi had the acute hearing of a wolf. Molly paused outside the open doorway to the apartment. "I was just going upstairs."

"What are you doing home? Come on inside for a minute."

Molly walked through the doorway and into a room so dim it was almost as if the gas company had had another blackout. Heavy drapes closed out all but a narrow crack of light. Four lit candles, one in each corner of the room, gave the surroundings an eerie glow. The plaintive sound of the flute floated on the still air and mingled with the scent of burning incense. Her aunt sat with her eyes closed on her yoga mat in the knee to ankle pose, the palms of her hands turned upward.

"Something's wrong. I can sense it. Come over here and tell me about it."

Molly had forgotten about her aunt's moments of psychic visions. "I don't want to disturb your session. Maybe we can talk later."

Vi opened her eyes. "I'm making sand candles at Ocean Beach later. I'm down to my last three. Come sit next to me." She put the tape on pause.

It was useless to try to fend off her aunt. She'd taken on the job of surrogate mother years ago and had become Molly's confidant, friend, and chief advisor. She had a well-honed sixth sense and could cut right to the core of any problem and offer a viable solution. Many times Molly had cried on her shoulder. This wasn't about being called Little Orphan Annie by some jerk at school, though, and then wanting to chop off all her hair. This problem had zoomed right to the top of the seriously crappy list.

Molly sat down on the carpet. She slipped off her shoes and propped her arms on her bent knees. Then she took a few deep breaths and gave a more or less accurate account of what had transpired that morning and how it affected Nick's tenants.

"They're scattered all over the city by now. They could face weeks in a city shelter or an SRO hotel."

"It won't last forever." Vi patted her niece's shoulder. "They'll settle into permanent housing eventually. Maybe soon."

"That depends on Nick."

"I like him."

"You do? Why?"

"He struck me as a man who recognizes his duty and does it."

"You only met him one time. You can't know enough to make a judgment."

"I felt a connection to him."

Nowhere near as strong as Molly's. Moisture welled in her eyes, and she blinked it away. She agreed with her aunt, though, that Nick recognized his duties. The day they went to search out affordable apartments, he'd brought her along to his parents' house first. Another man might have bailed out of the post-wedding brunch with some lame excuse. But they'd expected Nick to show up, and he'd worked it into his schedule. That was when Molly first decided she liked him.

"You know I've never pried into your life. I've always trusted your judgment."

Molly guessed where her aunt headed. "I know."

Vi changed from the knee to ankle position. She lay on her back, stretched her legs up, and braced her heels against the living room wall. "You have strong feelings for Nick."

Molly nodded.

"Were you with him last night?"

Her aunt must have heard her sneak in around six that morning. "Yes."

"You love him." Not a question but a statement.

Molly nodded again. She bit down hard to staunch tears that threatened to pop up again. It hurt so badly to love a man who didn't love you back.

"Everything will work out."

"Is that your crystal ball speaking?"

"No, you told me."

"I told you it will work out with me and Nick? When did I say that?"

"You didn't in so many words. However, you've never fallen so hard or so fast over a man. It means that besides all his other . . . uh . . . qualities, the ones that get your juices running, you trust him. You believe he's ethical and that he understands right from wrong. You never would have fallen in love with him otherwise. Would you have wasted five minutes on him if you believed for a minute he'd cheat his tenants?"

"Well, no, but everything's different now." She had to wonder about those other things, too. Maybe they were just another vibe he'd sent her way to reel her in.

"Listen, Nick will come back into your life, and in such a way it will make Romeo and Juliet look like a kindergarten crush."

"Oh, great. The last I read, nothing good ever came out of their relationship."

"Yes, but they had a heck of a ride along the way."

"I suppose." Molly rose to her feet and slipped into her shoes. As she climbed the stairs to her apartment, she wondered if she'd already been taken for a ride by Nick.

Chapter 25

Almost two weeks passed before Molly dredged up the courage to drive down the street to where Nick's construction site loomed. Rather than sit home and brood, she preferred to stay late at the clinic and work on her next event. She didn't need the pain that crimped her heart every time she thought about him. Still, she couldn't totally crush her desire to be close to the place where he spent so much time. Dominique would have called it spirit transference—if you can't be with the one you love, then hover in his shadow. She used to think it all a bunch of nonsense. Yet, here she was, cloaked in the fast-approaching dusk, seeking out his aura. Even in her teens, she'd never done anything so sappy.

Chances he hung around this late were slim to zilch, so she felt confident her little foray would go unnoticed.

Dusk slid into night as she approached the site. Nick's car was parked at the corner across the avenue. How odd. He'd always used the slot alongside his trailer. She crossed the intersection, skulked down in her seat like a spy, and cut a sideways glance at the hybrid in the rearview mirror. The last time she'd played detective, she'd followed him home. Tonight nothing could make her stop. Well, maybe if he waved a white flag and vowed to surrender his heart. He'd also have to furnish proof he'd found safe housing for his tenants and planned to hand over a big payoff. That had about as much chance of happening as the Niners winning the Super Bowl. If she had to choose, she'd put her money on the Niners. Anyway, the car was definitely unoccupied.

She went around the block again and returned to their street and crawled along at a speed slow enough to make a snail happy. Nick no longer had his trailer parked in its usual spot. He'd moved it out onto the street. Since no light showed through the two small windows, she had no way to determine if he was inside. Work at the site had stopped for the day, so she couldn't imagine why he'd hang out in the trailer. Unless he still kept tabs on his building site to forestall any future "accidents." She pulled in front of the trailer and cut her lights. She let the engine idle.

Ever since the foundation had been dug in the vacant lot that comprised the third parcel of Nick's project, work had progressed on the condo units above. Wood and steel beams outlined five floors of lofts. Dead center, where the apartment building once stood, a gaping hole scarred the earth. Everything had been totally obliterated. Molly sucked in her breath and didn't release it until her head buzzed from lack of oxygen. It didn't seem possible. The building was gone, expunged like a tumor. Sadness enveloped her.

She put the car into park and leaned back against the headrest. The corner condos showed even more progress where once there had been only naked wood and steel. They climbed five stories above the street. Metal screens sheathed the front section of each unit. Reflected in the glow from the streetlamps, they shimmered like silver. What she imagined would become clear glass walls waited to be installed behind them. The design was innovative, the form simple. She had to give Nick credit. When all the condos were finished, they'd add something new and interesting to the area.

Across the street, the Blackstone Group had made progress on their project, too. They'd advanced well into the demolition stage. Eventually, their buildings and Nick's condos would change a seedy area into something exciting. Molly ached for the tenants—*her* tenants. She'd heard nothing from them. She could only hope that Nick would keep his promise to somehow make it right. She drove away in a funk.

That night, she slept fitfully. Her dreams were a tangle of confusion and, as usual, revolved around Nick. In one, he stood in the middle of the street. As she drove toward him, he shouted something and waved her away. In another, a platform stretched across the yawning hole. Music, sweet and muted, drifted on the air. She and Nick stood together on the sidewalk. She wondered why he'd brought her there. When she asked, he took her hand. Then his image faded as if he stepped into fog.

She was drained and listless all morning, and doubted she'd ever excise Nick from her heart.

Ten days later, the same thing. She was drawn again to the construction site. Like a magnet sucks iron to its core, she made the turn from the parking lot around the corner and headed away from home and toward Nick's aura. Lately, she'd become more invested in Dominique's hocus pocus. Dark clouds clustered under a dusky sky. It would be full-on night in minutes.

Once again, his car was parked across the avenue and away from his office trailer. Molly slowed to a crawl, slid into her spy slouch, and continued on. He wasn't inside the vehicle. Weird. Why did he park here at night? Was he somewhere nearby? If so, where? Except for a down-on-its-heels residence hotel, an all-night bodega, a laundromat, and two low-rise claptraps on the next street, everything else was shuttered for the night. Her head began to throb from playing detective.

She continued down the street, hooked a right, then three more, and pulled in behind his trailer. She glanced above the security fence that stretched across the front of the property and gazed at the spot where once the apartment building stood. In only a week and a half, beams had formed new doorways, walls, and ceilings. They rose five stories and ended under a flat roof. No complete facade yet. Brick sheathed the first three floors around openings where, eventually, glaziers would insert the glass. Also, no sign of Nick. Frustrated, she fought the urge to slam out of her car and bang on his trailer. Except a sixth sense—another newly found awareness—screamed it was vacant. Her hands clenched the steering wheel. She worried about him. She cut the engine and flicked off her lights.

She opened her purse and rummaged inside until she found her cell phone. There was no need to check his business card for either of his numbers. She'd memorized them from all the times, late at night, she'd tried to convince herself to call him. She dialed his home number even though she didn't expect an answer. She had to do something besides sit out here in the deserted street.

After the fourth ring, his voice came over the line.

"This is Nick. Leave your name and number and I'll get back to you."

Molly pressed the phone to her ear. She hadn't heard him speak for over three weeks. She missed the sound of him almost as much as she longed for the sight of him. She jumped when the message signal beeped in her ear.

"Nick . . . I saw your car . . . It's Molly . . . I'm worried about you . . . I . . . oh, hell." She slammed the phone shut. What was that all about? Why leave a message? How would that locate him? She sounded worse than a fool. She slumped down in her seat.

The site loomed dark and deserted, eerie, like an abandoned property left for time and the elements to devour. At least she supposed it was deserted. Unless Nick was concealed somewhere inside. The silvery screens that sheathed the almost-finished front of the corner building made it impossible to tell. He'd fired the security guy, so maybe he'd set a trap for the person bent on sabotage.

She leaned across the console and peered out the passenger window. Misty fog turned the night gray. Silence deadened the air as if a great cosmic shroud blanketed the earth.

She snapped open her phone and dialed his cell. No answer. She closed her phone and shoved it into her purse.

"Where are you, Nick?"

She clenched her teeth in worry and frustration. She'd even welcome the yowl of a cat if it livened the bleak night. Her concern deepened. What if he encountered an Incredible Hulk wannabe, the kind who could separate a man's body into a hundred pieces? What if the Hulk caught Nick off guard? A whack with a tire iron and he'd be blotto, or worse. She pictured him crumpled on the floor, comatose, bloody, his body hidden under a tarp in some dark corner. He'd lie there until the workmen arrived in the morning. She bit down on her thumbnail. The question was: Should she take a quick peek? She knew the answer. Of course she shouldn't. Then, again, she couldn't *not*. She loved him that fiercely. Women in love did all kinds of stupid things. Just look at Helen of Troy. She'd started a whole war.

She popped the lever that unlocked her trunk and slid out of the car. The streetlamp across the way should have cast a glow but didn't. Had the bulb burned out? Had someone tampered with it? Using the light inside her trunk, she rummaged through her purse and checked for her can of mace. She worked late some nights and never knew who she might meet on the way to her car. The small spray can provided an extra measure of safety. She jammed the mace into her pocket.

She raked through the box of earthquake supplies in her trunk until she found a flashlight. Since she never thought to check the batteries, she muttered one of those quick, "Oh God, please let it work," prayers and clicked the button. A pale yellow circle, little bigger than a drink coaster, illumined the ground. Not great but doable.

She combed through the box and found a worn black cotton hoodie and a pair of running shoes. She traded in her heels and suit jacket, slipped into the hoodie and pulled on the hood to conceal her hair. Her chocolate brown linen trousers, along with the hoodie, made her inconspicuous. She tossed her purse into the trunk. Quietly, she closed the lid and headed for the chain link fence, thankful Nick had kept the combination to the gate lock simple. She clamped her ridiculously inadequate flashlight tightly between her teeth and put in the numbers. The lock opened and she rolled the gate aside just enough to squeeze onto the site.

She moved over uneven ground and loose stones. When she approached the central area, the one where the apartment building once stood, she shone her light into the void that eventually might serve as a lobby. An indentation along each side suggested housing for an elevator. With five stories, that was a necessity. A ladder led to the second floor. She bypassed it. Her plan didn't call for a broken neck. Plan? Did she even have one? She paused for a moment. The most logical place for Nick to stay concealed was on the ground floor behind the screens that sheathed the partially finished condos. She had to walk across the central area to gain access. She headed there.

*

Nick sat on an air mattress in the dark and watched and listened for the saboteur. The condos had risen fast, thanks to the overtime the guys put in. The cost to keep his crew on the job from early morning until dusk, including weekends, ate up profits. It was worth the expense, though. That compressed the timeframe for whomever was set out to ruin him. It compelled that person to make another move. So, just like he'd done for the past few weeks, Nick waited, primed to catch the son of a bitch.

That first night, when he'd hunkered down in this ground floor unit, there was nothing between his butt and the bare wood floor but the seat of his pants. Intent to begin surveillance, he hadn't taken the time to plan ahead. He figured he'd give himself away if he moved around, so he'd stayed in one position too long. His joints had become stiff and his muscles knotted from the cold. The following morning, he'd hit a store that specialized in equipment designed for camping and extreme outdoor adventures. It didn't matter that he had a ceiling and wall board for shelter. He considered his adventure extreme enough. Blasts of cold air whistled through openings, and his perch in the urban wilderness was about as isolated as any in the real world.

He'd purchased an air mattress, a small battery-run heater, and a super economy-sized thermos. They made the next few nights more bearable. He'd also eyed a down-filled jacket but passed on it. Bulky clothing would impede his ability to wrestle down the creep if he ever went *mano-a-mano* with some burly thug. He'd settled for a down-filled vest that he could shrug off in seconds.

He leaned against a back wall and uncorked the thermos. The aroma from the blackest, strongest coffee available at the nearest all-night bodega diminished the smell of raw wood and night mists. He poured a cup, took a deep swallow, and waited for the first jolt to hit him. Half a thermos of the stuff usually kept him wired for hours. The only chance to catch any sleep was when the sun rose and the neighborhood started to hum with life. After an uneventful night, he'd drag the air mattress into his trailer and crash until his foreman banged on the door and another day began. He'd considered hiring another security guard, but faced with the possibility of serious bodily harm—to the guard, not a determined saboteur—he'd chucked it. Since the danger had escalated, he believed only he should deal with it.

He became a night creature, which made him acutely sensitive to sound: footfalls, the close of a car door, the flap of a bird's wing, the whir of the wind. Once, when he'd heard action out by the security fence, he'd crept to where he had a better view of the sidewalk. It was a man walking his dog. When the animal had raised its leg, it had made contact with the fence. A month ago, he'd never have heard such an indistinct sound. Now his hearing was acute.

Boredom set in as he sat and waited. He no longer tried to read in the miniscule light thrown off by the heating coils. Most nights he had only his thoughts for company. The fate of his project was uppermost in his mind but ran neck and neck with Molly.

He shifted on the air mattress so the blood circulated in his butt. To sit for long periods made him restless. Thoughts bounced inside his head. He poured another cup of coffee. One sip and he put it aside. He was already too wired. He got up and paced off five steps, turned, and repeated it. If he calculated correctly, in less than a month the initial units should be ready for occupancy. He'd already earmarked one ground floor loft—the one in which he squatted—as the furnished model. His goal loomed within reach. At least, he hoped it did.

He was about to sink down on the air mattress when he heard a faint sound. Quickly, he turned off the heater and moved close to the side wall. If anyone came through the adjacent doorway, he'd let him get a few feet inside, then step in behind and block the exit. Surprise was paramount, along with a quick one-two punch to the jaw. He shrugged off his vest and kicked it aside.

Chapter 26

Each step brought Molly deeper into the project. Except for the tiny circle of light from her flashlight, a curtain of mist shrouded the area. Her back brushed against wooden beams that outlined a doorway. She played her light on the wooden flooring beyond and stepped onto it. The silence unnerved her. Numbness crept into her feet, cold gripped her hands. She tried to whisper "Nick," but her lips froze.

Maybe this wasn't her best thought-out move. It ranked right above the time she'd added an ingredient to cake batter fifteen minutes after she'd slid it into the oven. Luckily, the bakery had still been open, and no one at her aunt's sixtieth birthday celebration had suspected the truth. Not with all the compliments she'd received. Anyway, Nick could take care of himself. What did he need her poking around like Nancy Drew? This might be a good time to dig out her mace.

Her hand went to her pocket. Then something flew at her and knocked her down. She lay sprawled, her face pressed into the naked wood. Her flashlight bounced across the floor, flickered, and died.

"Umph." The air whooshed from Molly's lungs.

A heavy weight ground her hips into the floor. Rough hands sank into her shoulder blades. She tried to wriggle free but was pinned down. Then the weight lifted momentarily, and she was tossed onto her back. A dark shape loomed above her, straddling her thighs. It had the configuration of a man dressed head to toe in black. Her hands were held together in a tight grip above her head and her hood was yanked off. Her heart smacked against her chest like a mallet pounding a piece of beef. A light at least a million times more powerful than hers shone into her face.

"Molly?"

She blinked and turned her head to the side. Her breath wheezed as if she'd run up the steepest San Francisco hill—*twice*. She squinted sideways up at Nick.

"What the fu . . . " He stared down into her face long enough for her fright to slowly ebb. He released her hands and turned her face toward him. Their eyes locked; mortified, Molly grimaced. What she hadn't thought out was how she'd react the first time she bumped into him. Even in a city of three quarters of a million, it was possible they'd meet somewhere. Maybe she'd develop a sudden craving for tacos, or he'd get beaned at the construction site and carried into the clinic. What she'd never expected was to find herself lying under him—oh, God, don't go *there*—with a beam of light heating her face and probably a scowl distorting his.

For a moment, his knees tightened against her hips. Then he eased off her, stood, and pulled her to her feet. "What the hell are you doing here?"

He sounded anything but happy to see her.

She squinted into the light. He lowered it and flicked it off. He put it off to the side but kept his grip on her arm. "Pretty bad idea, huh?" She tried for a laugh and almost choked.

"What's this about, Molly?"

It's about love. Was he too dense to see that? Well, apparently so.

"I saw your car parked . . . you know . . . " She pointed vaguely toward the corner across the avenue. "I was worried." She shrugged. How lame did that sound? If only she could have said, "I worried because I love you and miss you and was afraid someone might have hurt you badly enough for your folks to debate whether to pull the plug at the hospital." Too bad she couldn't say that. Instead, she gave a spot-on impression of a jackass.

"I parked away from the site because I didn't want anyone to know I was here."

She bit down hard and grimaced. "Oh, I should have . . ." She did a side to side motion with her head and her hands. A habit she'd developed in childhood, when words failed.

"I don't know what concerned you. Or why you thought it was a good idea to prowl around in here."

Was he dense with a capital D?

"You're right. It was an impulse."

"Impulses like that can get you hurt."

Hurt. Lately, she'd learned a lot about that.

She nodded.

"It could become dangerous."

"I wasn't afraid."

He shook his head and exhaled, making an exasperated sound. "Well, you should have been."

Was he worried about *her*? Was he sending a signal he cared, at least a little bit?

"Try not to advertise the fact that I hang around here at night."

"Oh." He didn't care about her. He was angry she could have drawn attention to him.

"Go home, Molly. Don't do anything this . . ." She knew he was about to say "stupid." "Don't do anything like this again."

"I'm sorry, Nick." He picked up her flashlight and handed it to her. At least she hadn't maced him.

He took her elbow and led her toward the doorway. Before they reached it, he stopped dead.

"Oh, shit." The words were barely audible. Then he looked at Molly. She'd never seen deeper concern on a man's face. "This could be trouble."

"What?"

Nick clamped a hand over her mouth. He pulled her back and led her to where a sleeping bag lay on the floor. He removed his hand and put a finger against his lips, a signal for her to remain quiet.

"Don't move," he mouthed.

Molly froze and listened for whatever had caused Nick's sudden caution. Then, through the dead air that blanketed the site, footsteps. They came from what would soon become the central lobby, then stilled.

Nick pointed and in a whisper got the message across that he intended to investigate. He dug a cell phone out of his pocket and handed it to her. He put his lips against her ear and said, "Thirty seconds. If I'm not back, call nine-one-one."

As soon as Nick moved through the doorway, Molly left her safe position and crept close to the opening. The encroaching night kept her shrouded but she could still make out Nick's silhouette. A scrape and then a thud sounded, as if someone had set down a heavy object. Nick moved quickly toward the sound. A dozen feet from him, a dark shape crouched over the faint outline of what resembled a two-gallon sized gasoline can. The man unscrewed the cap. Nick dove at his back and the two men hurtled across the wood floor. The guy was easily six feet in height and burly with hard, knotted muscles that filled out his dark sweatshirt. Before he had a chance to scramble to his feet, Nick hooked one arm around his waist. Molly watched, paralyzed. Then the man shook him off and charged at Nick. Nick raised his arms and covered his chest. The blow grazed his bicep, and he moved in and landed a punch to the guy's nose. From the crack, Molly assumed he'd broken it. That didn't stop the intruder from countering with a full-out body assault.

Molly flipped open Nick's phone and dialed 911. Her heart beat a discordant rhythm against her chest and she spit out the message they needed help. Address? What address? There was none yet. She gave the location along with the two cross streets, snapped the phone closed, and dropped it into her pocket. Then she moved through the doorway. In the central area, Nick and the other man rolled about and kicked at each other. Arms flailed and fists made contact with any of the other's body parts. The strong odor of gasoline hung in the air. A dark puddle spread across the floor. A can with a spout lay on its side. Nick had intercepted an arsonist.

Molly searched for a board or a tool, something to get in a whack if she had the chance, but found nothing. Nick's elbow jabbed the man's ribs. It created an opening for another swing. Like boxers, they circled each other. Fists darted. Nick pummeled his adversary hard in the ribs and managed a couple of elbow jabs to the face. He landed a punch that connected with the man's jaw, then took one. He stumbled back a few steps and into a wall. Molly dug her mace out of her pocket.

The thug swung in her direction. Blood smeared his face. It wasn't Duncan Serk. He began to stalk toward her.

Nick vaulted away from the wall and charged at the man's back. He locked an arm around his throat and grabbed a fistful of hair. Molly raised her can of mace.

Nick's eyes went to the canister. "What's that?"

"It's . . . it's mace."

He yanked the man's head back. "Use it. Now."

As Nick ducked his head, Molly clenched her teeth and let loose with a full-powered spray. The thug's yowl rang in the dead air and his hands flew to his face. Then Nick threw a punch that connected solidly to the side of the man's head. He sagged, and Nick threw him face down to the floor and twisted his hands behind his back. He pulled off his belt and used it to secure them. He kept one knee jammed into the saboteur's spine.

The shrill whine of a police siren slashed through the night. As it drew closer, Nick said, "I want you out of here, Molly. Right now."

She couldn't seem to process his words, no less move. The siren screamed louder.

"I don't want you mixed up in this." His tone turned more forceful. "Don't argue. Go home."

Finally, her head cleared. "If that's what you want."

"Yes, damn it."

"Okay." Molly backed away from him. "Okay."

"You're a gutsy woman, Ms. Molly."

She slipped through the gate opening.

Was she? She stumbled to her car, ripped open the door, and slumped behind the wheel. Or was she just another fool in love?

Chapter 27

"Okay, this is the final round. Let's make it dealer's choice. Molly, what would you like to play?" Vi passed the deck to her niece.

Molly glanced at the picture on the top card—a young Elvis tricked out in combat gear and toting a rifle. "Oh, whatever." She'd wrestled with her concentration all evening. The last hand, she'd laid down what she'd thought was a winning flush, only to discover a club mixed in with the spades. That had cost her thirty-five cents.

"How about seven card stud, threes and nines are wild and fours give you an extra card?" Dominique suggested. "We haven't played that since the first round."

"Sure." Molly shuffled and dealt the first cards. She was in no mood for poker tonight. She would rather have curled up on her sofa in her nightgown and robe with a chilled glass of Chardonnay—make that three glasses—and some mindless TV junk. She was in a funk but didn't want to disappoint the others.

"Don't you think you should call him?" Dominique checked her two hole cards. "He might have gotten killed last night."

Nick.

That morning, the Bay Area section of the *Chronicle* had featured him on the front page. The picture was taken outside the construction site. In it, Nick leaned against the fender of a police car. He had an ice pack pressed against the back of his head.

"He might have suffered a concussion," Vi said.

"Or escaped with only a bump." Molly had told no one about her foray onto the condo site. Forget that the man she loved had tackled her and thrown her to the floor like a sexless sack of lawn clippings. She had bruises on her hips that matched Rorschach test patterns to remind her. When she'd reached home that night, she'd felt like inflicting further damage on herself for leaving the security gate open. At least when she'd read the article the next morning, she'd discovered the thug had come equipped with a bolt cutter. The police found it out by the fence. So even if she hadn't forgotten to close the gate, he still would have had the means to gain access to the site. She tried not to imagine the consequences without quick thinking on Nick's part and a good aim on hers.

"Even a bump can cause serious problems," Dominique said. "That's reason enough to phone him."

"Forget it." Molly dealt herself an ace. Together with two wild cards in the hole, it gave her three of a kind. "I bet a dime."

Her aunt and cousin each dropped ten cents into the pot.

"The newspaper article pointed out the man Nick caught trying to burn down his project had a long criminal record," Vi said. "All he had to do was strike one match and good-bye condos and maybe even Nick. You really ought to call him, Molly."

And say what? *Good thing you ducked in time or I might have maced you instead?* Was he so dense or disinterested he couldn't guess what had really prompted her to go onto the site? She'd already said "I love you" one time, which was exactly one time too many. Now it was his turn to say it. Right. She didn't need another session with Ouija to tell her what she already suspected: he'd moved forward with his life.

"So . . . what do you think?" If prizes were awarded for persistence, Dominique would possess a case full of trophies.

"No." Molly dealt everyone another card.

"He might have amnesia."

Molly stared at her cousin. "Then why should I call him? He wouldn't remember me."

Vi gave a soft laugh. "Molly's right. We ought to let her decide."

"Maybe it's about time she took a risk," Dominique said. "Man-wise."

Molly thought she already had—when she'd let Nick make love to her.

"Molly's thing with Nick reminds me of an old black and white film I saw on AMC about a month ago." Dominique checked her cards and bet a nickel. "Instead of taking a chance, the heroine let the guy she's interested in slip away. What a dumb move. She spent the next forty-five minutes of the movie regretting it."

"I remember that," Vi said. "It was what they called a screwball comedy way back then."

"I didn't find it funny," Dominique said.

Molly ignored them and dealt two more rounds of cards. When a nine turned up in her hand, she bet a quarter.

"I suppose people considered it funny in nineteen thirty-six." Vi added twenty-five cents to the pot. "In the beginning, she thought he came across as arrogant and opinionated."

"Like you thought about Nick, at first." Dominique nodded at her cousin.

"No, I didn't." Molly already had a rotten ending to her story. What she didn't need was to climb into her lonely bed at night thinking she'd fallen in love with a full-blown jerk.

"By the end of the movie, the heroine agreed he had a heart and a conscience," Vi added.

Molly thought Nick fit the same description. He never did evict his tenants. Legally, he didn't owe them a buyout, but he'd offered one anyway.

"That's when the female character wised up and chased after him. Everything worked out just fine," Dominique said. "Love prevailed."

Molly groaned. She was up to her nostrils with the Romeo and Juliet syndrome.

"Do you still have the newspaper articles?" Vi asked.

Molly hated to admit it, but she'd saved the Bay Area section with Nick's picture. She couldn't bear to recycle him along with the rest of the newspaper. He'd looked heartbreakingly handsome even with an ice pack pressed to his head and a bunch of cops and EMTs swarming around him. She'd folded and unfolded the newsprint so many times it began to fray along the creases. At least she hadn't rushed over to Kinkos and had it laminated. "Why do you want the articles?"

"Who turned out to be behind all those attempts to wreck Nick's project?"

Molly paused as if she had to think about the answer. She'd read the story so many times, she practically had it memorized.

"The former owner of the property was responsible. He sold Nick the three parcels to raise cash to invest in another venture. In the end, that didn't fly. He found out the Blackstone Group was soon to break ground with their project and realized how much more valuable his former property had become. He hired that thug to do enough damage to cause serious and costly delays. He never expected Nick to turn him down when he offered to buy back the property. That's when he stepped up the ongoing sabotage that started as thefts and vandalism. He ordered the creep to set fire to the place when everything else didn't work."

"The urban renewal South of Market makes the area much more desirable," Dominique added. "Nick's in a great location. He ought to come out of it with a heck of a profit."

"I suppose." Molly wondered if that would put him in the mood to share with his former tenants. He said he wasn't motivated by money. Then why didn't he prove it?

"Have you heard anything from Mrs. Z or the other tenants?" Vi asked.

"Not so far. I left two messages at social services, but no one's gotten back to me yet. I'll try again in a few days."

Molly dealt the last card face down. She checked her hand, which contained four wild cards, and bet fifteen cents.

"I'll keep you honest." Vi added a dime and a nickel to the pot.

Molly had dealt herself the best hand ever, but it might as well have been a pair of deuces for the way her enthusiasm nosedived.

"I'm out." Dominique slumped in her chair. "I couldn't put together anything more than a pair."

"You'll do better next week," Vi said.

Next week. Molly loved her family but hated the idea her social life was still relegated to Friday night poker. She glanced down at the hand she'd dealt herself. Six aces. Didn't someone once say lucky in cards, unlucky in love? Could anyone be more unlucky than that?

Chapter 28

Molly rose from her office chair and stretched her arms above her head. Knots pulled at her shoulder muscles, and her back ached from sitting hunched over her desk too long. Her fingers cramped from making copious notes on a yellow scratch pad. She needed to plan her next event and still hadn't made any decisions. She'd wracked her brain for an idea totally different from anything else she'd sponsored, something that, besides sounding exciting, held wide appeal. She'd scratched off the Fun Train to Reno. Even though she knew she could have the train ride catered for almost nothing, everyone didn't share a desire to gamble. Without a car, what else was there to do up there?

She'd already run through ten different ideas. A weenie roast at Ocean Beach raised goose bumps on her arms—since the event was scheduled for mid-December. Then just the thought of bobbing out on the Bay—even if she could wrangle a huge discount from the operators of the Blue and Gold Fleet—made her want to reach for a seasickness pill. Nothing seemed to jell. Her mind had turned into a desert—arid and vacant.

Only one possibility caught her interest—a western-themed event. The mayor often promised to make City Hall available for her fundraisers on a night the Board of Supervisors didn't meet. She'd never taken him up on the offer, but now might be the right time. She envisioned bales of hay and savory barbeque. Maybe even a lassoing contest. A couple of mimes she knew would work for about a hundred dollars apiece. Cowboy boots, a western shirt, hat, and jeans and they'd have all the costume they needed. She knew a fiddler she could round up pretty cheap. He could also double as a caller for square dancing. That would lend a buzz of excitement. It sounded like fun and might generate as big a profit as her auction.

Her auction. That thought took about a second to put her in a funk. The whole thing with Nick had started that night.

Nick.

She thought the worst thing that could happen had already happened until her aunt imparted the latest news from the mole. Trudie had spread the word about Nick to her friends in other areas of the Hall of Records and had hit a mother lode. Nick had bought the corner property adjacent to the clinic, the one with the empty ground floor and units above. The deed was already issued and Molly figured demolition would soon begin.

A few days later, workmen had swarmed over the building. She'd put in a call to her "angel," the man who owned the clinic property, but he was out of town for two weeks and unreachable. This time she asked her aunt to give Trudie the green light to snoop. Even an angel might sometimes shuck his halo when someone dangled a profit in front of his face. Would her landlord sell the clinic site to Nick if Nick decided he'd like to add to his new corner property? If that's how it came down, there was nothing Molly could do.

She tried to jackhammer Nick and his urban renewal plans out of her mind and focus on cowboys and mouthwatering slabs of barbecued ribs. That didn't last long. He kept slipping back inside her brain. Could any man better fill out a pair of jeans and a cowboy shirt? None she'd ever encountered.

Frustrated, Molly pulled at her hair. She was wound tighter than a spring in a knock-off Rolex. She needed to relax if she hoped to make any progress on a plan for her next event. Every time the phone rang, she was certain it was bad news. Nick was *her* new landlord and about to serve notice on the clinic.

Her yoga mat sat in the bottom drawer of her desk. She dug it out, spread it over the floor, and closed her office door. She dimmed the overhead light. She kicked off her shoes, hiked up her skirt, and assumed the lotus position. That usually stilled her inner turmoil. She held the pose for a couple of minutes then stretched her arms behind her and interlocked her fingers. She tipped her head back and drew in a deep breath. As she exhaled, she brought her forehead to the floor and her hands toward the ceiling.

"Does something like that have a name?"

The deep male voice sliced into her near trance. Her head jerked up, bringing her chin a few inches off the mat. She stared at a pair of tasseled polished brown loafers and the bottom few inches of neatly creased tan dress slacks. As she dropped her arms and straightened her upper body, her eyes climbed up and over a brown leather belt to a chocolate brown dress shirt and gold tie with little red squiggles. Finally, her eyes glommed onto the face of the man silhouetted in the open doorway. Nick.

The peace she'd managed to achieve evaporated.

She stared up at him. He stared back. One corner of his mouth twitched as if he was laughing. As if? He *was* laughing, but had the good sense to try to play it cool.

"Well, what do you call that?"

Molly unlocked her hands and slid her feet off her thighs. It took a few moments to get a simple answer out of her head and onto her lips.

"It's the lotus position."

"It looks like a bone cracker."

"Not if it's done right."

He smiled.

It occurred to her she should yank her skirt down. All she wore underneath was a pair of French cut white satin and lace panties. But her hands weren't in a cooperative mood. It didn't matter, though. He hadn't looked up her skirt. His eyes remained locked on hers.

"Do you need help getting up?"

She stared at him.

"Here, give me your hand."

Without waiting for her to decide one way or the other, he reached down and took both of hers. He drew her to her feet.

The space between them became compressed to an area normally limited to nothing thicker than a paperback book. Her hands felt good in his, like they belonged there. Since they didn't, she withdrew them. She stepped back and adjusted her skirt.

His eyes strayed to the lined yellow pages and Molly's scrawled notes. "Are you working on another fundraiser?"

"Yes, a western theme. Maybe." She hadn't felt this awkward since her eighth grade graduation party, when she waited for a boy to ask her to dance.

"Sounds like a good choice."

He appeared completely at ease. Probably because he'd already forgotten the last time they were together. She had regularly scheduled nightmares about it in which she missed the thug and sprayed Nick senseless. He'd no doubt forgotten exactly twenty-six days before, he'd made love to her. Three times.

"Do you have a few minutes?"

"Uh . . . I guess so." She wished her stomach would quit its climb into her throat.

"Most of my project is finished. It's completely sold out, the part that's for sale, anyway."

She smiled, barely, and only because it would be spiteful not to wish him well. Just because it hadn't worked out between them didn't mean she relished throwing a hex on his condos. She braced herself for him to drop the bomb and tell her he'd bought the clinic property.

"I'd like to show you a couple of the finished units."

Molly took a few seconds to think about all the bad karma headed her way if she spent any time with him. Even if the news wasn't as bad as she imagined.

"You had a lot to do with the completion of the project," he said.

"Me?"

"You know . . . " He raised a hand, made a fist, and pumped his index finger. "With an aim like that, the Giants could use you in the bullpen."

"You would have done fine without me."

"We'll never know. We made a pretty good team."

The smart thing was to make this snappy and get him out of her office.

"So what do you say?" The wattage in his smile could have caused a surge at the electric company. "Can you spare thirty minutes?"

She wanted to close her eyes and then, when she opened them, he'd be gone.

"We could probably do it in less than thirty."

"Sure." Why not get it over with like a bad case of measles? "Whenever you say."

"How about right now?"

"Right now" didn't sound like such a good idea, but to put it off sounded worse. The anticipation would totally wreck what little emotional balance she'd managed to achieve. "Okay, thirty minutes."

"Also, I'd like your advice on something."

If he thought she knew anything about decorating, he should see her apartment. Half of her furniture had come out of a secondhand store. She retrieved her shoes and slipped them on.

"My car's outside. I'll drive you back to the clinic later. We can save time that way."

That worked for Molly. The block was so long, it would have taken over ten minutes to walk to the other end of it in her wedge heels. She slid into her jacket, grabbed her purse from under her desk, and followed him into the reception area. Cynthia wore the same bemused expression as when Nick had first barged into the clinic.

Molly rolled her eyes. "I'll be back shortly."

She folded her body into the passenger seat of Nick's car. Her brain scrolled through the "car menu," like earlier it had done with the sex thing. Could her fourth time in the bucket seat be a charm? Could she change a chocolate kiss into the real deal? No way.

He fired the motor and eased away from the curb. "Do you do that stuff often?"

"What stuff?"

"The lotus thing."

"Not as often as I'd like."

"What's so great about tying your body up in knots?"

"Actually, it's very soothing. It's a great stress reliever." The beginnings of the benefit she'd just achieved from her yoga session gave way to tension that tightened the muscles in her neck and shoulders.

He slowed when they neared the corner. He squeezed the car into a barely recognizable parking space, which would have taken her ten tries to achieve. "I've had too much stress lately."

"Maybe you should try it."

"What?"

"Yoga. I could . . . " She almost blurted she could show him a couple of body-friendly positions but remembered in time that today he was strictly meet and release, not a permanent catch.

"You could what?"

"Um . . . you could find a beginner's manual at the bookstore. To, you know, help you relieve your stress."

"A beginner's manual." He laughed.

Well, it wasn't that funny.

He cut the motor and popped the locks. That spared her having to pursue the whole stress thing. They got out of the car and stood for a few moments in front of his building. It appeared divided into three distinct sections, with the five stories of condos at either end sheathed in the innovative screens. The late morning sun cast a silvery glow onto them. The central building seemed like a separate entity. The brick façade only rose three stories and did not follow the screen motif. Here were windows large enough to let in ample light. Above this section, the screen motif continued for two floors.

"I really like it," Molly said.

"I hoped you would."

A pair of heavy glass doors, interspersed with scrolled ironwork, led to a marble entry. To one side of the doors, a brass plate anchored a double row of bells along with an equal number of slots for occupants' names. No names were inscribed, so Molly assumed the new owners hadn't moved in yet.

Nick inserted a key into the lock and held open the door for her. They crossed the entryway where a shiny brass plate bolted to one wall was sectioned into individual mailboxes. Then they climbed three marble steps to another door that matched the first.

"You have great security," Molly said.

"Yeah, I planned it that way, even though the neighborhood will soon change for the better."

Across the street, the Blackstone project had made additional headway. A small park provided a grassy area with benches and a central fountain. Shade trees, their roots still encased in burlap sacks, waited for landscapers to plant them. The steel skeletons of two buildings took shape on either side of it. Maybe before too long a row of town homes would rise. Also, she remembered mention of a planned hotel and office complex.

Once in the marble lobby, Nick rang for an elevator, one of two. Molly did some quick surveillance while they waited. Three wood-framed openings, two on either side and one at the rear of the lobby, appeared ready for exterior doors. What appeared of the finished interiors suggested apartments, not lofts. A stairway cut into the wall adjacent to one of the elevators. Fire stairs, she supposed.

"Let's check out the third floor first," Nick suggested.

"Okay." The elevator arrived, and they entered the car. As it rose, Nick jammed his hands into his pants pockets and jiggled loose change. She wondered if that signaled some anxiety. Interesting since her nerves had calmed once they'd arrived at the complex. Her curiosity had superseded her awkwardness. Maybe she could spend a little time with Nick without her stomach twisting into knots.

They exited the elevator on the third floor. There were also three standard openings here, none of which had doors. A faint smell of paint hung in the air.

"Let's check this one." Nick took Molly's arm and led her into the unit that faced the street. "When the Blackstone project is finished, it'll have a nice view of the park."

The dimensions seemed right for a one-bedroom condo. She mentioned it to Nick.

"The units in this section aren't condos, and they're not for sale. They're rentals." He ran a hand through his hair and laughed softly. "Actually, it you want the truth, they're more like giveaways."

"Really." Why would he give anything away?

"The layout pretty much replicates that of the old building."

"What old building?"

"The one we took the wrecking ball to. It used to stand right here."

"You mean the apartment house?"

"That's what I wanted to talk to you about. I'm almost ready to move my tenants back in, but I'm having a hell of a time getting the run-around at social services."

Chapter 29

Molly's mouth dropped open. Cool air dried the saliva on her tongue.

"I get stuck in menu hell whenever I phone over there. When I finally make connect with a human, I'm shunted to another department. I went down Friday, spent a good part of the day, with the same result. When I tell them I need to locate some people, I'm directed to yet another office. It's the same runaround."

"You're moving your tenants back in?" Molly could hardly believe it.

"Well, yeah. Isn't that what you wanted? What we both wanted?"

Tears glistened in Molly's eyes. She balled her hands into fists and squeezed hard.

"It is, isn't it?" he said.

"You wanted it, too?"

"Yeah. Maybe I should have taken you over to social services with me. You know the people. You might have had better luck navigating the bureaucracy. But I wanted everything perfect before I brought you here."

Molly, a lapsed believer in perfection, thought he'd come close enough.

"Can I count on your help?"

"Sure. I'll do whatever I can."

"Good. First, we need to locate my tenants."

We.

Exactly how much time could she spend with him before her emotions plunged into free fall?

"Then we need to get them ready to move."

She wanted to hug him but couldn't. Well, maybe just a small one. She put a hand on his shoulder and quickly withdrew it. "You thought of everything."

"I did my best. We can work around your schedule, whatever's good for you."

How about some heavy petting followed by the most incredible sex? She wondered what he'd say to that. "My time is flexible."

"In that case, can you spare a few more minutes? I'd like to show you one of the lofts on the fifth floor."

All the talk about rentals and lofts reminded Molly about the building Nick had purchased next to the clinic. "You know, you never did fully answer my question about the rumor that's been floating around on the block."

"What rumor?"

"Hmmm . . . the one that you . . . ah . . . might buy the empty building next to the clinic and . . . ah . . . maybe even the clinic." *Especially the clinic.* She didn't dare tell him she already knew he's purchased the corner property.

"Yeah, since I lost space here, I figured I'd make it up down at your end. The corner spot stood empty. I put a small office building I own up for collateral and arranged financing. One of the better restaurants in town is ready to expand and sign a lease for the ground floor. Once I earthquake proof the place, I'll start on the units above. What I make selling them should offset some of what I lose on the rentals I'm saving for my tenants."

"And the clinic?"

"That's never been part of my plans."

Molly breathed a sigh of relief. "I'm glad."

"How do these rumors start, anyway?"

Molly shrugged.

"So, would you like to see one of the lofts?"

Since she'd discovered she could actually occupy the same planet with him without her heart swing dancing in her chest, she agreed.

They stepped into the hallway. With the touch of a button, the elevator door quietly slid open. Molly preceded Nick into the car. Brushed steel, shiny brass accents, and polished wood moldings made up the enclosure. Mrs. Z would have no more steps to climb even if she wound up on the third floor again. Still, Molly thought Nick would agree to situate her on the ground level. She made the suggestion.

"Sure. I suppose they'll still want a tenants' association. She can field their complaints. One plus, though. Duncan Serk won't join them any time soon."

"That's good news." Molly couldn't blame Nick if he excluded him from the building.

"He wound up caught in a sting when he tried to sell drugs to a DEA agent. I read about it in this morning's paper. It's not his first arrest. Anyway, I didn't plan to spend any time locating him. I would have offered him a couple of thousand to go away permanently if he were to find out about the new arrangement. There wouldn't be anything he could do about it. Now, even that won't be necessary."

The ride to the fifth floor took seconds. Nick used a key, and a separate door opened directly onto an entry foyer. A few steps took them into the loft.

"This is convenient." Now she understood why the elevator had two sets of doors, one opposite the other.

"There's only one loft per floor, with five floors anchoring each end of the project and two above the center rentals. Twelve lofts in all."

Molly wondered about the purchase price. When she'd glanced at the real estate section of the *Chronicle*, she'd noticed new lofts in the South of Market area generally sold in the seven hundred thousands and up. Her haphazard search hadn't come across any ads for Nick's units. Since he'd carved out three floors for rentals, his profit must have seriously nosedived. She felt a momentary pang of guilt. She wondered if he resented her costing him so much money. At least he had good financial prospects for the new corner property.

"There are no exterior hallways. It should be pretty quiet," Nick said.

Molly followed him to the front of the unit where four floor-to-ceiling glass panels created a wall. Nick pressed a button and the aluminum screens that sheathed the exterior rose. The park, along with the completed Blackstone project, would provide a great view.

She turned away from the windows and toward the interior of the large space. Polished steel columns, most likely structural, created a sleek modern look. Someone with decorating savvy could turn this space into a fabulous home.

"It's wonderful. It's so open. Once furnishings are in place, creating all kinds of cozy nooks, it should be very comfortable."

"I thought so, too. That's why I've considered buying one." He laughed. "I'll have to offer myself a pretty hefty discount, though."

"You want to move here?"

"I've thought about it. I'm ready for something different. I've spent my whole life in the Marina District and Pacific Heights."

Molly thought about his present apartment. They'd made love there. She'd given him more than her body there. She'd given him her heart.

"Yeah, I'd like to live down here for a while. If I'm going to do it, though, it had better be soon, before I get married. I suppose after I have a kid or two, it'll be suburbia for me." He grinned. "Though maybe not. You never know. A nice Victorian, like your aunt's, might be in the offing."

Nick is getting married. Why did it come as such a shock? The shock was he'd remained single so long.

"Have you set a date?" She didn't want to know, but the nasty little trickster who squatted inside her brain screamed for the details.

"About moving?" He shook his head. "I haven't one hundred percent decided to relocate here."

"No, I mean for your . . . wedding."

"My wedding?" For a moment, confusion settled in his eyes. "Oh that. No, no date's been set. If it were up to me, we'd jump in the car and drive over to the courthouse and do it now. The woman I have in mind is pretty traditional, though. She'll probably want the whole big scene."

I wouldn't. Molly knew she'd be happy with a handful of people and the mayor officiating. Or even one of his minions. It would take less than nothing to make her happy if she had Nick.

He reached into his pocket and drew out a velvet pouch. He opened it and a ring slid out onto his palm.

Molly's eyes widened. The center stone was a rich green emerald embedded into a gold band and surrounded by a swirl of tiny diamonds.

"It's beautiful." Emerald was one of her favorite stones, rich without too much glitz.

It was exactly what she would have wanted.

Nick held the ring out. "Here, try it on."

"I can't."

"Why not?"

This had to be his first engagement. Why ask her anything so silly, otherwise.

"Your . . . fiancée should be the first woman to wear the ring. I mean, after a while, she might let her girlfriends try it on. They would probably want to—I tried on my cousin's—but it shouldn't be that someone else wore it before . . . you know." Why, in awkward situations, did she have to babble? She wished the concrete floor would crack open so she could jump head first into the crevasse.

"Molly, you're still the most stubborn woman I know." He took her hand. He slipped the ring onto her finger before she could pull away. "I figured this was the right one for you."

"Me?"

He took her face in both his hands and kissed her as deeply and as long as he'd done on the night they made love. Finally, they broke apart. "Maybe I should have asked you first if you still feel the same way about me."

"Same . . . way?"

"You told me once you loved me. At least I thought you did."

"You were supposed to forget anything I said . . . along those lines."

"That's something a man doesn't forget. Not when he's in love with the woman who's saying it to him. I love you, too, Molly. More than I can ever show you. I want to marry you."

A grin spread across Molly's face.

"I woke up Friday morning and realized, not for the first time, how empty my life was without you. I love you. I wanted to tell you then, but I didn't have a ring or even a plan. I was afraid if I called you, I'd just blurt it out. It was important to me that I ask you to marry me in a place that had meaning for us." His eyes swept the room. "This is what brought us together."

Molly's heart filled with the best kind of ache, and she blinked back a sudden spurt of tears. "I'm glad you waited."

"I hope you haven't changed your mind." He tipped her head back and gazed into her eyes.

The muscles in Molly's face cramped from holding a broad smile.

Nick took her in his arms. "I'm probably not going about this the right way."

"Yes, you are." Molly put her hands on his shoulders. A note left in the hollow of a tree would have worked if it contained a marriage proposal.

"Maybe I should get down on one knee."

"That's not necessary."

"Okay, then. We'll forget the bended knee and I'll just get right to the proposal. Will you marry me?"

Molly looked at the ring on her finger. So much happiness filled her heart. She could barely speak; though, she needed to find only one word. "Yes."

It was Nick's turn to grin. Then he let out a long breath and followed it with a soft laugh.

Relief came in many guises, she supposed.

"Okay." He kissed the tip of her nose.

"Nick, will you tell me you love me again?"

Without hesitation he said, "I love you. I love you. I—"

"Don't say it again."

"Why not?"

"I figure each 'I love you' must have set you back . . . What do these lofts sell for?"

He shook his head.

"No, I'm serious. To give up three floors must have cost you plenty."

"It brought me a better than good return. You."

Tears glistened again in Molly's eyes. Happiness had a way of doing strange things to her.

"While we're on the subject, what do you think about living here? At least for a while. It's up to you. I'll do whatever you want."

"Whatever I want?"

"Absolutely and forever."

The absolutely part she might stake her meager bank account on. Knowing Nick, as to forever, she'd have to wait and see.

She wound her arms around his neck. "There's only one thing I want right now." She stood on tiptoes and kissed him with all the passion she'd held inside. Her heart swelled and told her she was the luckiest woman in the entire western hemisphere.

When the kiss ended he said, "I have my apartment until the end of the month."

"Hmm. I'll bet you still have furniture there."

"Are you thinking what I'm thinking?" he said.

"How about you drive me to my car?"

"How about once we get there, you follow mine? I know all the shortcuts to my place." He tousled her hair, and she didn't care if the curls stood out like bed springs.

"My, you're eager."

"Baby, you don't know the half of it."

Maybe not, but she had the rest of her life to find out.

About the Author

Carolann Camillo is a recipient of the Coffee Time Reviewer's Recommended Award for her historical romance, *Moonlit Desire*. A native New Yorker, she lives in the San Francisco Bay Area with her college professor husband.

In the mood for more Crimson Romance? Check out *No Secrets in Spandex* by Toni Jones at *CrimsonRomance.com*.